About the a

I'd always been into sports, knowing my mind drifted off with ideas, especially out jogging!

Any form of writing interested me: school, work reports, diaries, cards for family and friends.

I've been a paperboy, window cleaner, customs clerk, manager, terminal and security controller, unemployed and a postman.

This is a prequel to *Laura Come Back To Me*, my first of four novels linked by the characters.

I'll be eternally grateful for the opportunity that allowed me to achieve a dream of becoming an author.

Here's hoping you enjoy book two, *Four Becomes the One.*

FOUR BECOMES THE ONE

Michael Dowle

FOUR BECOMES THE ONE

Vanguard Press

A CIP catalogue record for this title is
available from the British Library.

ISBN 978 1 78465 636 2

*Vanguard Press is an imprint of
Pegasus Elliot MacKenzie Publishers Ltd.*
www.pegasuspublishers.com

First Published in 2020

**Vanguard Press
Sheraton House Castle Park
Cambridge England**
Printed & Bound in Great Britain

Dedication

This is for my mum, who loves reading.

Also, my brother, Richard and his wife, Maureen, along with my sisters, Jeannie and Barbara. Plus, my grown up sons, Sam and Josh, who've questioned me endlessly throughout the process!

Here's hoping you enjoy reading this as much as I've loved writing it.

Without your support, this may never have happened.

This story is dedicated to all of you. Thank you.

ACKNOWLEDGEMENTS

May I say a special thank you to the following, for your invaluable help: Gayna, Margaret, Deb and Suzanne. You have helped me with this novel more than you will ever know.

Also, to John H, Andy M, plus Gary and Bev. I'd like to say a big thank you, for listening to me yet again!

Plus, my family and friends too many to mention; you all know how I can talk and talk and talk! Thanks again to you all for being there.

Finally, to my publishers, Pegasus. This wouldn't be happening if not for you, so thank you for making my dream come true, you all know who you are.

1
The Beginning, 1954

On a cold night in late October, a cry was heard to come out of Bishopstone Hospital, as a baby boy was born. That baby was later named Peter. Peter Johnson.

His long blonde-haired mother, Brenda, had given birth to three older children already, all boys, just like him.

When he arrived at Bishopstone in Manchester, his three older brothers were at home with their father, Jim, a tall slim man with jet black hair.

It was a difficult birth, Brenda being told that due to complications, it was unlikely she would ever be able to have any more children. After being given the news by the doctor who delivered her fourth son, she was not upset, but relieved.

She'd had four sons in six years and it was exhausting her. When she was given that news, she smiled inside. No more pain. Life will get better now, she hoped. This made her decide to devote all her time to bringing up their four sons.

After a traumatic birth and recovering for six days in hospital, she was allowed to go home with her new-born son, Peter. Her husband Jim had visited only twice in those six days, having to look after their other children. On his two visits without their other boys, she noticed he only held Peter once, for a minute or so. She wanted Jim to come and see him every day, but he told her it wasn't possible, having to look after their other boys. They only had Brenda's parents to rely on, who lived some distance away, to look after the children while he came to visit her and their baby. Plus, the hospital was miles away, and they had no car.

She knew that he hadn't bonded with the baby. But, he had already become the apple of her eye. She loved her new-born son with all her heart. It was the strongest bond she had felt with all of their children. As he was likely to be their last child, she knew deep down she'd give him more attention than his three brothers, albeit unintentionally.

Throughout those six days, she gradually became stronger, breastfeeding him instantly, which she'd done with all of her other sons. She had an excess of milk for him, so was comfortable and happy feeding him this way, just as she had with the other boys.

Jim had convinced her that breastfeeding their other three boys for a couple of months was enough. But, she was determined this time – if it was to be her last baby – to continue much, much longer.

With her energy levels getting better and Peter in good health, she was discharged on day six. With no car, nor phone, she had no choice but to get the trolleybus, which a few years earlier had replaced most of the tram system in and around Manchester. It was late afternoon now, and likely to be almost dark by the time she arrived home.

Getting on board at the hospital, she travelled the four miles to their house, on the outskirts of Manchester. It took almost an hour when normally it would have taken half that time.

Whilst on the bus she noticed there had been a riot of sorts as there was a police presence outside the shops, not far from where she lived. The road they'd been travelling on, had been blocked, so they were diverted. It must be the rationing of food that they'd been rioting or protesting about, she thought to herself, hoping that there was enough food for her family when she finally arrived at their home. But then again, she remembered that rationing had ended only a few months ago back in July.

Not being overly concerned about the troubles, she wanted to get home with her new-born son, so that he could meet his brothers. So, after the longer than normal journey, she arrived at the end of their street, getting off, walking the two hundred yards to their house from the bus stop. Not having her key to the front door, she knocked and waited for a reply. No answer. Knocking again, much harder, she sat and waited on the doorstep.

After a short time, she knocked again on the door. This time after a few more minutes, it was answered by her husband. Brenda was still sitting on the step; it was cold, but not raining.

Without turning to see him, she said, 'Did you not hear me knocking, Jim?'

'One of the boys heard you,' he replied. 'I've had them all in the bathtub in the kitchen, you know it's always noisy at bath time; just got them all dressed.'

They had no bath, using the bathtub once a week to bathe the boys, with the toilet also being outside the house.

Brenda got off the step standing now directly in front of Jim, so he could see their new-born son.

'Come on then, you big lump! Let's get indoors. I've been sitting here for a while now getting cold,' she said, smiling at him.

'Sorry. C'mon love, in you get, the boys are in their pyjamas dressed for bed already, waiting for you to come home with their little brother.'

He stepped aside so she could get in, then closed the front door, following her into the living room where she saw the coal fire burning, then down some steps into the kitchen where the other boys were sitting on chairs, waiting for them.

She saw the bathtub still in the middle of the kitchen floor, full of the water the boys had bathed in. Jim opened the back door, then grabbed the tub full of water, taking it outside, throwing the water down the drain. He hung it up on a hook on the wall outside, behind the toilet, before going back inside, closing the back door to try and keep the warm air inside.

Still holding Peter, she said to her other sons, 'Come here, you three, see your little brother.' All three of the boys jumped off their chairs, as Jim had just got back into the house.

It was no wonder she was so tired, with their other boys all under six years old. Jim junior was known as Jimmy, being a few months past his fifth birthday in July. The twins named Stan and Joe were three-and-a-half, having been born in mid-May.

'Has Dad told you his name yet?' she asked them all.

'Peter, that's what Dad said,' answered Jimmy.

'That's right. Little baby Peter Johnson. Would you all like to hold him and say hello?'

'Yes, Mum,' said Jimmy. Stan and Joe both nodded in unison.

'Okay, then. Come into the living room, we'll all sit by the fire on the settee. You can take it in turns to hold him; then I'll feed him, as it looks like he's waking up.'

'Just going to get the dinner on, while you all pop by the fire,' said Jim. He'd already cooked a joint of beef – thanks to the end of the rationing – knowing that Brenda was due to be coming home with their baby. Plus, vegetables and potatoes, as he was preparing a roast dinner, which would only take another hour or so.

In the living room, Jimmy held his brother first, then Stan, and finally, Joe. They were all smiling at him, not knowing what to say, until Stan spoke. 'He's really small, Mum, isn't he?'

'Yes, he is. So we have to be very careful with him, until he gets a bit bigger like all of you. Do you think you can help me with him, whenever I ask you?' she questioned all three of them as one.

'Yes, Mum,' said Jimmy.

'I will too, Mum,' said Stan.

'And I'll be extra careful as well,' piped up Joe, louder than his brothers.

'Okay then,' said Brenda, laughing at Joe's raised voice, pulling him in towards herself, giving him a big hug. Then she did the same with the other two boys as well, before saying to them all, 'Good. Now, I just want to tell you all, that I love you very,

very much. I missed you all while I was in hospital having your baby brother. And, I'm very pleased you're all ready for bed.' She paused before continuing. 'So, Jimmy, can you put the radio on please, I'd like to hear some music. There's no radios in the hospital, and I've missed my music, as well as all of you.'

'Will do,' he said, turning it on so they could all hear it.

'Ah. My favourite just now, good old Don Cornell,' she said, knowing it was his number one song 'Hold My Hand'.

Peter was waking up, for a feed. Brenda was not embarrassed at all with breastfeeding him, as she'd done exactly that with the other boys as well. She explained to them, that it was the most natural thing in the world for a mum to feed her baby for a few weeks when first born. But it was something that she mostly did in the privacy of their own home.

Jimmy got up from the settee they were all sitting on, before saying, 'Going to help Dad in the kitchen.'

'Good boy, thanks, Jimmy,' replied Brenda.

'What can I do to help, Dad?' he asked as he went down the three steps into the kitchen.

'Well, you can lay the table in the living room for me, son. D'you remember where the big cloth is, in the drawer?'

'Yep, sure do, Dad. And the plates are in the cupboard, shall I get them out as well?' Jimmy questioned, pointing to the cupboard near the back door.

'They are. Put them here on the table two at a time, then you can get the knives and forks out of the tray in the cupboard afterwards and put them on the living room table.'

'Okay, Dad, will do.'

Jim knew that his oldest son was clever. He'd started school only a month or so ago, already being able to write his name in full. Plus, he'd been good at numbers. He knew Brenda liked to test them all. While he'd had a few days off work to look after the boys, he set them little quizzes himself, while they listened to the radio. He wanted them all to have a better life than he had. His wasn't bad, although he worked long hours on the Manchester ship canals.

Jimmy set the table for them all, while Jim continued with the dinner they were to have shortly. It was all nearly ready, when he left the kitchen to join the rest of his family in the living room, to see their newly-born son.

He sat next to Brenda, squeezing between Stan and Joe, as she finished feeding Peter, passing the baby to him. He smiled, looking into her eyes as he did so. She knew that he wanted a daughter, but their conversation before she went into hospital told her that he didn't mind either way, as long as it was healthy. And little Peter was, so far, a healthy boy.

She noticed that he didn't kiss his latest arrival, just stroked his head gently, saying, 'He's a lovely little fella, Brenda. Very nice.'

That was not the reaction she'd expected at all, as Jim stood up, still holding Peter for a moment, before handing him back to her.

'Right, I'll get the dinner sorted and dished up for us. Boys, you sit with your mother while I get everything organised, okay?'

'Okay,' they all said, sitting with their mum, as she held their baby brother, winding him after his feed.

At least he cuddled his baby son, she thought to herself. But, he seemed distant. Maybe it was because he had dinner to do. She didn't dwell on it, thinking it'd pass.

Peter fell asleep within minutes. She placed him in the carry-cot they'd used for all of their children in the first few months of their lives, before transferring them to a bigger cot, having to borrow one from a neighbour when they had the twins. Peter would sleep with his parents for a few months, whilst their twins shared a bedroom, Jimmy having a room of his own to sleep in. That would continue until they decided where Peter would be sleeping, in their three bedroomed house.

'Dinner's ready!' shouted Jim. 'Get yourselves on the chairs, boys, I'll bring it in for you all.'

Brenda checked on Peter briefly, to ensure he was sleeping after his feed.

'This looks lovely, Jim,' she said, as he began bringing in the food.

They were all now sitting around the table apart from Jim, who was carrying his own dinner in from the kitchen to join them, smiling at Brenda. The twins were sitting on wooden blocks shaped on top of the chairs Jim had made, allowing them to reach the table to eat. Jimmy had progressed to sitting on his knees on the chair, to eat his dinner.

The boys had already started eating as Jim sat down and spoke. 'If you can't use the forks and knives, you two, use your fingers,' he said looking at Stan and Joe.

'I can use them properly now, Dad,' said Jimmy.

'I know, son. Your brothers will get the hang of it soon, just like you,' replied Jim. 'And if you eat all your dinners up, there's a pudding as well.'

'Oh, nice,' said Brenda. 'Is it a surprise?'

'No, just an apple pie and custard. Thought it'd be a treat for us all.'

'Thanks, love,' said Brenda.

There was some chattering then from the boys, whilst they ate their dinner, knowing there was more food to come.

Now they'd become a complete family, Brenda thought to herself. She knew it was unlikely there'd be another child. No daughter after all...

2
Peter's Early Years

For the next eight months, Brenda continued to breastfeed her baby, whilst also looking after their twins; Jimmy carried on going to school in the day time. Then she began feeding Peter with much the same food as they all had, other than it was mashed up for him.

She noticed that Jim hadn't spent much time with Peter, in comparison to their other children. He was still a baby, so that may explain why. Plus he worked long hours. It still did not overly concern her, knowing how tired he was from working.

His job at the moment, was on the lock gates, meaning it was physically exerting. He was waiting to get a promotion, where other lock gates had become automated. That may take a few years, he'd told her.

Working six days a week, the only day off he had was a Sunday. His routine was to have a lazy morning that day, with a lay in bed if he could. This had been the case, since they were first married and had their first son, Jimmy. He'd always worked six days a week; it was the only way they could survive. At least he didn't have to work night shifts, Brenda said.

Their parents were friends. Since they'd first met as children, Jim and Brenda became besotted with one another. Once the war was over, they began dating, even though Jim was fifteen and she was fourteen. Saving all their money, they married quietly three years later, in a registry office in 1948. Although young, they had the blessing of Brenda's parents and Jim's mother. His father had been killed in the war when he was twelve years old.

It was 1949, when Jimmy arrived. Then eighteen months later, Brenda had their twins. Now, in 1955, she thought with Peter and the complications, she'd finished with childbirth.

Brenda always loved Jim, from when they were children playing together, right up to today. Both of them always enjoyed their time together. Jim used to say to her "let's make the most of each day". That's what they did before she had Jimmy. They'd go walking along the canals. She watched Jim playing amateur football; he'd tell her about his job and how he'd have to wait a while to get a promotion and more money.

In all this time, he'd never drank alcohol. Jim always said he never felt a need for it.

By the time Peter was one-year-old, Jim realised he'd neglected his youngest son. His first birthday happened to be on a Sunday. When he awoke that morning – after his usual lay in – Jim decided he had to tell his wife the reason behind his neglect of their youngest child.

He spent the day playing with their boys, including Peter, who was now toddling about himself. Late in the afternoon, as darkness was falling, Brenda called them all into the living room from the front room where they'd all been playing. Dinner was ready.

I'll tell her tonight, when the boys are all in bed, Jim thought to himself. It wouldn't be his wisest decision, but he knew in his heart he had to do it.

They put the children all to bed, Peter sharing Jimmy's room now, in his cot. Then they listened to the radio. Jim wasn't as keen on music as Brenda, but tolerated it for her sake. They went to bed at nine o'clock. Jim got into bed next to Brenda, knowing he had to tell her.

'Listen,' he said, pausing for a big breath. 'I've got something to say to you, Brenda, that you won't like, but I have to say it anyway.'

'Jim? What is it?'

There was a silent pause before he spoke. 'Okay. I know Peter's my son. You know I've had trouble bonding with him. I'm sorry. But I feel as though he's not my son. From the day you came home with him, it's been difficult for me to have feelings towards him. The truth is, I wanted a daughter. I know that sounds selfish, but I'm telling you now, because I can't hold this in any longer.'

Brenda put her hand over her mouth, stifling a scream. 'NO!'

'I'm so sorry,' he whispered.

'This is wrong, Jim!' There were tears in her eyes now. She was devastated, after a few seconds of silence, adding, 'You don't mean this, do you?'

'I've tried so hard, but all I can think of is I'll never have a daughter. I don't understand why. I just want to be honest with you about this. I'm sorry.'

They were both sitting up in bed now. Jim said nothing more. Brenda was sobbing, with her head in her hands, crying quietly so as not to wake their children. Wiping her eyes, she stopped a few minutes later, saying to Jim, 'If you can't love Peter, then you cannot love me!'

It was now his turn to feel devastated. He loved her, and their four sons, but he just couldn't find strong feelings towards Peter.

'You cannot sleep in this bed with me. It's not possible,' said Brenda.

Jim didn't reply. There was no need. He'd jeopardised their marriage, everything they had. His honesty may have just ruined their lives. They would not sleep together as husband and wife again, maybe forever, he thought. They had a settee in their bedroom, which became his bed. It was all his fault.

The boys never knew what happened. They did not suspect. How could they understand, they were just children.

He tried his hardest over the next few years to bond with Peter. It didn't happen. Brenda, on the other hand, gave Peter more attention than his three older brothers. It did not go unnoticed by Jim.

There were many arguments over Jim's attitude. He thought that Peter was not his son, even though he looked like his siblings. She told him time and again, that he was the father. He only had to look at him to see that all of the boys looked alike, although Peter had more of his mother's features.

Throughout his first seven years, he never laid a hand on his youngest son in anger; nor did he to the others. For this, she was eternally grateful, knowing that Jim had a vicious temper on him. She had seen him in action when they were first married, when he knocked out a chap who was chatting to her after they'd had their first baby.

She knew also first hand of his temper. He had punched and slapped her a few times when they argued, mostly over Peter.

Every time, he always said sorry. She accepted his apologies because she knew it was better for her to accept the violence than any of her boys.

With his mother's love and attention, Peter became what was known as a "mummy's boy". His three brothers were more boisterous. They played in the street often with an old laced football, while Peter was happy to watch them. Sometimes he'd be the referee when they played with the other kids in the street. He did not think it different that he preferred playing with the girls just as much as the boys. Even though he was just seven years old, he felt comfortable in the company of girls.

In school, he sat next to a girl named Elly Baxter, becoming good at all of his subjects. The only thing he wasn't keen on was sports. He could play just as well as the other boys and girls, but he wanted to watch instead of getting involved directly.

And in his friend Elly at school, he had a challenge. She was the most intelligent girl in his class. He wanted to get higher marks than her in all of their subjects. Peter really liked her and they quickly became good friends. She helped him, not knowing that he wanted to be better than her when it came to the tests the teacher set them.

He had ambition, drive from somewhere. Maybe it was from his hard working dad, who never seemed to have time for him. Or his mum, who was always telling him as he grew up, he could be the best at whatever he did. He believed her.

It was good that Elly only lived a couple of streets away from his house. From the day he was placed next to her in class, they remained friends. He thought she was different to all the other girls, not just because she was clever, she was bossy too! Maybe it was because they were both tall for their age.

There was a game that he was good at and liked playing. The girls always played it, but he joined in. It was hopscotch; Elly showed him how to play. It consisted of chalking nine boxes on the ground, then throwing the piece of chalk into one of them. Then, you have to hop and skip from one to nine, not standing in the box with the piece of chalk in it. Peter liked it because he had fun playing it, as well as helping him with his balance. He was flexible and liked numbers. Plus he could stand on one leg for ages, much longer than any of his brothers or his friends!

A few days before his eighth birthday, Elly said to him as they walked home from school, 'Hey, you're going to be a birthday boy soon, aren't you?'

'Yep. I'll be eight. Mum said I can have a party the Sunday afterwards. She said I have to wait until I'm actually eight years old, so it's a few days after.'

'Oh, that'll be nice. Never had a party on my birthday when I was eight a few weeks ago.'

'You didn't tell me you'd had your birthday. When was it?'

'Back in September. The twelfth. You can remember that for next year.'

'Okay. I will, it's just after my mum's.'

By this time, they'd reached Elly's house; the quickest way was going under the railway bridge at the end of their respective rows of houses. They said goodbye as she went inside, knowing that Peter would be back again the next morning to walk to school.

3
Eight Years Old

In October 1962, a few days before his birthday, his mum told him that he could invite one person to his party, which was going to be in their house. He knew who that would be.

When they walked home from school together the Thursday before his party, he asked her, 'Err, Elly, I've got a question for you.'

'What is it, Pete?' she replied, always calling him Pete.

Avoiding her eyes, seeing her long dark brown, curly hair all around her pale face, he asked, 'Well, you know it's my birthday party on Sunday?'

'Yes, I know that. Your birthday was Monday, the twenty-second.'

'Mum said I can invite somebody.' He paused and took a breath before asking her. 'I'd like you to come... if you want to?'

'Ooh, yes please!' she almost shouted, as they reached the front door to her house.

'Good.'

'What time shall I come round?'

'Err... not sure. I'll ask Mum. I'll tell you tomorrow. Probably in the afternoon.'

'Okay, lovely. Thanks, Pete.'

'That's okay. Well, I'll see you in the morning then.'

'Yep, see you then.'

He turned away from her smiling face, as his was doing the same thing. She was his best friend, he thought to himself. As he walked home, he knew there was nobody else he wanted other than Elly coming to his house for his birthday.

The next day at school, he told her he'd come round for her at one p.m. and they were going to have food and drink, so she didn't need to have any lunch at all.

On the following day, Saturday, Peter went with his brothers – who were to look after one another – and their mum, into town. Jimmy, being thirteen, was in charge of the money and list their mother had given them, as they walked along one of the canals towards town. It was a long hike for them all: at least it was dry, although cold. They'd often go out together to play football in the street, or wander around the ship canals, or go to the park on their own. Their mum trusted them, once she'd shown them where to go on previous trips. But today, she accompanied them all; it wasn't very often she had the chance to be out with all four of her boys. As it was Peter's birthday, she was going to the salon to have her hair washed and cut. This was a rare treat.

Her relationship with Jim had become increasingly strained over the last few years. They had arguments every now and then, as he still had issues bonding with his youngest son, even though she noticed that at least he was trying more recently. She still would not allow him to share their marital bed. Jim never forced himself on her, although he did verbally abuse her in the privacy of their bedroom, taking out his frustrations on her this way. He hadn't hit her for many years. If he apologised for what he said about Peter – wanting a daughter and not another son – there was a chance for them to resume a full, loving marriage, she told him.

Leaving the boys to get the shopping for the party, Brenda went to the hair salon. A couple of hours later, she met them all. It was getting dark now, so they walked swiftly home, knowing that tomorrow was the day of the party.

As they did, she saw headlines in some of the shop windows which showed "Cuban missile crisis averted". Jim had told her about it, as they'd heard it on the radio. Apparently the Russians had missiles in Cuba, thinking the USA didn't know; but the American president did know! Jim's boss had a television and told him about it. She knew that it could have led to another world war, starting on Peter's birthday. Everyone they knew was talking about it. Now, thankfully it was over.

They'd got the ingredients for the cake, plus sweets for them all. Jim had told Brenda he was getting a special present for Peter. He didn't say what it was.

Waking up the next day, Jim didn't have his lay in. He was up at seven thirty.

'Can you get the party organised please, Brenda? I've an errand to run this morning. I'll be back by one o'clock. I won't be late,' Jim said as he ate some toast.

'Well, I'm sure I can cope. The boys will help.'

'Good. Good. I'm off to get Peter's present. You'll know what it is when I get back. Sorry for not telling you, I want it to be a surprise for everyone.'

'Go on with you! It'd better be good?'

'I hope so. See you in a few hours,' he said, kissing his wife on the cheek. They'd not been intimate for years Brenda thought to herself; it was unusual that he'd even kissed her. She hoped maybe he'd changed his attitude towards their youngest son.

Jim knew he had a long walk ahead, due to the recent bus strike, which was still going on. The present was in a shop on the other side of town. They had no car yet, so walking was the only option. The shop owner was opening specially for him.

Peter was already awake, coming downstairs after getting himself dressed. Stan and Joe were sitting at the table eating toast. They'd heard what their dad said. Jimmy was still in bed.

'Psst,' said Stan, looking at Peter.

'What?' he asked.

Whispering, Stan said, 'Dad said he's going to get your present. Don't think we were supposed to hear him. He said it's a surprise. Mum doesn't even know.'

'Oh. Crikey, he's gone early. Wonder what it is?' said Peter.

'No idea,' said Joe, still whispering, so that their mum couldn't hear them.

'Just have to wait and see then, won't we?' said Peter, smiling.

'Yep,' said the twins together.

Brenda brought some breakfast in for Peter then, from the kitchen. 'What are you all whispering about, don't you know it's rude to whisper?'

'Sorry, Mum. The twins just told me Dad's gone out to get a present for my birthday. They heard you and Dad talking.'

'You boys don't miss a blooming thing, do you?' she said laughing and then smiling. 'Before you ask, no I don't know what it is, he wouldn't tell me either.'

'I'll wake Jimmy up in a minute,' said Joe, 'see if he wants to go and play footie with us.'

'Well eat your toast first all of you and drink your tea. You go and have a game with them, Peter, when you've opened the cards on the sideboard.'

'Will do, Mum. Thanks.'

'Then you can go round to Elly's. See if she wants to come round early and help with the cake.'

'Okay,' Peter replied.

That's exactly what he did. They had a kick-about, but it started raining after a while. So, they went back indoors, where Jimmy got out the snakes and ladders game.

'Off you go then, go and get Elly,' Brenda said to Peter.

He smiled at her, put on his jacket and walked round to Elly's house to bring her round early. It was now eleven thirty.

Returning, the two of them went into the kitchen to help his mum bake the birthday cake. The twins and Jimmy continued playing snakes and ladders. Time was going by, as Brenda finished off the cake, putting it into the oven, knowing it'd be about an hour before it was baked. Then she could put the icing on it. She'd prepared the food for a Sunday dinner, which was usually the case for them all, especially in winter time. The radio was on and there was an announcement again about the Cuban missile

35

crisis ending. Knowing Jim would be back soon, she would tell him the news, even though it was happening on the other side of the world.

It was now almost one o'clock. 'Boys, can you clear the table, lay the cloth and put the cutlery out please. One extra place for Elly as well.'

Jimmy put away their game into the sideboard drawer, where the cutlery was kept and the tablecloth. 'All done, Mum,' he shouted to her when he'd finished, with the help of the twins. Peter and his guest were sitting on chairs in the kitchen still, sniffing the smell of the cake in the oven, chattering away.

'Come on then, you two, we'll put the food on the table, you can all help yourselves to whatever you want for dinner, seeing as it's your birthday, young man!' Brenda said, smiling at Peter.

He took a bowl of hot roast potatoes with a tea towel wrapped around it up the few steps out of the kitchen, placing it onto the table. Elly followed him, with a bowl of vegetables. Then his mother followed with what Peter knew was a giant-sized chicken she'd chopped up.

'Now, over there on the settee Peter, there's a couple of presents for you.'

Oh, thanks, Mum,' he said, opening the two presents. One was a big notepad. He liked drawing. The other one was colouring pencils.

'Hope you like them?' questioned his mum.

'Yep, lovely Mum. Better than a football!' he said, laughing.

'Huh! Not if it was me,' said Stan.

'Well, it's not your birthday yet, Stan, so shush,' his mother whispered in his ear.

They never had many presents for birthdays or Christmas, any of the boys. None of them minded, though Brenda realised that Jimmy had made comments on each of the other boy's presents. She knew why. He was growing up fast. And, he was the one who was the spitting image of his father.

Then, with the table laid and Jimmy bringing in the squash for them all to drink with their dinner, there was a knock at the door. Then the doorbell rang as well; the new doorbell Jim had fitted a few months earlier. Strange, Brenda thought, putting the gravy dish on the table. If it's Jim, he would've come straight into the house.

'I'll answer it,' said Brenda adding, 'you all start helping yourselves to dinner,' as she went down the hallway.

When she opened the door, it was Jim. 'Shush!' he said, putting his finger to his lips for her to be quiet. Then he put his other hand over Brenda's mouth, so that she couldn't speak.

'Listen,' whispered Jim, pausing before continuing, 'sorry I've been so long, but I realised what a fool I've been. Brenda, I'm sorry. I love you, and all of our children, including Peter. Truly, I do.'

'Oh, Jim. I'm sorry too,' she said, after he'd taken his hand from her mouth.

She had tears in her eyes. So did Jim. Very unlike him, she thought. As she stared, he wiped his eyes; it'd been a long time since she'd seen him cry.

'Okay then, here it is,' he said, walking away from their front door just a few feet away. He came back with the present none of them could have ever expected.

'No!' she shouted. 'How could you afford this? It's so expensive.'

'Who is it, Mum?' shouted Jimmy from the living room.

Before she could reply, Jim said, 'It's okay. Get the kids into the hallway. I'll close the front door, then ring again in twenty seconds. Make sure Peter has his hands over his eyes. No, tell them all to put their hands over their eyes.'

'All right,' she said. And for the first time in a long, long time, she kissed her husband on the lips. Maybe, he'd come to his senses. The present was incredible, she thought, as she shut the door.

'Kids!' she shouted. 'All of you into the hallway, now please. Come on, hurry up!'

They all scrambled out of their chairs, not sitting on raised boxes like years ago, all bigger now.

'What is it, Mum?' asked Peter, as his brothers pushed him forward, with Elly standing right next to him.

'Right,' she said, 'close your eyes all of you, your dad's here with your present, Peter. Keep your hands over your eyes until I say you can remove them.' She could hardly speak, her voice excited with emotion, already knowing what the surprise was.

They all shut their eyes, putting their hands over them, as directed by Brenda.

She opened the door before Jim rang the bell, not waiting for him, saying, 'No peeking any of you!'

He walked past Brenda, tapping Peter on the shoulder. 'Okay, son, you can open your eyes now. Just you. The rest of you, count to five, then open all of your eyes.'

Peter opened his eyes, looking at what was directly in front of him, with the front door now closed. Standing in the hallway, being held by his mum, was a GLEAMING, SHINING, BRILLIANT BLUE BICYCLE.

'What!' Peter shouted. 'Is this for me?'

'It sure is,' said his father. 'Well, do you like it?'

'Dad, it's fantastic! Is it really for me?'

'Yes, of course it is.'

He raced towards his father, hugging him so tightly he almost knocked him over!

'Wow!' said Jimmy.

'I don't believe it!' said Joe.

Stan just looked open mouthed, lost for words, which was not like him at all!

It was Elly, who took them all by surprise when she spoke. 'Bloody hell! It's a bike. Crikey!'

The boys rarely swore, expecting Elly to get told off. Instead, Jim and Brenda laughed, as she went red in the face, realising what she'd just said.

'Elly, it's fine. We're not going to tell your parents,' said Brenda looking at her, then Jim for approval of what she'd said, as he nodded in agreement, smiling.

'Sorry,' she replied. 'I don't know anyone who's got a brand new bike. Flipping heck!' she shouted, putting her hand to her mouth so that she couldn't say any more.

This time, they all laughed. Peter took Elly's hand from her mouth. Red faced, she joined in with the laughter, before Jim spoke after a few seconds. 'Come on then, you lot, I can smell dinner. Let's go and eat. Maybe later, Peter can let you all have a ride on his new bike; you included Elly,' he said, smiling after he spoke.

Looking at his bike before going back to the living room, Peter touched it with his hand. It was his. It really was. A bicycle all of his own, though he knew he'd have to share it with his brothers.

Fantastic, he thought, as he walked into the living room, with his dad's hand around his shoulder.

This would be the one birthday above all, he always remembered. They had a lovely dinner. Played snakes and ladders, again! Then hide and seek. It was simple pleasures back then. Plus, of course, there was the majestic bicycle nobody ever expected to see on that day. After going out on his bike, being shown how to ride it by his father with Elly looking on, he knew then, that it was the best day of his life.

His brothers would be allowed to try out his bike on another day his dad told them. Today was Peter's birthday.

When they came back after an hour or so, Jim said to Brenda, 'He's a natural on the bike. Even Elly had a go and got the hang of it quickly.'

'Great,' said Brenda. 'Now, sit down all of you, it's getting dark. We've got a cake to eat between us all!'

She went into the kitchen, collecting the cake which now had eight candles on it. As she came up the steps into the living room, nodding at Jim, he knew she meant to turn the lights out.

As he did so, Brenda started to sing. 'Happy birthday to you.' Everyone else joined in with the rest of the song, 'Happy birthday to you, happy birthday dear Peter, happy birthday to you.'

41

They all clapped loudly, as Elly gave a loud shout of 'Woohoo, wahey, happy birthday, Pete!'

Jim was smiling, as was Brenda. He put his hand on Peter's shoulder and said, 'Come on then, blow those candles out, you.'

He took a big breath, blowing hard on the candles for a few seconds, managing to blow them all out, as another cheer of "hooray!" rang out, with more clapping.

'Right, let's get this cake all eaten then, you lot,' said Jim. He looked at Brenda after saying this, smiling at her. There hadn't been a great deal of happiness between them both for some time, unknown to the children, as he watched her cut the cake into pieces for them all to devour.

As it was dark outside now, Brenda suggested that Jim and Peter walk Elly home soon. They did. It was a cold evening as they said goodbye to Elly, turning to make the short walk home.

'Dad, I'm really tired.'

'Come on then, up here, you,' Jim said, grabbing Peter and placing him on his shoulders, saving him from using his weary legs.

It was another memory Peter remembered, being in his recollection, the first time his dad had carried him on his shoulders.

When they got home, he slipped Peter off his shoulders, carrying him in his arms, walking straight through to the kitchen to speak to Brenda. 'Hey, this little fella looks tired. D'you want to go to bed, son?' Jim said, looking at his wife.

'Pyjamas on first, Dad. Yep, I'm knackered. Oh, sorry, Mum,' said Peter, knowing his mum didn't like bad language.

'That's okay,' she replied, smiling, 'we'll let you off; it is your birthday after all. No bath tonight, we can do that tomorrow. Let's have a bit of music on, then all of us can get ready for bed. Okay, Jim?'

'Good idea, luv.'

There was a bit of cake left, which the boys all shared, with a drink of milk before Peter and the twins went up to bed, followed by their dad, who was going to read them a story.

Jimmy stayed downstairs as he was older, helping his mum to tidy up after the party. The bike stayed in their hallway.

When Jim came back downstairs, he hugged his oldest son, thanking him for helping all day long. Listening to the radio, after an hour or so had passed, Jimmy started yawning, taking himself to bed.

With the radio on quietly, Brenda finally sat down with Jim to listen to the music. 'Jim,' she said, pausing. 'What you did today was amazing. You seem like a changed man. How did you manage to afford the bike?'

'Well. You know I got that promotion at the beginning of the year, working on the lock gates?'

'Yes.'

'Every day for the last six months, I've worked through my lunch break. You know the job's easier as the gates I'm working on are automated.'

'So, you saved for his bicycle.'

'Yep. Wanted it to be a complete surprise. Tried to figure out a way to make up for being the arsehole I've been towards Peter. I'm sorry for not letting you know. And, I'm sorry for the way I've been for years now. I hope this goes a little way towards making it up to you. To all of you.'

'Oh, Jim. I know you're a good father. There's time to make it all up. It was great seeing you with Peter today; and the other boys too.'

'I'm a lucky guy, Brenda. You're a special lady for putting up with me.'

'That works both ways,' she replied, as Jim leant towards her, kissing her for the first time in ages; she could see tears in his eyes. 'Tea?' she asked, getting up to go to the kitchen.

'Yep, thanks,' he replied, quietly.

After finishing the cuppa, whilst listening to the radio, he got up to go and lock the front and back doors as usual. Then, as Brenda had already earlier changed into her dressing gown, she got up, yawning. He saw her, saying, 'Right, bed time for us.'

Going into the bedroom, he got into his bed clothes to go onto the settee. He always slept naked before, until Brenda banished him from their bed years ago. He put his head on his pillow, saying goodnight to Brenda, not knowing what was to happen next.

'Jim,' she whispered. He could hear her voice quivering, not knowing what to expect, as he raised his head to listen. He'd got so used to sleeping on the settee, he thought it would never change, secretly hoping that it would. He'd never told a soul about their sleeping arrangements.

'For the first time today, I saw you bond with love towards Peter. You know he's our boy, not just mine. Thank you for being his father. I've always loved you, Jim. God knows, you've been patient over these years. I wasn't sure this day would ever happen. But, I think it has. It was wonderful to see you playing with the kids today, especially Peter. I love you.'

She looked over at him, laying on the settee, as he watched and listened to her words, with a small smile on his face, not being able to speak, as she continued. 'Today, of all days, has been and will be, I hope, a day for all of us to remember. Especially us and Peter. Please, Jim. Please, come to me?' he heard her questioning, with her voice still quivering, and her hand outstretched towards him.

He didn't feel excitement at that moment. There was no excitement in his loins at all. He'd practically forgotten about having sex with her, knowing what he'd done years ago, was, in essence, his mistake.

Moving from laying on the settee to sitting on it, he stared at her for what seemed like an eternity; it was in fact, just a few silent seconds. He didn't speak. Rising, he stared at her, in the dim light of the bedside lamp, transfixed, staring directly into her eyes.

Climbing into their bed, he felt the soft sheets around him for the first time in many years. Knowing that they'd both enjoyed love-making, he was unsure after all this time, if he'd be able to perform and satisfy her. There was no need for him to worry.

As soon as Brenda touched his face and kissed him, she let her other hand slip down his body, stroking him gently, laying down underneath him. Slipping his pyjamas off his lower body, she lay directly underneath Jim, taking him in her hand, guiding him inside her.

It'd been a long time since they'd made love. She wanted him now, just as much as he wanted her. As he slid inside her with her help, he was gentle.

Releasing a gasp, she whispered, 'Oh, Jim, I love you so much.'

'And I love you too, Brenda.'

They said nothing more, as he continued to writhe on top of her, knowing that he'd not be able to control himself for long. In a matter of minutes, he'd finished...

'Jim, it's fine. I want you again tonight, when you're ready,' she said, as he breathed heavily, still on top of her.

They held one another tightly in their arms. They were only in their early thirties, having plenty of energy still; even with having to run around after their four children.

As their night in bed wore on, they made love again and again, with Jim managing to last longer, trying his best to satisfy Brenda, until they fell asleep with their arms entwined.

They'd had discussions years before, knowing that it was very unlikely that she'd become pregnant again, due to the complications of giving birth to Peter.

For the next few weeks, life was idyllic for them all. Although the weather was cold, they had a couple of Sundays when Jim was off work, travelling to Blackpool on the bus for a day out by the seaside. They didn't care about the cold. His new job meant they had a little extra money for treats. And Jim said they could afford a television, which they had delivered at the beginning of December.

She'd managed to get Christmas presents for all of the boys, hiding them away in the loft space when they were all at school, keeping Jim informed.

Then, a few days before Christmas, Brenda dropped the bombshell that neither she nor Jim thought possible…

4
It Happened

It was the seventeenth of December 1962. Brenda was in the kitchen, listening to the radio. A new group from Liverpool had released a record a few weeks earlier she liked. It was called "Love Me Do". She knew all the words to it now, singing it to Jim when it came on the radio. The group were The Beatles. She asked Jim if maybe one day they could go and watch them, as they were not too far away. He'd already said yes, liking the music too.

As she was singing along, the house was empty other than herself. She was feeling ill again... just like she had been for the last few days. Jim was now only working every other Saturday in his job, so there was more time for the children of a weekend. Their lives were turning a corner: a little more money and time together.

Knowing what could be wrong, she was going to the doctor's before the boys came home from school. There'd been terrible weather for the last couple of weeks, heavy snow, so she went in the late morning, catching the bus.

Arriving wearing wellington boots because of the snow, she went into the surgery having to wait half an hour to be seen. Her appointment was with Dr Martin Prebble, their family doctor, who she'd met on many occasions, trusting his judgement.

Finally, seeing her doctor, Brenda explained to him, what she thought.

'Morning, Doctor. I'll come straight to the point,' pausing before adding, 'I think I'm pregnant.'

'Oh? That is a surprise, Mrs Johnson. I know from our other conversations and your visits, that it was highly unlikely, due to complications with your last child, that you could ever be pregnant again.'

'Yes, I know that. I'd been told when my youngest son was born. But I have the symptoms: sickness, tiredness, weight gain, and my upper chest is sore and swollen,' she said looking down at her breasts.

'Well, as I say, there is evidence here stating that damage to your uterus, womb, back then, was such that only constant rest over a period of time would enable any pregnancy. Also, your cervix had become contorted, twisted, which would technically make any fertilization practically impossible.'

She understood her body, realising that it was the lack of love making over the years with Jim, which may have led to the recovery of her inner self.

'Doctor, I think once you've examined me, you'll see I'm correct. My reason is that my husband and I have had no... no, intercourse for many years, until recently. There seemed no need to take precautions.'

'I see,' he said, raising his eyebrows briefly. 'That could indeed explain why and if you are pregnant. The lack of sex and penetration inside your body could indeed, allow your body to self-heal.' He paused before continuing. 'Now, may I examine you, Mrs Johnson, if you'd like to pop onto the bed please?'

'Yes, Doctor. Do you need me to take my boots off? You know how bad the weather is out today.'

'No, thank you,' he said, smiling, before adding, 'All well I trust, with your husband and children? I've not seen you here for quite some time?' he said, proceeding to examine her, pressing her lower stomach gently.

'All fine, thank you, Doctor. Our youngest one is already eight years old. I'd believed this couldn't happen again.'

Then he placed his stethoscope in several places around her waist, before saying, 'I have a relatively new piece of equipment here that we are trialling. It's called a Fetal Doppler. May I use it to listen for the heartbeat?'

'Yes, of course,' said Brenda as he placed the small monitor around her lower stomach.

'Okay, if you'd like to pop down off the bed, and get dressed again, we'll have a chat about the results.'

'Right, thank you again,' she replied pulling her clothes back around her, before sitting back on the chair at his desk.

'From what I can feel and hear, there is a very faint heartbeat in there. I'd like you to have a urine test to confirm the diagnosis, Mrs Johnson, just to confirm you are indeed, pregnant.'

Brenda's jaw dropped. Although she'd suspected, the confirmation was a massive surprise. 'Phew! Err, thank you. And I thought it was never possible?'

'As we discussed earlier, the lack of intercourse may have given your cervix, and womb, time to rest. And ultimately, heal itself.'

'I understand. So, I must be around seven or eight weeks pregnant then, Doctor?'

'Correct. Probably eight weeks. That would be my estimation. I will not allow an X-ray due to the radiation towards the baby, nor to see if there is unknown damage to your cervix. My assumption and belief is that your body has unusually righted itself over the years. A urine sample should be sufficient to confirm. You're now, let me see, thirty-one. Not too old for childbirth. Let's see how you go. But, please, if possible, try and rest when you can. I know that'll be difficult with your children. Do, please try though, Mrs Johnson.'

He handed her the slip for the urine test.

'How long will it take for the results?'

'Approximately two weeks. There'll be a delay due to Christmas being almost upon us, so come to the surgery around, say, the tenth of January. I'll chase up the hospital to ensure we have the results by then.'

Brenda got up, putting her coat on. 'Thank you, Doctor, merry Christmas to you,' she said, leaving the room.

'And to you too. See you in the new year.'

Closing the door, Brenda did not know whether to laugh or cry. She felt it was some kind of miracle. Why now? Jim had a better job, they'd completed their family, or so she thought. How would he react? Getting onto the bus home, she was in a daze. Tomorrow she'd go to the hospital, not enough time now, she had to get home for the boys. Then later tonight, tell Jim. She was worried, seriously worried. They'd been getting on so well in the last couple of months, after Peter's birthday. Now this.

Going through the motions when the children came home from school, they got themselves ready for bed by seven o'clock, when shortly after Jim came in from work, cold, from the snowy evening outside. Once the boys were all in bed by nine, they watched the television on their own for half an hour.

'Come on you, bedtime,' she said to him.

'Yep, I'm knackered. Did overtime today, extra money's always handy.'

'True,' she replied, adding, 'you doing the doors?'

'Yep, be up in a minute.'

Joining her in the bedroom shortly after, getting into bed, he leant over to kiss her. 'Good night, luv.'

'Jim, got some news for you.'

'Oh? The boys okay, anything happened at school?'

'Nothing like that. Listen.' She paused as he stared at her leaning on one arm, looking down at her face. 'Only one way to tell you really… I think I know how it's happened… I'm pregnant.'

'What! It's impossible, isn't it?' he said, open mouthed.

'Not exactly,' she said staring back at his face. 'When I saw the doctor today, he explained, after I told him that the lack of… you know… sex… has probably healed me inside. And now we've been going at it like, well, rabbits, we're going to have another baby.'

'Bloody hell!' was all Jim could say. Then he smiled. He wasn't angry. He kissed her, before she spoke.

'I've to have a urine test first. You're not angry, Jim?'

'Why would I be? This is terrific. Amazing. I've got a better job. I know I made a mistake, but you've stuck by me. I love you, Brenda, always have. Always will. It'll be tough, but we'll be fine. I know we will.'

She put her arms around his neck, kissing him, whilst pulling him on top of her. 'Might have to stop doing this soon you know?' she said, stroking his face, smiling at him.

'You sure this is okay?'

'Yes. We carried on until I was almost ready to drop before Peter was born, remember?'

'Oh, yer. If you're sure?' he said, smiling back and laughing at her.

'I didn't know how you'd react after everything that's happened. Jim, I love you; so pleased you're happy about this. It is a bit of a miracle after all, don't you think?'

'I reckon so.'

They began kissing again, before making love, falling asleep in one another's arms afterwards.

5
School Reports

The next few months flew by for Brenda and her family. Due to the snow and freezing cold weather, schools were closed, with people being advised to stay in to avoid accidents due to the snow and ice on the pavements and roads. It was the same all over the country, their television told them.

So, Brenda, with Jim still working as usual through the cold, decided to leave the urine test until the weather was better. She knew she was pregnant, and they'd told the boys on Christmas Day.

Their schools opened for a week in February, but closed again, due to the big freeze. As there was no school after this until early March, she decided, with Jimmy's help, to educate the other boys as best she could. They had writing books to use. Brenda did well at school herself, so to stop the boredom, she gave the boys lessons in lots of different subjects. They could all read and write, but none, Jimmy apart, were very good at maths.

Knowing this, she began working with them all as a group in the morning. In the afternoon after they had a sandwich for lunch, she took it in turns to test them individually with spelling and maths. Knowing their mum was having another baby, the boys, who still had their arguments, knew they had to behave. And they did. Jimmy always kept them in check, being the oldest.

They took it in turns to help with dinner. By the time they'd all returned to school, all of them could cook a full roast dinner, bake cakes and make a shepherd's pie. It was unknown to Brenda whether they'd improved at their schooling; they would only know when they went back, at the end of March.

Jimmy and Peter especially, shared her love of music. Some days, the radio was allowed on when they were doing their lessons. The group Brenda liked, The Beatles, were becoming well known. They had an album Jim bought for her.

They were allowed to stay up later in the evening, which she told Jim was a treat for their good behaviour. Watching with their parents, they saw programmes such as *The Price is Right, The Lucy Show, Bonanza, Gunsmoke, The Flintstones* and *The Ed Sullivan Show.*

It was on the last one they saw The Beatles. When they came on, girls were screaming and going crazy in the studio. The songs could hardly be heard, but it didn't matter. They'd seen them on television a few times. All the boys loved them, as did Jim and Brenda. They knew the words to all of the songs, as the group became increasingly popular.

Finally, they all went back to school. Brenda missed them. It was later when Easter arrived, the boys came home with their school reports; she expected little improvement due to the bad weather shortening their time there, but was pleasantly surprised as she opened each letter. None of the boys had tried opening them. As Jimmy, Stan and Joe were at secondary school, Jimmy was given their reports in a separate envelope, for safekeeping. Peter had his own in his bag.

They'd all improved in their maths and writing classes. Jimmy had a glowing report; Brenda was impressed. He only had another year or so left at school, with it being suggested that he be given additional tuition. Jimmy was way ahead of all his classmates in maths, his report advised.

Stan was top in their spelling test, with Joe second. The roles being reversed in maths. There was an additional letter in the envelope addressed to Mr & Mrs Johnson.

When reading it, she was flabbergasted! The headmaster requested to see her, being very interested in all of their improvement at school. When the holiday term was over, he'd asked her to go to school, at her earliest convenience, to discuss it. Furthermore, it read they'd all said their mother had been teaching them and it was a lot of fun.

Peter's report was last. She didn't expect much from him. How wrong she was! He'd come top in English and spelling. And, he'd been singing beautifully.

None of them knew what the reports said. They knew the results that they'd all come top in some lessons, but everyone had glowing, wonderful comments about their behaviour, kindness and helpfulness. She was indeed very happy, tears rolling down her face as they all sat around her on the settee; other than Jimmy, who'd gone to make them drinks in the kitchen.

'Mum, you okay?' asked Joe.

'Yes. Yes I am. You've made me very, very happy and proud,' she said, pausing to raise her voice. 'You too, Jimmy.'

'Thanks, Mum,' he shouted back from the kitchen.

'You two twins. I'm over the moon with both of you. Brilliant!'

'Hmmm,' mumbled Joe, smiling.

'Thanks, Mum,' said Stan, going slightly red in the face.

She put her hands out, waving them towards herself. They both leant into her, having a cuddle.

Jimmy came in with their cups on a tray, putting it on the living room table.

'And you, Mister Jimmy Johnson. Fantastic. I'm so proud of you,' she said with tears on her face still as he leant down to give her a hug. Jimmy was about two inches taller than his mum now, nearly as big as his dad.

Then she let go of him, turning to Peter. 'You as well! Crikey, singing and top of the class in a couple of subjects!' He smiled as she hugged him.

'Must've been your teaching, Mum,' said Jimmy.

'Yep,' said Stan. 'That's what we told our teacher; that you started teaching us yourself.'

'Well, I did, but you all remembered it. That's wonderful.'

So, what was in the other letter, Mum?' asked Jimmy.

'Oh, that. Blimey. Think it's me who's in trouble with the headmaster now, not you lot!' she said, laughing.

'What d'you mean, Mum?' questioned Stan, as she looked at the letter.

'After the holidays, he wants to see me. Not sure quite what for; just wants to talk about how much you've all improved and why, I guess.'

She told them everything in all of their reports, letting them read their own ones. Then, they passed one another's around, all commenting about how well they'd done. At the bottom of Stan and Joe's letters, it stated they'd been selected for the Manchester Counties football team.

'And you two,' she said, ruffling the hair on Stan and Joe's hair, 'almost forgot to say well done on getting in the county football team. You knew your dad was a keen footballer; never took it seriously enough to get anywhere. But, maybe you boys can?'

'I'd like to be a footballer, Mum,' said Stan.

'Yep, me too,' said Joe.

'Well, let's wait and see, boys, shall we? Just do your best, that's all I ask of you,' she said, looking at all four of them in turn.

'Right,' said Jimmy, with authority. 'Think we have to thank Mum somehow, guys, don't we? Anyone got any ideas?'

'Yep,' said Joe. 'We all know how to cook, thanks to Mum. Let's all do dinner this evening. Mum, what time's Dad home, about six thirty?'

'Err... yes, should be about then.'

'Okay, right,' said Stan, 'let's get to it, men!' smiling after he spoke.

Peter looked up at his mum still sitting on the settee, tugging her arm, saying, 'Leave it to us, Mum. We can do it.'

'Too right we can, Pete. Come on, fellas, I've got a plan. Mum, roast chicken, with some veg? Followed by an apple pie?' asked Jimmy.

'Yes. Yes please,' she said, smiling broadly, knowing he was turning into a young man, his features strikingly like his father's.

'Pete, you want to see if Elly wants to come round for tea? Go out on your bike for an hour if you like, then bring her round before it gets dark. That okay, Mum?' asked Jimmy.

'Good idea, Jimmy. Yes, do you want to do that Peter? Then you can see which subjects you beat her in. I know you've wanted to do better than her for ages now,' said Brenda.

'Cor blimey, yer! Is that okay, Mum?' he asked.

'Of course it is. Off you go now. No longer than an hour though. You can get back and help the others with dinner. I'm just going to sit here, listening to the radio,' she said laughing, as he shot off upstairs to go and put some playing clothes on.

And that's what she did; as Peter went out to play, the others sorted out dinner. She fell asleep. The boys worked quietly, knowing that their mum must be tired. That's what Jimmy told them.

Waking up later, the door opened. In came Peter and Elly. Jim arrived about an hour later. 'Smells nice, luv?' he said, as he saw his wife sitting on the settee.

'The boys are making dinner, Jim. You need to sit down, then read all of their school reports, plus the extra letter for us.'

'Got you a cup of tea, Dad,' said Joe. 'Sit yourself down next to Mum, take it easy!'

'Err, okay, son.' He was smiling as Brenda handed him the school reports and letter. She kissed him as he took the reports from her.

As he read all of the reports, Peter and Elly laid the table for dinner. Finishing reading them all, Jim rose from his seat, going down the steps into the kitchen; Elly, Peter and Brenda followed him.

'What can I say, guys. This is all fantastic. I'm just, so proud of you all. And, your mum too. It's bloody brilliant!'

'Thanks, Dad,' said Jimmy, 'dinner's almost ready.'

Jim had left the forms on the sideboard. He walked over to Jimmy first, giving him a massive hug. He did the same with Stan and Joe. Then he picked Peter up, saying, 'Singing as well, little man. Bloody fantastic!' whilst hugging him.

He turned towards Elly then. 'So, Elly, did you get a good report? I know you usually do, your dad tells me.'

'Yes, sir. I did. Got beaten for the first time by Pete. I think I've been helping him far too much, but not with the singing though!'

They all laughed as Brenda walked over to Elly, giving her a hug. 'Come on then, let's have dinner.

Jim, let's me and you get out of the kitchen. We're having dinner made for us tonight!'

'Okay.'

Going into the living room, the table was already laid, a jug of squash was there with glasses for all of them. Nothing for them to do, other than sit down and have dinner. Jim didn't bother getting changed, as nowadays his work clothes didn't get as dirty as they used to.

He turned to Brenda as she was about to sit down. 'Hey you,' he whispered in her ear so the kids couldn't hear him, 'you're fucking wonderful you are. Just got to tell you that. I love you, Mrs Johnson.'

'I love you too. You're not so bad yourself,' she said, quietly.

They kissed, then took their seats next to one another.

It was a lovely dinner, Brenda told them all afterwards. They were all chattering away. She didn't want it to end.

'Peter, it's getting late now. It's about time we walked Elly home,' said Jim.

'Okay, Dad. You ready?' he said, looking at Elly.

'Sure am.'

'We'll wash up, Dad,' said Joe, knowing they'd already agreed in the kitchen they would.

'You and Mum watch the telly when you're back, we'll sort it all out,' added Jimmy.

'Thanks, guys,' Jim said, getting up to leave with Peter and Elly.

When they returned, it was all tidy. Brenda told him that she'd said the boys can stay up late. It was school half term and a Saturday tomorrow, Jim being off too.

Easter came and went. The weather improved after months of bitter cold and snow. When they returned to school, Brenda went with them to go and see the headmaster.

6
A Job Offer

Walking Peter to school with Elly, Brenda carried on past, along with her other three sons, to their school, only a further hundred yards away. The letter asked her to come to school along with the children first thing on the first day of term.

Going into the playground, her three older sons said goodbye, meeting up with school friends, as she went directly into the entrance nearest the headmaster's office. Glancing at the letter, she continued up the stairs to the offices, where Mr Andrew Crawford, the headmaster, was waiting for her.

'Good morning, Mrs Johnson, thank you for coming. Welcome to our Croxton Secondary School,' he said, in a well-spoken voice, reaching out to shake her hand. He was a slim man, almost as tall as Jim, she thought, but much older, with a bald head and round glasses.

'Hello, Mr Crawford, good morning,' she replied.

'Shall we go into my office?' he asked, putting his hand out to usher her into the room. She nodded and smiled as she went in before him. 'Please, take a seat. I've asked for some drinks, if that's okay with you?'

'Oh, yes. Thank you.'

He sat down at his desk when they arrived, pouring for them both. 'Milk and sugar, Mrs Johnson?'

'Just milk will do, Mr Crawford.'

He smiled at her, passing the cup to her before speaking again. 'Okay. So, why did I ask you here? I'll try not to take up much of your time.'

'I am intrigued,' she asked.

'Well. You know that your three sons had pretty remarkable results in their half term tests. And your other son next door too, at his primary school. Quite splendid. I made a point of asking your three here, if there was any reason they'd improved so much. Their class teachers had all realised it, speaking together in the teachers' room,' he said, pausing to sip his tea before continuing. 'My colleagues told me they'd all said you had been home schooling them due to the inclement weather. So, I asked the boys, who confirmed this to be correct.'

'Yes, that's true. When I was a young girl, I used to keep the score for my father and his friends in the pub when they played darts. I was always telling them what they had left to finish the game, before they knew themselves!' she said, smiling.

He laughed out loud at her comment, saying afterwards, 'So that'll explain the improvement in all of their mathematics results. Seems they've all had their eyes and brains opened to an aptitude you've doubtless always had.'

'I wouldn't have put it like that myself; though I've always liked my numbers. Especially when I was at school myself. Never pursued it at all. I always used to work out my father's expenses, now my husband's and mine, every week. We met very young.'

'Jolly good. I'll come straight to it. What I'd like to know is, and if, would you be prepared to train as a mathematics teacher. There is a huge demand all over the country for teachers. Presently, it's a two year course. Do you have any formal qualifications in the subject, Mrs Johnson?'

She was taken aback by his idea. 'Err, well, no. I don't. It's not something I ever talk about. I didn't take the 11+. It was implemented when I was nearing the end of my education in 1944, I think.'

'You're correct there with the date. Spot on. Now, I'm aware that you're a mother, of course. This would take up two years of your time, though there is much time allowed for study, which you could do at home. Also, there is a college here in Manchester, so there'd be no need to travel. What do you think, Mrs Johnson?'

'It's a lovely idea, thank you. But… but, not practical. I'm pregnant with another child, so my time will be limited. I don't think I'd be able to afford the tuition fees I imagine are required. Maybe in a few years?'

'I know of a bursary, a type of grant, that would give you all the funding you need. It's available now and if accepted, you'd not need to start for up to seven years after the award is given. After what you've achieved with your sons in a very short space of time, I believe you could be a terrific teacher. Specifically in mathematics. What do you think?'

'Well, it's the sort of opportunity that could change our lives. This is quite a shock, Mr Crawford. I'll have to discuss this with my husband first, and my children. To leave it for up to seven years means nearly all of my children would have left school, other than the one I am carrying now.'

'I understand. Please give it some serious thought. By all means, discuss it with your husband. I'm aware it is a very big decision for you. Believe me, when I tell you, from what I've seen in your boys' results, you can do this. I will back you every step of the way. Being extremely selfish, I'd love to welcome you back here as a teacher. There is talk that our school, is going to be turned into a comprehensive and moved to bigger premises in a few years. I intend going nowhere until I retire, which is quite a few years away. This makes me aware of the need for good quality teachers. Like I said, please give it some serious thought.'

'I will. It's a very kind gesture, Mr Crawford. Thank you for even thinking of me.'

He stood up, going to the door, before continuing. 'My belief is that people like you do not come along very often, Mrs Johnson. You have time on your side. This can be, and is, a rewarding career. Thank you again for coming to see me.'

Brenda was up and out of her chair, shaking his hand as he opened the door for her. 'It may be a while,' she said patting her stomach, 'but I'll think long and hard about this. Thank you so much.'

'Good luck with your baby. I will wait for you to contact the school when you're ready. In the meantime, I will do all I can for Jimmy with the additional tuition.'

'That's wonderful. Goodbye, Mr Crawford. I will be in touch.'

'Please do. Goodbye for now.'

Leaving his office, she made her way across the now empty playground to catch the bus into town, before going home, knowing that this was a chance in a lifetime to do something for herself. But, with the children and being pregnant, it would be impossible right now, and maybe for the next few years. Still, she'd speak to Jim later.

When he came in from work and the boys were home, she discussed it with them. Jim had already known she was good at numbers, not realising how gifted she really was. The boys knew now, after their brief spell of home learning.

But, Brenda knew it wasn't possible. Not yet. She went to speak to Mr Crawford a few weeks later, to tell him she would apply, with his help, for the bursary. He was delighted. However, she could and would not take up the training for at least three years. It would not be a problem, he told her. The money would be sitting in an account waiting for her by then. That was that. She would become a teacher, with Jim's blessing... but not for a few years. That was the plan.

Plans change. One evening in early June 1963, when Brenda was almost eight months pregnant, everything changed...

7
Too Soon

After tea on this warm June evening, Peter asked to go round to Elly's to play, on his bike. Jim was working late on overtime. Yes, he could. Brenda forgot to tell him not to be late home, which he often was, always chatting with Elly. Jim would normally go round and collect him. Peter was as bright as a button, but never a good time keeper, she thought, laughing to herself.

Jimmy was out. Now fourteen, he'd a girlfriend, Dotty. The twins had gone up to the park with some friends; they were due back by nine o'clock before dark, so Brenda would go herself. She left a note on the front door, to let the twins know she'd gone round to collect Peter, just in case they arrived when she was out.

It was starting to get dark as she walked past the other houses in their street, seeing just three cars parked. Not many people had one. Going under the railway bridge, she turned right past the big grass bank, then right again towards the street Elly lived in. Then, it happened.

In the haze of day turning into night, Brenda walked on the path under the bridge before turning the corner to walk towards Elly's house. She didn't see him.

With no lights on his bike she thought she saw Peter riding straight at her! Trying to side step away as he got closer, she saw it was her son. But he hit her! He couldn't stop in time. Peter caught his mother with the handlebar of his bike as he tried to swerve off the path, knocking her over! Falling off the bike, which stayed on the path undamaged, he crashed to the ground, rolling into the road.

Brenda looked over at him, shouting, 'Get up, Peter, there's a lorry coming. Now! Run here!' Fear gripped her voice. She didn't think about herself, as she tried to struggle to her feet.

The lorry didn't see him as it sped around the corner. 'NO!' shouted Brenda. In that instant, Peter looked up, seeing his mother laying on the pathway. Looking back ahead of him as he lay on the road, was the lorry. He saw the driver smoking a cigarette, he was that close. It didn't look like the driver had seen him. Only one thing he could do…

He pulled himself up off the road knowing one of his legs was hurting like hell! Just one chance; he saw it.

The grass bank was a few feet away. He could jump. Hop and jump, just like in the game he played with Elly. It was all he could do with one leg. Jump Peter, jump, he shouted at himself, hearing his mother shouting like he never heard before.

'STOP! STOP!' Brenda shouted, waving her hands furiously while still laying on the ground.

One, two, three, four, he counted in his head, jumping to the numbers as fast as he could. Then, he fell onto the grass bank beside the path.

He heard a screech of brakes. The lorry driver must've seen him. The next moment, a man was pulling him up off the grass. 'You okay, little fella? I didn't see you until the last second!'

Peter said nothing for a few seconds. He stood on his good right leg, looking down at his left one. There was blood all over his knee. Looking back up at the man, he said, pointing in the direction of his mother, 'My mum, she's fallen, over there.'

'Okay. You sit back down, little chap, I'll be back in a moment.'

'No. I can hop over. I'm good at hopping.' It was all he could think to say.

The man left Peter and ran over to his mother, who was still on the ground.

'You okay, luv?' said the man.

'Not sure. Not sure. Is my boy all right?'

'Yep. He's hurt his leg, but I reckon he's otherwise okay.'

'Think I might need to go to hospital. I'm pregnant. I think the fall hasn't helped me.'

'Listen. There's a phone box at the end of this street. I'll call for an ambulance straight away. You stay there, don't move,' the man said, leaving her, racing to the phone box.

'Okay, thank you,' she said, as Peter hopped over to her.

'Mum, Mum! I'm sorry. I didn't see you until it was too late.'

'Hey, it's okay,' she said cuddling him, as he started to cry. 'It's not your fault. It was just an accident. Now go and collect your bike. The man in the van's gone to call for an ambulance.'

'Okay,' he said, hobbling over to his unmarked bike, Brenda waving him to return to her as she lay on the ground.

'Listen,' she said. 'When the man gets back, I need you to be brave. Really brave, okay? How's your knee?'

'Sore, Mum. I can be brave.'

'Good. Get on your bike, ride really fast. I want you to go fast this time.' She smiled at him, stroking his face before saying, 'Go home, see if Dad's back from work yet and bring him here really quickly. If he's not, get the twins to come here with you, straight away.'

Just then, the man, who had a flat cap on, came running back towards them. 'Called 999. Ambulance on the way. You're bleeding on your head, luv, I've got a handkerchief here, use that to stop the bleeding.'

'Thanks. Now go, Peter, go! Hurry back.' He nodded, jumped on his bike and sped out of sight.

'Is your little fella okay, lady, nasty gash on his knee there?'

'Should be okay I hope. He'll be back with his dad or brothers shortly. We only live around the next street.'

'Well, I'm going nowhere. Staying right here with you, lady. My name's Larry. Larry Williams. Sorry about this.'

It's not your fault. I'm Brenda. I should be thanking you for missing my son.'

'I could just see what he did. He saved his own life. Never seen a kid hop like that so fast in my life. Where the heck did he learn that?'

'Strange really. For some reason, he likes hopscotch. Never thought it'd be useful.' She tried to laugh, but he knew there was pain by the sound of her voice, as she sat on the ground now.

'Incredible kid. Look, you'd best stop trying to talk, err, Brenda. Just stay there. I told the 999 lady that you're pregnant, she said not to move you.'

'Okay, Larry. I'll be quiet. And thank you again.'

'Not a problem,' he said, smiling at her. 'I'll just go round the corner, see if it comes that way.'

She nodded, as he ran off, sitting on the ground leaning on one hand, in extreme discomfort. She had bad pains in her stomach. Now she'd been left alone for a minute or so, on the cold ground, it was getting dark all around her. She began to cry, knowing that it was too soon to have the baby. Wiping tears from her face, she could see in the dim light figures running towards her; it was Jim, followed by Peter and the twins.

'Oh, Jim, I'm sorry. I didn't see Peter, then the lorry!' She started crying again. He wrapped his arms around her as she sobbed.

'It's okay, Brenda. It's okay,' he said softly. 'It's nobody's fault. Peter told me some of what happened. You can explain it all later. Right now, we've to get you to hospital.'

Stan shouted, 'Here comes the ambulance, Mum!'

There was a police car following it up the road.

Larry came running back up the road again, pointing the ambulance in the direction of where Brenda was.

The driver pulled up, whilst the other guy jumped out of the passenger seat, running to the back of the vehicle, coming over with a stretcher.

The driver raced straight over, followed by the police officers, as the chap with the stretcher said, 'Hello. Bad fall by the looks of things. Are you dizzy at all, young lady?'

He must have been in his fifties, Brenda thought. It'd been a long time since she'd been called that. 'No, bashed my head on the ground. I'm pregnant, due in a few weeks. I've got a lot of pain all around my stomach and back.'

'Okay, let's get you on the stretcher to hospital as soon as we can. You the husband?' he said, looking at Jim.

'Yes,' said Jim, nodding.

'Come with us in the ambulance. Give us some information about your wife.'

'Yep, will do.' Jim said, turning to speak to their sons as one. 'Boys, go home, wait for Jimmy to arrive, he'll be home soon. Get yourselves ready for bed. Tell Jimmy we'll be at the hospital.'

'Okay, Dad,' they all said over one another's voices.

He hugged them all, as Brenda was lifted gently onto the stretcher and taken into the ambulance.

The police were having a conversation with Larry Williams as Jim walked over to them.' I owe you a debt of gratitude, sir,' Jim said to Larry.

'Not exactly. You've got a son there who could hop for England. I swerved to avoid him as he pretty much jumped on one leg away from my van. Never seen a kid move so fast in my life.'

'Well, thank you. And for looking after my wife, and calling an ambulance.'

'It's what anyone would do,' said Larry.

One of the policemen interjected then. 'Actually no, Mr Williams, it isn't. What you did was above and beyond what most people would do. Well done.'

'Thanks,' said Larry.

'We do need to take some details from you, Mr Williams, nothing to worry about at all,' said the police officer.

'Yep, sure thing.'

'Think you'd best be getting into the ambulance, sir,' the policeman said to Jim.

'Yes. Thank you, Officer. And thank you again, Larry,' Jim said, shaking his hand.

He nodded, as Jim turned away to get into the ambulance, which quickly sped off to hospital, as the police continued to question Larry Williams.

The boys had already gone home, as Jim got into the ambulance. 'You okay, luv?' asked Jim.

'Not sure. Don't feel too good, Jim, I'm scared.'

'Mrs Johnson,' said the medical chap, 'I'm Dr Davis. My driver is partly medical trained to assist me. We'll get you to hospital as quickly as we can, assess the damage to your head, and more importantly, check on your baby.'

'Okay,' she said, her voice trembling.

'I've a few questions to ask, whilst I examine you,' said Dr Davis.

She nodded.

'This isn't a regular request, but on a scale of say one to ten could you tell me how much pain you are in, with ten being the worst?' he asked, holding her stomach gently with both hands.

'Nine. It's absolute agony, to be honest,' she replied, wincing and glancing at Jim.

'And you are about eight months pregnant, right?'

'Yes.'

'I'm going to listen for the heartbeat now, if you can lay as still as possible.' He placed the stethoscope on her body for what seemed an eternity. 'Hmmm. Need to do that again I'm afraid.' He paused before adding, 'Right,' leaning over her, pulling the partition panel open to speak to the driver, 'quick as you can, please, Tom,' who nodded.

Feeling a burst of speed, Jim held on tightly to the rail in the back of the ambulance.

'What is it, Doctor?' he questioned.

'Not one hundred percent sure. Need to get to hospital as fast as we can to check. Your wife has lost some blood here,' he said pointing to the stretcher bed she was laying on. 'And fluid too. It's likely her waters have been damaged and broken in her fall.'

'And?' Jim shouted at him.

'Mr Johnson,' he said looking at Jim. Then turned towards Brenda. 'Mrs Johnson, it's very likely you'll be going into labour shortly. Early. We need to get you to hospital to the delivery ward.'

'But, I'm not due yet?' Brenda questioned.

'I know. That's why we must get there, to avoid upsetting you and the baby in case there are complications. I am trying to be as honest with you as I can.'

'Yes, I know that, Doctor,' said Jim. 'But will my wife and our baby be okay?'

'Let's get there first. Then we'll have the equipment that can let us know.'

'I'm feeling faint, Doctor, is that the loss of blood?'

'Yes, that's very likely. I'm going to put a drip in your arm now, Mrs Johnson, to give you fluids. Try and stay awake if you can.'

'Jim, I'm frightened,' she said, crying again.

'We're in good hands. We'll be there soon. Just try and stay calm, I'm not going anywhere,' whispered Jim.

She smiled at him, as the doctor put the needle in her arm to administer fluids. She was in pain, her face was contorted. Jim could see it. He hoped that Brenda was going to be okay. And the baby...

Brenda was rushed into the hospital when they arrived, with Jim at her side. 'Don't leave me, Jim,' she pleaded.

'I won't,' he said.

And he didn't. Over the next two hours, unknowingly, their lives would change forever...

8
Birth Time

When they got her into the operating theatre, after checking Brenda's abdomen for a pulse several more times, she had an idea that something was terribly wrong. She was induced by another doctor, although Dr Davis was there throughout. Two doctors, two nurses and an anaesthetist.

Pushing after an hour, Brenda began crying. Jim was holding her hand. It was rare for a father to be at the birth in 1963. But, he promised her he'd be there.

Within another half an hour, the baby was born. Naturally, just like her others. But there was no cry. No noise. No movement. Just silence.

'Where's my baby?' shouted Brenda. 'Jim?'

He looked at her, then Dr Davis. Jim knew. 'Brenda,' Jim whispered to her, moving his head from side to side.

'NOOO!' screamed Brenda. She put her hands over her face, sobbing.

'I'm so sorry,' said Dr Davis.

One of the nurses was holding the baby.

'C-c-can I h-hold the b-bab-y?' asked Jim, hardly being able to say the words, through a croaky, stuttering voice. The nurse nodded.

Brenda had taken her hands from her tear-stained face. 'Jim. I want to see. Please.'

Jim pointed the nurse towards Brenda, to hand the baby to her first. She kissed it on the cheek, knowing what it was, seeing her baby now, closely in her arms. 'Oh, Jim,' she said above the silence in the room. 'I'm sorry.'

He leant over her, kissing her forehead. No words came out of his mouth, as he cried. He stroked the baby's head. It had lots of black hair. Now he knew too.

She passed the baby to him after a few minutes. The doctors and nurses said nothing until the baby was in Jim's arms. He cried, uncontrollably then, just as Brenda was doing. 'Why? Why? It's not fair!' he shouted.

One of the nurses came over to him. He kissed the baby as the nurse stood in front of him, with her arms outstretched to take the baby.

'No,' Jim said quietly, turning to Brenda as she lay in the bed, sobbing. Stroking the little head of the baby, kissing the forehead, he passed it back to Brenda again.

They had another two hours together with the baby. That's all they had to say goodbye to their stillborn child.

A girl. Their daughter.

9

The Impact

In those two hours, they both felt the warmth of their little girl. They knew she was dead.

'What shall we name her, Jim?' sobbed Brenda, holding her.

Jim was sitting on a chair now, next to Brenda, still in the delivery room. He didn't know what to say at first, just sighing. Taking a deep breath, wiping his eyes yet again, he said, 'You know, I never thought of a name at all. I guessed it'd be another boy. Never dreamed we'd finally... you know... have a girl.'

She whispered back to him, 'Something different. I've had a name in mind for a while. Martha. Do you like it, Jim?'

'Perfect,' he said, quietly.

The nurse came back in then, asking them both if they'd like more time. She was very apologetic and sympathetic. 'Would you like to have a photograph with your baby?' she asked.

'Yes, we would, wouldn't we, Jim?'

He nodded in agreement, saying 'And c-can we take s-some hair?' stuttering through the words.

'Of course. I'll arrange for the resident chaplain to come in to see you shortly. We have a camera in the hospital. I'll fetch that as well. Would you like a drink?' she said.

'Please, yes. Thank you,' said Jim, who'd now stood up from his chair.

They didn't speak for a few minutes as Brenda continued holding Martha. 'Jim. Why us?'

'I don't know, I just don't know.'

'It's not bloody fair!' she shouted, crying again.

He leant over and stroked their daughter's face again as the nurse came back in.

'Here's some drinks for you both. Mrs Johnson, I've the camera here, would you like me to take a photo of you all now?'

'I know it sounds silly, but do you have a mirror, so that I can tidy my face a little please?'

'Of course. Sorry, I'll fetch one,' she said, leaving them.

A few more minutes later, she returned. 'Here you are. I've a hairbrush for you.'

'Thank you. Would you like to hold Martha for a few moments?' she said to Jim.

Brenda passed the baby to him, the nurse already having given him a mirror for his wife to use.

She did the best she could under the circumstances. 'That'll do,' she said, covering her hair over the cut on her head.

Jim passed Martha back to her in silence, as the nurse picked up the camera saying, 'Would you like one of Martha on her own first?'

'Aha. Please,' said Brenda, nodding.

She took two pictures of Martha on her own. Then two of Brenda with her, then two more of all three of them. They couldn't smile. A moment later, she pulled an envelope from her pocket. 'Would you like me to take some of her beautiful black hair?'

Brenda nodded again.

'Yes please,' said Jim, hardly being able to utter the words.

Taking the scissors from her pocket, she gently cut some hair from her head, placing it into the envelope, handing it to Brenda.

'Thank you,' she said, sighing loudly.

'I'll ask the doctor to come in shortly,' the nurse said, before turning to leave the room. Jim nodded, sitting back down in the chair.

When Dr Davis arrived, he explained what would happen. Death certificate. Release to the funeral parlour, who can arrange a service.

Jim wasn't really listening. He was, but none of it was sinking into his brain. When the doctor left, he asked if he could come back soon to take the baby. Brenda and Jim nodded, not speaking.

When he returned, he took Martha from Brenda, in silence.

They were alone now. No baby girl. She'd gone for good. Dr Davis told Brenda she must stay in hospital for a few days, to be checked over.

'Jim, the boys. You'd best get back home to them.'

'Yep, I know.'

'They'll put me on a ward shortly. You go, it's way past midnight now. I'm sure Jimmy would've sorted them all out, but all the same, you go. Come back in the morning. Go and get some sleep. There's nothing either of us can do now,' she said, stifling tears, with her voice croaking.

'Okay,' he replied despondently, stroking her face. Then he kissed her, saying, 'We'll get through this, won't we?'

'Yes, somehow, we'll find a way.'

'I'll find the nurse, check where you're likely to be. I'll be back in the morning once the boys are off to school.' She nodded, as he left the room.

Finding the nurse, she told him what ward Brenda was likely to be in. He'd be back in the morning. He saw the clock at the nurses' station; it was one thirty. What a fucking nightmare, he thought.

Leaving the hospital, knowing there'd be no buses at this time, he decided to walk home. Didn't want to speak to anyone. He thought about the last few hours of his life. Everything that'd happened. If he'd not worked overtime, Brenda wouldn't have gone to pick up Peter, who was fortunate with the lorry, though he'd hurt his leg. After knocking his mother over, maybe he deserved that. Jim told himself not to think that; Peter was his son. But, this thought ate away at his brain as he walked. It was Peter's fault…

Arriving home, Jimmy was asleep on the settee. 'Hey, Jimmy. Come on, son, time for bed.'

Rubbing his eyes, he said, 'Hey, Dad. Mum okay?'

'No, son. Well, yes, your mother's fine. Listen, I need to talk to you man to man. I'll tell your brothers in the morning. Are they all in bed?'

'Yep. What is it, Dad?'

'Difficult, Jimmy. Difficult,' he said, hugging his son as he got up from the settee, tears welling up in his eyes again.

Jimmy had never seen his dad cry. 'Dad. Sit down. What is it?'

'I have to tell you…'

Staring at his dad as they sat down, Jimmy raised his eyebrows, waiting.

'Bad news, son. The worst. When Mum had the accident, it hurt her badly. So much... so much that...' he had to say it. Taking a deep breath, Jim continued. 'It hurt the baby much more. Your mum is going to be okay. But, the baby. The baby, didn't make it...' Jim started crying again. Jimmy was open mouthed, before putting his arms around his own father. He began crying too.

They sat there not speaking for a minute or so, before Jim told his son the rest. 'Jimmy, after Mum was knocked over by Peter, you know she hurt her head. Well, like I said, she's going to be okay, I hope. But, she lost the baby due to the fall. It was an accident, we know that. We've just said goodbye to your sister. We've had some photos taken, not sure when we'll get them, but you'll all be able to see her. I'm sorry, Jimmy. She died,' he said with his voice hardly able to say the words.

'Fuck! No!' said Jimmy. 'Sorry, Dad.'

'That's... okay.'

'When can we see Mum?'

'I'm going back in the morning when you've all gone to school.'

'No, I'm coming with you, Dad. I'm old enough to understand this, y'know.'

Jim nodded, hugging his son again. 'Yep, I know. Right, let's try and get some sleep. Don't tell your brothers if they wake up. I'll tell them together in the morning.'

Going to bed, Jim couldn't sleep. He tossed and turned, thinking what if some things had been different. Waking at six o'clock, he walked round to the phone box to call work, explaining why he wouldn't be in today.

Telling the other boys was hard. They all understood. They all cried. He told them to go to school as normal and if anyone asked they should tell the truth. Martha, their sister, didn't survive. He'd take them to hospital to see their mum after school.

Getting on the bus, they arrived at the hospital going straight to the ward the nurse said Brenda would be in. She wasn't there. He found Dr Davis, who took him into a waiting room.

'Mr Johnson, I take it this is one of your sons, I can see the likeness.'

'Yes. What is it, Doctor?'

'After you left last night, I wasn't far behind you. Arrangements have been made with a funeral service on your behalf. There is no fee whatsoever, for your information. But, there is a further problem with your wife.'

'What is it now, Doctor?' said Jim, in a whisper.

'There are internal complications due to your wife's previously twisted cervix some time ago. I'm afraid that she has started bleeding overnight.'

'So what can you do?' Jim said, louder.

Jimmy was staring at his dad, waiting for the doctor to continue.

'I'll come straight to it. I believe the only way to avoid any further damage to your wife is for her to have a hysterectomy. You understand what that means, Mr Johnson?'

'Yes, no more children. And you need my consent. I've heard it's a big operation, is that right?'

'It is. Would you like to see your wife now? She's on a drip to keep her fluid levels up. She is aware of the requirement for the operation, though she is sedated at the moment.'

'Okay, let's go. Come on, Jimmy, you come too.'

'Follow me please,' said the doctor.

He led them into a private room. She looked pale in comparison to last night, saying, 'Jim? Jimmy?'

'Hey, Mum.'

'Dr Davis told me about the operation,' Jim said after kissing her.

'It's for the best, Jim,' she said in a slow, faint voice, with teary eyes. 'They need you to sign the form.'

'I know. I will. Just want you better and home.'

'It'll be several weeks I'm afraid, Mr Johnson, before your wife leaves hospital. We need to act as soon as possible. There is a possibility of blood poisoning if we don't,' said Dr Davis.

'I understand. Have you got the forms for me to sign, I'll do it now.'

'Yes, would you like to follow me, please?'

Jim nodded.

Jimmy was standing listening before he said, 'I'll stay with Mum while you sort that out, Dad.'

'Okay, thanks, son.'

They left to sort out the paperwork. Dr Davis told Jim it's likely the operation would be later today or tomorrow at the latest.

Jim asked if he could bring his other sons in to see Brenda before the operation, which the doctor agreed to.

Leaving the hospital after spending half an hour with Brenda, Jim and his oldest son went home, before going to the two schools to collect Stan, Joe and Peter. Peter's gashed knee was bandaged up by Jimmy when they got back to their house after the accident. It wasn't as bad as it looked. He was walking around straight away after, with just a sprained ankle.

They all saw her that afternoon.

The next morning, she had the operation. Jim had to organise leave from work. His boss said to take as long as he wanted; he would pay him for as long as he was off. Jim knew this was his boss's way of repaying him for all the overtime he did.

After the operation, Brenda was in hospital for three weeks before being allowed home. Her parents came to help Jim with the children, often staying overnight, Jim's mother visiting when she could to help out.

Coming home, there were strict instructions for Brenda. No lifting, no heavy work whatsoever. She was pampered by the boys, grateful for their help.

Jim arranged the funeral of Martha a month after Brenda came out of hospital. They had the photos by then. The nurse and Dr Davis came to the funeral, as did their sons, parents and close friends. It was not an easy day. Saying goodbye was the hardest thing Jim and Brenda had ever done.

But, it allowed them to move on with their lives. Knowing how tough it would be, they were blessed, Brenda said, having their boys.

Jim knew that the accident could have been avoided. Too many reasons why. The biggest of those, was Peter on his bike.

Try as he might, Jim couldn't get the image out of his mind, of Peter knocking his own mother over. It festered in him, when he returned to work.

For the first time in his life, he finished work before Christmas 1963, going to the pub with several of his work colleagues. They were all surprised, knowing he'd never touched alcohol.

It began a downward spiral for Jim. He enjoyed the alcohol he was drinking. A further promotion meant there was a little more money for the family and for him.

After Christmas, Brenda noticed a change in Jim. She bided her time, waiting a few months before confronting him…

10
Bad Attitude

It was a year since they'd lost Martha. This would be a difficult day, though their lives had returned to some sort of normality. Although they'd been sleeping together, there'd been no intimacy between them since losing the baby. It had been too difficult for Brenda, too painful. Maybe that's why Jim had started drinking, she thought. So, she waited until the school summer holidays to confront him...

'Jim. We need to talk.'

'I know.'

'Well? You've been so distant since... since we lost her. I get it that you want to drink to forget. God only knows I'd like to do that. It hurts me too, seeing what you're doing to yourself.'

'Yer, I know.'

'Come on. You have to shake yourself out of this! I mean, you haven't spent any time hardly with the boys like you used to. Especially Peter again, I've noticed.'

He was sitting on the settee with his head in his hands now. The boys were all out playing; Jimmy was at his girlfriend's.

'Say something, Jim!'

He looked up at her. 'Okay. Okay!' he replied, standing up before continuing. 'Drinking makes me forget. I'm sorry, but it does. It's become a habit. I like it.'

'You've got us. Your sons. Me. We need you!'

'You don't need me. You don't even want me! Do you?'

'Jim, you know why. After Martha, you know what happened. The hysterectomy. The pain I've had. It's still here,' she said, pointing to her heart.

'I feel it too!' he said, anger in his voice.

'Yes, I know. But you never talk to me about it! Please, we'll get back on track. Talk to me, Jim, like we always used to. I don't want this to break us up.'

There was silence for a few seconds before he spoke again. 'Right. Here's the thing,' he said rubbing his chin, calmer now. 'I know all that you've gone through. Wouldn't wish it on my worst enemy. I feel like I'm going through the motions. I can't see a light at the end of the tunnel any more. I used to want to grow old with you, I still do. But you're distant too. I don't mean sex either! You never ask me about work anymore. We've no time together, except when we go to bed at night. I need you, Brenda. I want the old you back.'

'Oh, Jim. My body's changed, I'm still getting used to it. The kids are growing up. Jimmy's likely to get a job soon, he's got an interview at that accountants in town, thanks to his maths work. We'll have time together. Let's make sure we do. I want to take them to Stanley Park and the beach in Blackpool, like we used to,' she said, almost pleading with him.

'Look. I'm trying my best at work, doing well. Might even be able to buy our house soon. I know I've been distant from the kids; since the accident, I've had this nagging feeling it was all Peter's fault. I know that's wrong, but I can't help it. I'm sorry.'

'Just try, Jim. I know you've struggled, I lost a daughter too. How do you think I feel? I'm empty inside. A part of me died with her. My heart was broken that day. I don't want it broken any more by you. Do you understand me, Jim?' she said, sobbing.

'I think so.'

'Do you? Do you really?'

'Yes! I do. It's my fault for working overtime that night. If I'd been home, I'd have gone to collect Peter. None of this would've happened. That eats me up every day. I have to live with that!'

'God, don't you think I know that. Stop feeling sorry for yourself. It's happened and we can do nothing about it now. Nothing!' Brenda was shouting at him, grabbing him by the arms, staring at his eyes.

'Okay. Okay!' he shouted back at her, putting his arms around her.

They both began to cry.

'Jim,' she said quietly through her sobs, 'talk to me. Please. I love you. Just give me some time, I don't know how long. But you've got to talk to me. I never want to go through anything like this ever again. Do you get me?'

Pulling his head away from her shoulder, he looked into her eyes. 'Yes. I'm sorry. I'll try and be a better father, I promise,' he said, with tears rolling down his cheeks.

'You've always been a good dad. Just try and spend more time with them, especially Peter.'

'I'll try. I will,' he replied, before kissing her.

'And one more thing… please, Jim. You don't have to stop, but cut down on drinking. You've been going to the pub nearly every night after work. I've noticed it on your breath, so don't try and deny it.'

He nodded. 'Sorry. I know. That's been my way of dealing with my feelings.'

'Talk to me. That's what we have to do, okay?'

'Okay,' he said, pausing, then added, 'how come you're always right?' smiling at her.

'Well, I'm a woman, we're always right!' said Brenda, smiling back at him.

He knew she was right as he kissed her again. She always was.

From that day, he changed, as did Brenda. They became the chatterboxes they used to be. That summer of 1964 was a good one for them all.

Jimmy started work at the accountants. With his help, they became one of the few families in their street to buy and own their house; the mortgage was only a little more than the rent they paid.

Stan and Joe continued to get into the school and county football teams. Jim couldn't have been prouder. And it didn't stop there.

Peter spent lots of time with Elly that summer, she was often around their house. Jim tried his hardest to forget the accident; but it was always there in the back of his mind, knowing their daughter was taken away by a tragic accident. He made the effort with Peter for years, sometimes crying in front of Brenda, as she did too, sometimes on his own. Would he ever get over losing Martha?

Jimmy moved out in 1968, getting married to his fiancée, Dotty. They'd been courting for years, since they were both fourteen. Jim hadn't drank for four years at all, until their wedding.

Stan and Joe were taken on as apprentice professional footballers at Middlesbrough, moving away to stay in digs initially, after their seventeenth birthdays in May that year.

When the twins left home, Peter was on his own. Jim tried his best to be a good father. It was a constant struggle. Peter was as tall as he was, though he was only fourteen, with dark hair just like his dad.

Leaving work on Friday the 20th of December that year, Jim, for the first time in years, went into the pub, having a Christmas drink, getting blind drunk. He didn't remember getting home, nor anything that happened when he did.

Brenda remembered. She told him the next morning when he woke. Somehow, he never got a hangover.

'You don't remember last night, Jim, do you?'

No. I don't,' he replied.

'Well, I'll tell you. It was awful. I told you about the drinking years ago!'

'Oh God,' he whispered.

'You pinned Peter up against the wall. Told him what you should never have told him. It was his fault we lost Martha. You're a bloody idiot, Jim!'

'Oh shit! I'm sorry. Where is he?'

'Probably still in bed. I had to pull you off him. He's your son for Christ's sake! You had him by the throat, he was terrified of you!' she shouted at him.

'I'm such an idiot! No more drinking, I promise you,' he said, getting out of bed to go to Peter's bedroom.

He wasn't there. It was the Saturday before Christmas.

'He's not there?' he said, coming back into their bedroom.

'Well find him!' she shouted.

Quickly he got dressed before going out in search of Peter.

11

All Alone

After his dad attacked him, saying what he did, Peter knew he wasn't wanted. He went to his bedroom, but didn't go to sleep. He couldn't get the vision of his father's face out of his mind: rage, anger, all being directed at him.

His mother said his father would be sorry in the morning. He was drunk, that's why he attacked him, she said. Peter's mother hugged him, told him that she loved him, as they went to bed after the altercation.

No way could he sleep. At eleven o'clock that night, Peter packed a bag with some clothes. He'd been saving his pocket money for no reason; now there was one. What could he do? It was impossible for him to stay in the house now, believing what his father felt towards him was not just a grudge, but hatred.

So, he crept downstairs after waiting an hour, making sure his parents were asleep, going to the sideboard drawer, taking his own birth certificate, knowing he may never come back. He would miss his mother. And his brothers.

Going out of the front door as quietly as he could, there was only one person he wanted to see. Elly.

Knowing which bedroom was hers, he went round to the back garden, throwing small stones up at her window. She looked out after a couple of minutes, as he waved for her to come down.

At the back door, he told her what happened.

'Look,' she said, 'it's the drink. That's all.'

'No,' whispered Peter. 'He's never wanted me. Since I was born, he wanted a daughter. He blurted it out when he had me by the throat. And when baby Martha died, he blamed me for the accident. I'm no good living there. I've got to go, Elly.'

'Oh, Pete. You can stay here.'

'No. I have to go. I just have to.'

'Where?' she said raising her voice.

'I don't know.'

'Let me know. I have to know you're safe, Pete?'

'Okay, I will. Wherever I am, I'll write to you. I'll always keep in touch with you, Elly.'

'You're bloody crazy, Pete Johnson, you know that, don't you?'

'Kind of always knew I was a bit of a weirdo!' he said, laughing.

'No, you're special,' she said, hugging him, kissing him on the cheek.

'My parents will wake up if you don't go. Dad's always been a light sleeper. Listen, let me know where you are. I won't tell anyone, I promise,' she whispered.

'All right. I will. Get in, it's bloody cold out here. Goodbye, Elly.' he said, turning away from her.

'Bye, Pete. Don't forget to write,' she whispered.

'I will,' he said as he turned away down the alley, waving to her.

Where could he go, he thought? Wandering into town, it began to snow. Reaching the bus station, he went inside. It was lucky he was tall for his age. Most people who met him thought he was a lot older than fourteen, with his black hair and deep voice. He thought about his mum; she always called him handsome. She'd be okay, he hoped. But the wrath of his father's temper meant he had to go; that's what was in his mind.

At the bus station, he looked up at the signs. Knowing he had to escape, there was only one place he thought was far enough away. Paying for his ticket, he had to wait another hour before it left. He was on his way to who knows where. No more school. He'd have to get a job. No turning back now. Sitting on the bus all alone, waiting for it to leave, he cried. There was no choice. The overnight journey would take him to a new start in life. He was on his way. To London…

12
No Streets Paved with Gold

When the bus arrived at London Victoria he got off, having been asleep for over four hours. It was almost daylight, with the big clock at the station saying seven o'clock.

Rubbing his eyes, he picked up a map that was laying on the floor. Where shall I go? Peter thought to himself. Looking at the map, he saw that Buckingham Palace wasn't far away. So, he decided to do some sightseeing. The building, when he got there, was massive. He'd seen pictures in books at school and on the television, but it looked bigger in real life. He'd never seen so many police officers in one place.

Strolling around, he began to feel hungry. So, leaving the Palace behind him, he went back to the station, getting a sandwich there and a coffee. He still had a few pounds in his pocket to last a while for food and drink.

Seeing a sign for the underground system, he asked a member of staff how to get a ticket. It was simple. After getting one, the map he'd found showed lots of different places he'd heard of, but never been to. He would investigate as much as he could today, travelling on the underground, finding different places to see, keeping out of the cold weather.

After using the underground system to see some of the sights of London, he remembered what his brother Jimmy had told him. He'd spoken about a place called Covent Garden. So, late in the afternoon, with darkness and snow falling, that's where he went to next.

There was an array of shops, with pubs and bars all around him. It was very busy, being a few days before Christmas; he'd never seen so many people, all rushing around.

People not much older than him were dressed in flowery clothing, both men and women. Nearly everyone was smoking. He could smell something strange in the air as he walked past many of the bars. It wasn't smoke, it was something else he'd never smelt before.

Reaching a large square, he saw some lights around a small stage. There was a man with a top hat on, dancing. He could hear the tapping of his feet as he got closer. At the side of the stage was a cap, with money in it. Peter realised that's how you can make money. He had no skills like the dancer, although his mum said he could sing; there was always hopscotch, he thought to himself and laughed! He'd have to learn something, or get a job.

As he wandered around for a few more hours with day turning into night, he became tired. He wasn't lost or lonely, he thought to himself, just alone. So, he found a side street away from the crowds, seeing a couple of people covered in cardboard to keep warm. That's what he'd have to do. Find some cardboard and wrap himself up with his other clothes in his bag.

After searching for a while, he found some cardboard, curled up in a ball to keep warm and fell asleep. He did the same thing for another couple of days and nights.

Waking up in the early hours of the morning, he knew it was a couple of days before Christmas Eve. Nowhere to go, other than to look for a job. Packing his bag with the clothes he'd laid over himself, he got up, walking into the first bar he came to. No jobs, he was told. Again, and again, it was the same answer.

He was about to give up, when he made his way to an area called Soho, late in the afternoon. Going into a club named Johnny's, which had red lights outside it, flashing that name, he was stopped by a man who was enormous.

'What you want, sonny?' the man said with a booming voice.

'Err, just looking for a job?'

'Not here, buddy.'

'Oh, okay.'

'Tell you what, wait there a mo. I'll get the owner, just had a thought.'

The giant man walked off into the darkness, through two big double doors, then another set of doors. Peter could just see a glance of lots of tables and chairs, all laid with cutlery. Must be a restaurant. He also saw a stage and a bar. Could be a nightclub, he thought to himself.

When he came back, the big guy had another man with him, smoking a big cigar. He was slightly smaller than Peter, stocky, with a mop of greying slicked-back hair.

'Hey there,' he said. 'You looking for a job, fella?'

'Yes, I am,' replied Peter, nervously.

'Okay. Come back here at six, got a job for you. It's only washing up in the kitchen, but if you show me you're keen, I'll keep you on. Tonight's just a trial, okay?'

'I'll be here. Thank you. I won't let you down.'

'I'm Johnny. Johnny Fenton. This is my club. You're in the right place at the right time, kid. How old are you?'

'Sixteen,' lied Peter.

'Good. You look older kid. What's your name?'

Better not tell him my real name, Peter thought. 'Paul, Paul Jenkins,' he lied.

Johnny thrust his hand out to shake his. 'Fine. Be here at six, like I said. Big Dave here'll show you where to go. You'll be busy,' he said, nodding at his colleague.

'Yes, sir. Thank you.'

Johnny turned and went straight back through the big doors, leaving Peter standing there with the man he knew now as Big Dave.

'Off you go then, kid, see you in a couple of hours.'

'Okay, thanks,' said Peter, turning away, smiling, thinking about his mum.

He'd got a job. Pleased with himself, he went and got himself a hot drink and a pie from one of the stalls back in Covent Garden. Then, when time had gone by, he went back to the club at six o'clock, like Johnny had said.

13
Johnny's

He was taken into the kitchen, still carrying his own bag of clothes. 'Can I leave my bag somewhere?' he asked Big Dave.

'Sort that out with one of the kitchen guys; Terry over there can help you with that,' he said before shouting, 'Hey, Terry! New kid here. You want to show him the ropes; he's trialling tonight.'

Terry came over, thrusting his hand out to Peter. 'I'm Terry, let's get rid of your bag, then we'll get you started.'

He wasn't as tall as himself, having short blond hair, dark rimmed glasses and looked older than he did, Peter thought. Terry showed him around the kitchen; it was enormous, having two sinks. Worktops were all around it. In the middle was a giant island, with more food on it than he'd ever seen.

'So,' Terry said, 'what's your name, kid?'

'Paul,' Peter replied, lying again.

'Well, let's see how you go. It's hard work, I can't deny that, fella. You'll be on your feet washing up until about midnight, maybe later. You can have a drink and something to eat when we finish. There's rubber gloves there. I suggest you use them,' he said pointing to a box on a shelf.

'Okay, thanks. I will.'

'Right, also, you have to make sure the water is always hot. I don't mean burning your hands hot, but when the water gets dirty or cooling down, change it. The boss hates dirty plates or cutlery and he'll let you know about it!' he said, raising his fist, laughing.

Peter wasn't sure if he was joking or meant he'd be in trouble, maybe getting hit. Knowing what that was already like back at home, he didn't ever want that again, nodding at Terry.

'Once you've washed up a batch of plates, bowls and cutlery, put them over there,' Terry said, pointing to a worktop a little way away from the sink. 'Once you've filled that up, dry them all, then put them over there, piled up neatly, with cutlery going in the pots there,' he said, pointing to another section of worktop, before adding, 'right, you're on your own, kid. Last fella doing this lasted two weeks. Nobody likes this job, it's shitty! Give it your best shot, okay?'

'Terry, I want to work. I'll do my best,' Peter replied.

Leaving him to it, Terry told him he's the head chef, pointing to his white hat on his head. At one corner of the kitchen were the double doors. Terry went through them, then through another set, which Peter guessed led to the restaurant and bar area.

For the rest of that evening, he never stopped until one o'clock, and didn't complain. Nobody spoke to Peter other than Terry to check up on him every hour or so. There were two other guys cooking as well as Terry. Both said hello, rushing around all evening. Peter lost count of how many waitresses came in and out. Not one waiter, he thought, only women.

At the end of the night, with the food area being cleared away, he was finishing off the rest of his job, when Terry came over. 'Well done, kid. Got to be honest, didn't think you'd keep up with all this. You want a drink? Something to eat?' he said, pointing at the array of food still there. 'Mostly it'll be chucked out. Bloody shame, but there you go. The punters pay top whack for this you know.'

'Yes, please. You sure I can help myself now?'

'Yep, you deserved it. I'll tell the boss you done a good job, ask him to take you on, even though you're a youngster.'

'Thanks.'

'Right, pile a plate up, help yourself to any drink you want over there. Have to wait a while to see the boss, he's still with some punters. Get a few famous people in here, y'know.'

'Really?'

'Yep, we get to meet them sometimes; they ask to see the chef, me, if they've had a cracking meal.'

'Blimey!'

'Go on then, get stuck in. Fill your plate up, before it all gets thrown out,' Terry said, smiling, putting his hand on Peter's shoulder, before going through the sets of double doors.

So, Peter sat with a plate full of all sorts of food, filling his face, washing it all down with two mugs of coffee.

Going back to the rest of the washing up, he finished, as Terry returned. The other chefs had already left at one o'clock. It was nearly two now, as Peter had another yawn.

'So, can you make it back here every evening at six? Five nights a week to start. We don't normally open on Sunday or Monday. But, it's Christmas, so we're opening specially this week. Told Johnny you did well. Keep it up and you'll have a job for as long as you want it, okay?'

'Great, thanks. I'll be here.'

'Okay. Nice one, kid. Monday tomorrow, the twenty-third. Nearly Christmas. Get yourself going. Johnny always pays us cash on a Friday every week, unless you've been here years like me, then you get a cheque each week.'

'That's fine by me,' said Peter, smiling.

'Right off you go then. See you tomorrow. It'll be easier the next couple of nights, it's Christmas party time here, only selected guests.'

Reaching out to shake Terry's hand, Peter said, 'Thanks again, Terry.'

'No problem, kid,' he said smiling, turning to go back into the club.

Peter walked out of the side door, collecting his bag on the way, not daring to follow Terry into the club itself.

He found some more cardboard that night, putting all his extra clothes on underneath his jacket. It was a very cold night. At least he'd had some hot food. That'd last him until he went back to work, he thought, hoping he would be able to eat every night. And he'd found a rubbish skip to sleep in with an old canvas sheet covering his cardboard.

The next couple of days flew by. Then everything changed when he went to work on Christmas Eve at the club…

14
What a Boss

On Christmas Eve, the club closed at midnight. It was easier work as there were only a few guests, like Terry had said. He'd found out that Terry lived above the club; there were rooms above it.

Johnny came into the kitchen, with a bottle of champagne at midnight. 'Right, kid,' he said. 'Seems we've got a bit of a problem.'

Peter was scared. He was slightly taller than Johnny, but knew he didn't have the strength of a grown man yet, like his dad.

'Err, sorry, boss. I thought I'd been doing okay?'

'Relax,' said Johnny. 'Get three glasses from the cupboard, you know, the flute type, so we can drink this bottle between us. Leave that washing up for a minute,' he said, winking at Terry who was sitting at the island table already.

He knew already they'd all started calling him "the kid". Peter liked it: he hoped they wouldn't have to know his real name.

Johnny opened the bottle, handing it to Terry to pour.

'Right, kid. Cards on the table. You tell me the truth now, I'll help you. You lie to me, I'll have the shit kicked out of you, understand?' Johnny said, with a stern look on his face.

Peter was scared; more so than when his dad pinned him up against the wall a few days ago.

'Terry, tell him about yourself.'

'Okay, boss.' Then, Terry told him how he'd been helped years ago, by Johnny. He'd lost his parents in the war. Johnny took him in; helped him train as a chef.

Terry didn't look as old as his own parents, maybe in his late twenties, Peter guessed. Johnny was older, maybe in his forties or early fifties.

'Listen,' said Johnny, when Terry had finished. 'This is your chance to come clean. I always have eyes on the street, so tell the truth. Right now!' he said, almost shouting at Peter.

Peter took a deep breath, feeling really scared. If he told them who he was they might take him back. Got to be honest, he thought to himself. He looked at Terry, then Johnny, taking a deep breath, before speaking.

'I came here from Manchester a few days ago. I've been sleeping wherever I can. My dad attacked me, so I ran away from home. I can't go back; he doesn't want me. Nobody knows where I am,' he said, wiping his eyes.

'Carry on, kid, there's more, isn't there?' questioned Johnny more quietly now, sipping his drink.

Taking a big swig of his glass, Peter continued, knowing he was crying. 'There was an accident, I knocked my mum over on my bike. I was only eight at the time. She lost the baby, a little girl. I've three older brothers, they all live away from home now. My dad was always distant towards me.' He stopped, knowing his voice was wavering badly, hardly being able to say the words, taking another deep breath before continuing. 'He was drunk when he went for me the other night. He told me it was my fault, Mum losing the baby… I had to leave. My real name's Peter Johnson, and I'm fourteen years old.'

Johnny got up from his chair. He waved his hand upwards, for Peter to get out of his chair. Peter got up, backed off, scared again.

No words were said as Johnny walked over to him, slowly embracing him. He was crying, couldn't stop, until Johnny spoke. 'You're a really brave young man, kid. Takes bottle to do what you did. You want to go back? I can help, if you want?'

'No, I can't. I'm sure he hates me,' Peter replied, his voice croaky.

'Well, think about it. I can help if you want me to,' said Johnny, who'd released his embrace by now.

'No, I can't. He'd take it out on me. It's better I stay away, especially for my mum's sake.'

'Okay. Thanks for being so honest. Now sit down, drink some more of this champagne. Probably the first time you tasted it, eh?' Johnny asked, smiling.

Peter smiled back, wiping his eyes again. 'Actually no. My oldest brother got married earlier this year, tried it there. Quite nice.'

'Terry, tell him what's going to happen.'

'Big Dave saw you at Covent Garden, climbing out of a skip. We know you've been sleeping rough but didn't know how long. Okay for me to tell him, boss?' Terry asked, with Johnny nodding at him, before he continued. 'We've got rooms upstairs. One of them is yours for as long as you want.'

Johnny put his hand up to stop Terry talking.

'Terry's been here years. Rent free. He's loyal and honest. Seems you might be the same, kid. So, you've got a room upstairs to stay in. Gratis. Free. You'll still be paid the same amount, I deduct nothing for you sleeping here; it's good for me to have someone on site,' Johnny said, before sipping his champagne again, adding, 'furthermore, show me you'll work hard, I'll see what I can do. Terry started off just like you. What do you say, kid?'

Peter was struck dumb. He couldn't speak for a few seconds. This was amazingly generous. Finally, he said. 'Johnny, boss. Terry. Thanks. I won't let you down. I promise.'

'That's all I want to hear,' said Johnny.

'Yep, me too,' said Terry, getting off his stool, putting his arm around Peter.

'Right then. It's Christmas Day, just,' said Johnny looking at his watch. 'Merry Christmas, you two. Terry, can you show the kid, Peter, to his room? I'm going home to my wife. You two have got a day off. We're opening Boxing Day, so see you then.'

'Sure thing, boss. Think we'll keep the name "kid", don't you?' asked Terry.

'Hmmm, yes. I like it. Terry, help yourself to a drink in the bar. You know I trust you. Make yourself at home, kid.'

'Thanks, boss. Merry Christmas to you too,' said Peter, stretching out his hand to shake Johnny's.

'Yes, merry Christmas, boss,' repeated Terry.

Johnny smiled and nodded, shaking Terry's hand. Turning away, he left the club through the double doors. Terry and Peter went into the club, Terry getting some bottles of beer, as they heard Johnny lock the outer doors to the club. Terry went to check that it was locked. He always did.

'Come on then, I've got a little telly in my room. We can see if there's anything on still. I know you're under age, kid, but you look a lot older. You can have a drink if you want to; it's up to you. We get coppers in here, so the boss knows we've got nothing to worry about on that score.'

He led Peter to a doorway off from the kitchen, going up two flights of stairs. There must've been about six rooms. 'Entertaining and meetings some nights up here,' Terry said as they walked down the corridor. At the end there was another door, leading to more stairs, which they climbed.

Showing him his room, he saw a bed, wardrobe, chair, bedside cabinet and a radio. 'Wow!' Peter shouted.

'Not bad, eh?' Terry said, continuing, 'Come on, let's go to my room, have a drink. Then crash out. I'll take you around some haunts I know in London tomorrow. That okay with you, kid?'

'Brilliant. Thanks, Terry.'

'Honesty is the one thing the boss asks for. We knew you'd come from up north, because of your accent. And, you smelt disgusting. I guessed you'd been sleeping rough, told the boss. No need to worry, he'll look after you, like he did me,' Terry told him, smiling.

Peter nodded, before Terry added, 'Right,' opening a couple of bottles of beer for them, switching the television on, adding, 'let's see if there's anything on the telly, shall we?'

'Thanks, Terry,' Peter replied. He'd never expected this; he'd broken down in front of them. Now, he had hope… a job and a roof over his head.

From that day on, he became part of Johnny's working family, whose wife Ruth often came to the club. They had no children of their own, Terry told him. His club and his wife, were his life, along with his niece Helen and her parents. Because Peter didn't want his father to find him, he asked them all to use his other name, Paul Jenkins. Johnny told him, no need. Everyone at the club will call him "the kid".

Johnny treated Peter like a son, just the same as he did Terry. For the next four years, he worked in the kitchen, mostly washing up. It was busy, but he was young, handling it well, helping the chefs in the kitchen sometimes. Terry couldn't believe he knew how to bake cakes. Peter told him his mum taught him and his brothers when younger. Terry showed him lots of places in London. It was always busy, working or going out on the odd night themselves, when the club was closed. They became the best of friends.

Peter wrote a letter to Elly in 1970. He couldn't face doing it before then, asking her not to let his parents know where he was, but said he would write to her again.

It was another three years before he put pen to paper again, after turning nineteen years old, in 1973...

15
Helen Armstrong

Christmas 1972 came and went. The following spring, Johnny told Peter there was a vacancy coming up behind the bar, in the club, as their barman was emigrating. He'd already started helping Terry in the kitchen cooking with the other guys. That's because they hired a girl named Helen as their washer up. Peter showed her the ropes. He liked her, a lot. She was tall, slim, with blonde hair, and had freckles. She was Johnny's niece, Terry informed him. Don't go there, was the warning. But, Helen had other ideas as well.

With Peter working in the bar now, he didn't see as much of Helen as he liked, but they flirted with one another when they could. Johnny arranged a taxi home for her every night, until she turned eighteen in the summer. When she passed her driving test, her parents bought her a car. After a party – no invite for Peter – on a Sunday in August, she turned up at the club the next day. Big Dave was there working the door, letting her in, even though the club was closed.

She went straight up to the rooms above. Johnny wasn't there. Knowing where Peter's room was, she knocked on his door. Helen was nervous.

Opening the door, Peter, who told her his false name of Paul Jenkins, stood open mouthed, dressed in shorts and T-shirt, listening to the radio. 'Hey there,' he finally said. 'It's the birthday girl. How you doing?'

Everyone had got used to his humour. They all called him "the kid" still, except Helen. She called him Paul: his false name.

'Listen,' she said, nervously. 'I've got my car outside. You've got a day off. My parents want to send me to university; I don't want to go. I need to talk to someone. That's you. I also know from my Uncle Johnny who let it slip last night, you're a man of mystery.'

'Err… well. C-c-come i-in,' stuttered Peter.

'No,' she replied. 'Get yourself dressed, or are you coming out like that?'

'Err, yep, like this,' he said slipping his trainers onto his feet. 'Let's go then.'

'And stop saying "err". I know you're nervous, so am I. Come on,' she said, smiling, leading the way out of the corridor, down to the car.

Peter didn't say a word. Big Dave winked at him as he walked out of the club's main entrance.

'Like my car?' she asked.

'Yep, it's great.'

'Get in, we're going away for the day. Lots to talk about.'

'Oh, right?' he said, climbing in. 'This is nice.'

'Yes, Mum and Dad got it for my birthday. It's a Ford Escort. They said I had to get used to driving before getting something bigger.'

'Well, this is lovely,' he said, admiring the bright red colour. 'Brand new?'

'Yes, it is. Right, put that seat belt on, we're going to the coast. And turn the radio on please,' she said, starting up the engine. It was a soft top, with the roof already down.

She smiled at him, as she drove off, putting her sunglasses on. He'd no idea where they were going, as he sat listening and singing along to the music.

'Good voice,' she said after driving for almost an hour.

'Thanks. Always liked singing at school; Mum always said I had a good voice,' Peter replied, smiling at her.

The wind was blowing around the car, as she shouted, 'Wait till we get there, I'll tell you what I want to talk about when we arrive!'

Nodding, he felt apprehensive about what was going on; had she found out who he really was? They sat in silence as she drove, until they reached their destination after a couple of hours, at the beach.

'Bognor Regis?' he questioned, when they finally parked.

'Yes. My parents have a flat here. I told them I was going to have a couple of days here with a friend. I led them to believe I was taking Kate, she's my best friend.'

'Oh. I'm honoured then?'

'Yes, you are. Now, out of the car. We're going to the beach. I've got a picnic in the boot for us.'

All he had on was his shorts and T-shirt. It was a lovely sunny day as they made their way to the pebbled beach.

'Right. I'll pour the tea, mister! The champagne might come later!' she said, smiling again. 'You put the food out.'

There was a silence whilst they did this. Peter listened to the crashing of the waves. Apart from the canals in Manchester, and the odd day at Blackpool, he'd never been to the seaside, other than a stroll around the Thames.

'This is great. I can smell the freshness and salty sea air,' he said, sniffing loudly.

'Good. Now, eat. Have a drink; then we'll talk.'

'Oh, okay,' he said, remembering not to say "err" to her.

After ten minutes, she spoke. 'Right. Listen first. I said I don't want to go to university. Never have. Uncle Johnny wants me to learn everything about the business; he says I'm like the daughter he never had. I've argued with my parents. That's why I wasn't at the club Saturday night.'

'I see.'

'Well, thing is, they all started drinking at the party last night at home. Uncle said the offer is still there for me. But I have to decide what I want, not what my parents want. He's a forceful guy, as is my mother, his sister.'

'And?'

'Uncle said I'd have to work hard to learn everything. I'm feisty like him and my mother, I know that. These couple of days are for me to make my mind up. But, there's a bit more to it than that.'

'There is?'

'Yes. He told me, Mum and Dad, about you last night. He was drunk and blurted out your name is not your real name. Said he took you in a few years ago. I want to know where you're from. And who you are? So start talking,' she said, lowering her eyebrows.

He could see how serious she was. Recalling what Johnny had said to him years ago, he was more grown up now and could handle his emotions better. But this would still be hard, he thought. Here goes… Taking a deep breath, he began. 'Okay. My name's not Paul Jenkins. It's Peter Johnson, but they all call me "the kid". Other than you. I ran away from home a few years ago – 1968 to be exact, and Johnny gave me a job. I've been working and living at the club ever since.'

'Why?'

'Bit of a long story there.'

'Tell me, please,' she said, staring at him, speaking quietly now.

'I lived in Manchester. Got three older brothers. When I was eight, there was an accident… I knocked my mum over on my bike, nearly got run over myself by a lorry; she was heavily pregnant.' He stopped for a moment, taking a deep breath before adding, 'Years later when I was fourteen – the night I left – my dad told me it was my fault she lost the baby; a girl he always wanted. He threatened me. I was… well, terrified. If Mum hadn't stopped him, I reckon he'd have beaten the shit out of me. So, I left.' He stopped again, his voice trembling. 'My brothers had all left home by then. The night it happened, I saw a friend, the only one I really had: Elly. Told her I was running away. It's been five years now. I've written to her once three years ago. I can't go back. He hates me,' he said, putting his hands over his face, stifling tears.

'Thank you, Peter Johnson. Nice to meet you. My turn again,' she said, brushing her hair out of her face, then putting her hand on Peter's arm.

'Okay, go on then,' he said, quietly.

'I will be running the club. That's what I want to do. It'll take a few years, Uncle said.'

'I guess it would.'

Helen took a deep breath herself, before saying, 'However, I am interested in something else. That's you. I know when I started, Uncle tried to keep us apart, moving you into the bar and club. I know why now. He probably thinks you're not worthy of me. Well, I don't care about what he, or my parents think. We're staying in the flat over there, just off the beach, tonight,' she said, pointing to a block of apartments not far from the beach.

'Oh. Oh, I see. Err. Oops! Know you don't like that word!' he said, laughing at her.

Laughing, she got to her knees. 'Listen, I've fancied you since I first met you. You've always flirted with me since I met you. I don't want to flirt any more,' she said, leaning over, kissing him.

'Nice!' he said as their lips parted.

'Is that all you can say?'

'Not exactly!' he replied, putting his arms around her, pulling her onto the pebbles, before staring into her eyes, lying next to her. Then he kissed her, closing his eyes.

A few seconds later, she smiled and said, 'Let's finish the picnic, then go into town, have a look around before we go to the apartment.'

'My first time on a beach and I get snogged. How good is that!' he laughed.

Then, she kissed him again. 'The kisses won't stop if you play your cards right, Mr Johnson!'

He continued smiling, saying nothing, sitting up. They both ate some more food, before putting everything away in the basket, returning to her car.

After strolling through the town, they went to the apartment. It was a two-bedroomed place, with a balcony overlooking the sea. They had a couple of drinks there, as the sun went down.

Shortly after, knowing the only clothes he had were the ones he was wearing, Helen went for a shower, leaving him sitting watching television. Returning, she had a nightie on and was ready for bed.

'Look,' he said. 'I know I'm a little older than you, but I've got a confession. Honesty's the best policy, right?'

'Only by about a year. What's the confession then?'

'Well, apart from having no… no protection, I've never… never had sex. Been waiting for the right girl to come along.'

'Good. Well, we're in the same boat, apartment, then!' she said smiling at him. 'And no need to worry, I'm on the pill, as of a couple of months ago.'

He turned the television off, walked over to her and kissed her, as she took his hand, leading him into the bedroom.

After a night of passion with Helen, he knew already that he was in love with her. He'd got to know her working at the club; he'd always fancied her, just like she did him.

Waking up in the morning, he was naked lying in bed. She leant over, kissing him, pulling him on top of her.

When they'd finished, he decided to tell her how he felt as they lay there. 'I love you, Helen.'

She snuggled into him again, before saying, 'I've waited a long time to get you. I'm not letting you get away now I know who you really are. And I love you too, Pete Johnson.'

He held her in his arms, before deciding to go and make a drink for them.

When they eventually got dressed it was midday. She took him to a small café, where they had breakfast. 'Got to keep your strength up you know!' she said smiling and laughing at him, as they devoured the meal.

Going to the car, it was another sunny day on the Tuesday, when they had to drive back to London for work.

'I'll drop you off so you can get changed for work, okay?'

'Thanks.'

'But do something for me soon, Pete?'

'What's that?'

'Get in touch with your mother, or Elly. You should let them know you're safe, well and above all, alive. I get it that you don't want to see them, well your dad; but your mum must be living in hell not knowing.'

'Okay, I will. I'll write to Elly. I can't tell them where I am though. I don't want to see him. He'll rake it all up again. I've got my own life now, with you.'

'We'll tackle my family together. Yes, you have got me. I've found the one I want in you,' she said, smiling at him.

Leaning over, smiling, then kissing her as she turned the key to start the engine to drive back, he said, 'Yep, me too. Me too.'

By the time he got around to writing to Elly, it was almost the end of the year. When they confronted her parents, they weren't happy. She told them everything about Peter. Johnny knew they were smitten with one another from the first day she arrived at the club. He tried to keep them apart, with the taxi every night until she passed her driving test. And, although there was a vacancy that he gave to Peter in the bar, he knew it may not keep them away from one another.

But, Peter did so well in the bar with his comic turns and jokes with all of the "clients" as Johnny called the customers, he knew he was onto a winner with "the kid". Everyone liked him. He was tall, handsome, but never flirted with any of the clients; not to Johnny's knowledge anyway.

So, he knew they'd gone away in Helen's car as Big Dave called him when they left the club together. He said nothing to her parents, who told Johnny that she'd gone away to think things over with her friend, Kate. The boss, of course, knew otherwise.

The pair of them, with Johnny's and his wife Ruth's help, got her parents' seal of approval. For the next two years, the club continued to be Peter's life. He still lived in the room above, Helen stayed at her parents'. They made time for one another on their days off. Whilst working together, they kept it professional. Her parents allowed them to go to Bognor whenever they wanted; they both loved the tranquillity of it, away from the hustle and bustle of London and its night life.

Peter, working behind the bar, always cracking jokes, still saw Terry as much as possible. Terry got himself a girlfriend, Alice, getting married in 1975, asking Peter to be his best man. It was a no-brainer: of course he'd be his best man. They had a quiet wedding in a registry office, telling Johnny he didn't want a fuss. Johnny honoured Terry's wishes, but he told him there was something he was going to do; put a deposit on a house for him and Alice. Terry had no choice, but to say yes!

Helen was replaced in the kitchen after advertising for two staff. She'd told Johnny it was too much for one person. How Peter had put up with it for years before she took over, was beyond her! The boss agreed, and they split the job in two. She suggested the club opened earlier at five until seven p.m., to attract "the suits" as she called them. He knew what she meant: people in the city who liked a drink before going home. They set up a separate bar area inside the front doors, especially for this time slot from Tuesday to Thursday only.

The two staff taken on for the kitchen doubled as bar workers for this time slot. It closed at seven p.m. sharp, Big Dave made sure of that. This meant that the main club and restaurant opened later at seven thirty p.m. on those days. Helen told Johnny and Peter they were making more money this way. Knowing how the kitchen ran already, she worked behind the bar, training alongside Peter, thanking Johnny for giving her the chance.

And, she helped with the accounts; even getting Peter involved, after he told her how his mum had home schooled him for a while, when he was eight.

A couple of times a year, Johnny and his wife drove to the Kent coast to catch a ferry. He'd heard about giant duty free shops in Calais, France. It gave them big savings on drinks, especially spirits. He'd taken Helen a couple of times, but couldn't take Peter until he got himself a passport. So, after he got his driving licence, having his proof of birth, the only document he took when leaving home, he got a passport in his real name. Peter and Helen took over the trips, but stopped in late 1975 after Johnny received a tip-off from one of his police clients. Clubs were being raided all across London. So, the trips stopped, as Johnny decided to go legit.

Johnny didn't take a back seat; he was mostly "front of house" as he called it. It was still his club; but he knew that as he was fast approaching sixty years old, he needed a replacement. Helen was that person, but she needed time, a couple of more years to get to know the "clients" and how to deal with their personal needs.

The one thing she had to know about was discretion. Peter had got to know many famous people who came into the club, but he never spoke about them outside of it. This is what he had to get

Helen to understand; which she would, with Peter's help. Although he was a joker, Johnny trusted "the kid" implicitly.

16
A Change of Job

After Terry's wedding at the end of 1975, there was another job vacancy that arose in the club, through unfortunate circumstances.

Johnny had a resident band and singer who spent three nights a week at the club. There was a comedian as well on another night, and also a drag artist.

He kept the same format for which nights they worked. Some weeks, he'd tell the band to have a break, then the comedian and drag artist would get extra work; and he got other acts to come in on Saturday nights, well-known ones.

Not long before Christmas in December on a wet and windy afternoon just outside London, a man was driving towards the club. He was the drag artist, Tommy Blythe. It was his first night back at work, as he'd asked for a week off which Johnny agreed to. Heavy rain was pouring down as he parked his car a few roads away from the club, near Carnaby Street.

He was well known, being a slight man in his late forties and going bald, still dressing in effeminate floral clothing. He was openly gay.

Getting out of his car, he saw a group of men coming out of a bar. He crossed the road to avoid confrontation. It didn't work. They followed him, as he picked up speed, running, turning towards the club, still two streets away.

Tommy was scared; he'd been the victim of what was called "queer bashing" a couple of years before with plenty of verbal abuse. Now, he looked over his shoulder, seeing the gang almost upon him. It looked like there were five or six of them, all white men.

He fell to the ground after being punched in the back, curling up in a ball. They shouted obscenities at him, as he cowered on the pavement. 'You fucking poof! Gay arsehole! Bender!' Tommy held his head in his hands, as they rained kicks and punches down on him.

After what seemed an eternity, he heard a whistle. There was one final kick to the back of his head, the last words he heard being, 'You fucking scum!' The whistle was from a policeman.

Tommy was unconscious. He wouldn't come round for two days. The policeman knew him. Everyone knew him in Soho; he wouldn't hurt a fly.

When an ambulance arrived to take him to hospital, the policeman went straight to the club. He found Johnny there, telling him what had happened, suggesting it might've been to do with a television show aired recently called *The Naked Civil Servant*, as there'd been incidents all over London like this.

Johnny was livid. He didn't care that Tommy was gay; he was his friend. The club opened that night; he managed to get another comedian to stand in.

That evening, Johnny was at Tommy's bedside, also going back the next day.

The day after, Tommy's partner Ken was there when he awoke, before Johnny and Ruth arrived, telling them his injuries: broken ribs, a fractured skull, internal bruising and a broken leg. Johnny knew it was likely he'd never work again, saying as they went to his bedside, 'Hey, Tommy. You took a real kicking. You know what I'll do if I ever find the bastards.'

Tommy put his hand out to him. 'No. You can't do that, boss.'

'Yes I fucking can!'

'No, please,' said Tommy, quietly. 'They've no idea what they did. Just let this one go, you'll never find them.'

'Look, you're one of my best friends, Tommy. I have to do something,' said Johnny, spitting the words out through a croaky voice.

'Do nothing. Not now. The police probably haven't got any clues. Let them investigate, go through the right channels. You've got coppers who're clients, remember?' said Tommy, stumbling over his words.

Johnny scratched his chin, glancing at his wife and Ken before saying, 'Good point. Good thinking. Anything you want, Tommy, you've got it, okay?'

'Thanks, boss.'

'Just get better, my friend,' said Johnny, in a hushed voice.

'When I came round earlier, the doc said I'd be here a while. Think you'll have to get a replacement, don't you?'

'Seems that way,' said Ruth. 'As Johnny said, we'll do anything for you, Tommy, you've been with us so long. You know you're like family to us, don't you?'

'Thank you. That means the world to me.'

It was late in the afternoon. They left not long after arriving, Tommy falling asleep. They'd been told he'd been taken off oxygen that morning, needing an operation on his leg, lots of rest for his ribs and his skull may take weeks or months to heal; only an X-ray could give the answer to that in a few days, Ken told them.

So, Johnny had a problem. Tommy was good at his job, but he'd need a replacement. As they drove to the club, Ruth had a suggestion. 'May not be the right time or place here, but I've got an idea.'

'Oh. What, to take his place?'

'Yes. Give it some thought when I tell you.'

'Who?'

'One person springs to mind straight away. He's funny, cracks jokes, the clients love him. And, he's already pretty much part of our family.'

'You mean "the kid"?'

'Exactly,' said Ruth.

'I know he's got the gift of the gab, great behind the bar. But, going on stage, doing a drag act?'

'It could work. With Tommy, he was good, but he's, well, you know... gay. With Peter, he's straight, obviously! That could work to his and our advantage. The clients know him. He is funny. Plus, a straight guy playing a woman is more appealing; well it is to me.'

'Let's get to the club. I'll have to think about this for a while. Don't tell him, or Helen. Or anyone else... not yet.'

Johnny left it until after the following week. They got by okay without a drag act, visiting Tommy in hospital, as did everyone else at the club, including all of the waitresses.

When he was released another week later, Johnny took him to his home in North Kent. His partner Ken was waiting at their house.

'Johnny,' said Tommy, as he was leaving, 'at my age, I don't think I'll be back.'

'Just think about it. I told you there's no rush. Take your time. I'll be in touch by phone. I've got the police on the case already, see if we can get a result.'

'Thanks, Johnny,' he said, shaking his boss's hand before he left their house, sitting down in an armchair.

'Good to be home,' Tommy said to Ken, who'd bent down to kiss him.

'Yes, glad you're back. Now listen. We don't need to worry about work. You know my job's well paid, we'll be fine,' said Ken.

'Okay,' replied Tommy, quietly.

'Just sit back and relax for a few months. I only work a mile up the road in the office, you know that. So, I'll pop back every day until you don't need me to,' said Ken.

'Thank you,' said Tommy. 'Now where's my coffee!' he said, jokingly. It was a running joke between the two men, that Tommy always bossed Ken around.

'On the way, boss!' said Ken, kissing him on the cheek, stroking his face.

It would be a long time before he fully recuperated, and returned to the club.

Whilst Tommy regained his health, he had conversations with Johnny every week. It was on the first of these calls, only a couple of weeks after getting out of hospital, he made a suggestion to Johnny. 'Listen, boss. You need an act to take over from me. I've been thinking; got plenty of time for that right now.'

'What and who do you think, Tommy? I've got someone in mind already.'

'The kid. He's got the chat, the jokes; and in all seriousness, he's straight. That could work to his advantage as a drag artist.'

'You been talking to my wife about this?' questioned Johnny.

'No, course not,' he replied, laughing.

'Funny that, it's just what she said about him. He's who I'm thinking of asking after Ruth suggested him as well.'

'You know him. He's family. Well, almost. And, above all, Johnny, you trust him. It's worth a go.'

'Well, yep, maybe. I know Helen can help him. It could be good, really good. But he'll need help.'

'I can show him lots of movements, mannerisms. Ask him, then send him down to me, if he agrees,' said Tommy.

'Okay. You and Ruth have convinced me. We'll give it a go. I'll be in touch, Tommy.'

'Excellent. All you've got to do is find a barman as good as him now!' said Tommy, laughing.

'Yep, one door closes, another one opens. Well, something like that,' said Johnny laughing.

'Absolutely.'

'Get back to you, Tommy. Take care. All the best to Ken. Goodbye,' he said, mulling the idea over in his head, putting the receiver down, ending the call.

It's worth a go, he thought to himself. The next day after discussing it with Ruth again, they spoke to Peter and Helen together. He wasn't sure, but Helen was, thinking it a brilliant idea.

First, they had to get a barman, who had the patter, like Peter. It was a good job, in a good club, Ruth had said. It may only be temporary at first; in case Peter was crap on stage, Johnny told them!

Johnny and Helen did the interviewing; they had fourteen applicants. Finally after a couple of weeks' deliberation, they settled on a guy who'd ran his own pub for a few years. A family man with kids. Ruth said he'd be reliable if they paid him a good wage.

Offering him the job, Arthur Francis said he was delighted, with Peter training him for a week. Johnny always liked to help staff settle in; Peter knew that, just like everyone else who worked at the club. The good thing was that Arthur was a happy guy and funny; Johnny said that always helped.

Peter and Helen went to see Tommy. 'He'll show you the ropes,' Johnny told them.

For the next week, Tommy showed Peter how to walk, talk and dress like a woman; even with his leg in plaster he could still pose! Helen was impressed, knowing all this herself, of course.

The bonus was that Peter could sing. Helen encouraged him, getting a tutor in to help with his breathing, remembering he was always singing in his room, or in her car.

So, in early February 1976, with Helen becoming his make-up artist, Peter took the plunge. They came up with a stage name. Petra Juno. It was short and sweet; he didn't want a long name, just something simple in case he fell flat on his face with his act. He couldn't have been more wrong.

It would be more than two years before Tommy came back to the club. The circumstances were not happy...

17
Onwards and Upwards

After practising in front of Tommy and rehearsing in the club, his first night live arrived. None of the audience knew it was Peter for weeks; not that it was a secret. He was introduced by Johnny as a new drag artist, Petra Juno. She'd arrived all the way from Las Vegas. Peter knew it was a white lie; but Johnny always liked to throw some sort of glamour into the shows, if he could!

Walking on stage gracefully as a woman, Helen watched from the wings. He'd perfected his voice, raising it and using a slight lisp to make him sound effeminate, even balancing well on the high heeled shoes he wore.

Dressed as a flamenco dancer in a long flowing dress – Tommy's idea – he cracked jokes at the crowd's expense; taking the piss out of women with beehive hairdos, fat men, thin men, bald men; telling a story about the winter Olympics, specifically John Curry who'd just remarkably won a gold medal, saying he fancied the pants off him. There were no cameras to record anything, so he got away with everything he said.

His timing was good, waiting between his jokes for the applause to die down. Then, he sang, with a piano accompaniment, his first song. It was "Walk on The Wild Side". He needn't have worried. As he began, the curtain went up to reveal the backing band.

He was only supposed to be on stage for forty-five minutes, but he over-ran, due to the incessant applause. Not one person heckled him. After telling some more jokes about Las Vegas where he'd not been working, he sang a second song, accompanied by the resident band. He chose it on purpose. It was "Homeward Bound"; he used to sing along to it with his mum.

Finishing, he curtsied, just like a lady, staying in character, saying, 'Goodnight to you all. I wish you all, a goodnight!'

The whole crowd at their tables rose in unison, clapping loudly. He took a second curtsey, then bowed, before walking off stage. Helen was waiting for him. 'Wow!' was all she could say. 'What a gig! If I was a man, I'd fancy you!' she added, laughing, then hugging him.

'Don't look too bad yourself, toots!' he said, laughing, still in character.

'Pete,' she said, quieter, 'that was amazing. Honestly. I'm not saying it because it's you. It really, really was.'

'Thanks,' he said, nodding his head. 'Wasn't sure about it working. But, I have to say, I really enjoyed it, especially the singing parts.'

'Well, let's see Uncle later. He's still at the bar, doing his thing with the clients. Go and get yourself changed, I'll see you at the bar.'

'Okay.'

He went off to his changing room, then back behind the bar to help Arthur, knowing that it was only a trial, hoping it would become permanent. It was nerve-racking he thought to himself, but he loved it.

Getting to the bar, the band were playing some numbers now, before the club closed. Some of the clients had left. Johnny told Peter to join him at one of the tables.

Getting a drink from the bar, he walked over to the table where Johnny sat; Helen joined them. 'Bloody hell, kid! That was great! You looked like a natural up there.'

'Thanks, boss. Bit nervous, but felt good once I got into my stride.'

'Blew me away. I was at the bar, listening to the clients; they all loved it. Think you've got a weekly spot here. You'll need to keep topical with your stories. Bloody good job, son,' said Johnny, who rarely gave compliments.

It was the first time Peter had been called son in a long time, as Johnny put his arm around his shoulder. He liked that. 'Cheers,' Peter said, raising his glass.

'Right, I'll sort out additional wages for you. See how you go. Maybe make it more than one night a week. You went down a storm there. Bloody terrific that was.' Smiling, Johnny raised his glass, before taking a sip.

'Right, you two,' said Helen, 'let's see how it goes.'

They both nodded at her, before Johnny went back to the bar. Helen smiled at Peter, before she got up to go and get them both another drink.

For the next few months, he polished the act, throwing in the odd Beatles song remembered from his childhood. They were all simple to sing, not too many high notes, just in case his singing voice couldn't handle it.

Then, in July of that year, Johnny upped him to two nights a week. The money was better than working behind the bar for those two nights, even though he was working less time on stage. He knew there was money to be made in this entertainment game.

Arthur was kept on at the club, slotting in well.

The club closed for a week in August. It was the school summer holidays, with a heatwave being predicted. So, Peter and Helen decided to spend a few days at Bognor, courtesy of her parents' apartment, who'd gone abroad. It was very hot this summer; luckily they both liked the heat.

Helen convinced him to write to Elly. He'd not done so for nearly three years. Her best friend Kate worked at the telephone exchange; there was a way to find out if Elly's family had a phone line.

So, he wrote to her, while they were away in Bognor, saying he knew their phone number and he would call on a certain day and time at the end of August.

That day came to make the call. Helen was by his side as he dialled the number from a phone box. She stood next to him as he held the receiver to his ear. 'Hello. Hello?' said a female voice. 'Pete, is that you? Is that you?'

He couldn't speak. Helen poked him in the ribs, jolting him back to life again. She could see tears in his eyes, knowing he'd not heard Elly's voice since they were children.

'Pete, is it you?' Elly asked again.

'Yes… Yes, it's me. How are you, Elly?' he said, struggling to say the words.

'Fine. Fuck, you've been away a long time! It's great to hear from you. It's 1976 you know, why the hell haven't you written for over three years?' she shouted down the phone at him.

He sniffed before he spoke again as Helen put her arm around him. 'Sorry. Been kind of busy.'

'No matter. You're well, are you? And safe?' asked Elly, calmer in her tone now.

'Couldn't be better.'

'Lucky you sent the letter. Listen, I told your mum. Had to. She's been distraught, Pete. Blames herself for you leaving.'

'It wasn't her fault. Please tell her I'm okay, Elly. I've met the most wonderful young lady. I've got a job, can't tell you what. But everything is fine with me.'

'I'll tell your mum. Got an idea so she knows you're okay. Send me a birthday card every year for her birthday. I'll get it to her, secretly, of course, if that's okay with you. You can send it along with mine too, if you remember the date?' she said, laughing.

He looked at Helen, as she nodded, then he replied, 'Yes, I will. Thanks. I'll send them both together. I know yours is a few days after Mum's.'

'Good,' said Elly, pausing before continuing. 'So, tell me about who you've met.'

'Her name's Helen, she's here with me now.'

'Can I speak to her?'

'Yep, sure,' Peter said, handing the receiver to Helen.

'Hi, Elly,' said Helen. 'Pete's told me all about you. How you both used to play hopscotch when kids, and being best friends.'

'He's a special guy, Helen, was always my best friend. You've got that job now. I've got someone in my life too. Her name's Jenny. Tell Pete, he won't be surprised. I always was a bit of a tomboy!' she said, laughing down the phone.

Peter heard it as he wiped his eyes, smiling, saying, 'Yep, course I knew. That's great.'

'Right then,' continued Elly, 'you send the cards, then I can pass your mum's on. Every year, without fail, Pete!' she shouted down the phone.

'Okay,' I will, he said, quietly.

'I'll make sure of it, Elly. When he's ready, we'll come up to see you. That's a promise,' added Helen, glancing at Peter, handing the receiver back to him.

'I'll hold you both to that. Oh, and Pete, your mum's a teacher now, just like me and Jenny.'

'Bloody hell! She really did it!'

'Yep, talk of the town your mum, for a while; not just because of you, either!'

'Thanks for telling me. I hoped she would do something to get away from Dad.'

'You want to know about your dad? He blamed himself, obviously, after what you told me the night you left.'

'Go on then. Is he still working the lock gates?'

'No, not any more. Stopped drinking the night you left, your mum told me. Then Stan and Joe got him a job at Middlesbrough football club about two years ago, as a scout. He looks for kids with talent; you remember he was half decent as an amateur when he was young?'

'Yes. Well, at least he's stopped drinking,' he said.

'And there's more, Pete,' she paused before continuing. 'I saw the twins a few months ago. They're always popping back to see your mum. Stan told me your dad took the job, as it's the only way he has a chance of finding you. He travels all over the country scouting for players. Plus, he goes looking anywhere he can trying to find you.'

'I can't come back, Elly. Not yet. I just can't!'

'Stan said he's never going to give up. He stays away all week in Middlesbrough, or travelling around the country. They gave him a car. He's hardly ever at your old home, always on the road looking for you.'

Helen looked at him, hearing the conversation, shaking her head, before saying, 'Pete, you have to get in touch.'

'No!' he shouted. 'He hates me!'

'Pete, he doesn't. I've seen him. He even told me he'll die trying to find you. Come home. Please, even if it's just to see your mum,' pleaded Elly.

'I can't, not now. Not yet, Elly. Sorry. I need more time to get my head round this,' he said, changing the subject. 'How's Jimmy?'

'Good. He's got a little son, Charlie, must be about five years old now.'

'Great! Is he still at that accountant's?'

'Yes. He's only the bloody manager!'

'Really?'

'Yep.'

'Great. Listen, Elly. I'll be in touch, I promise.'

'I'll make sure he does, Elly,' said Helen, leaning towards the receiver.

'Thanks, Helen. Sounds like you two are quite a team,' she said pausing. 'Make sure he writes. Don't forget. I'm going to tell your mum I've spoken to you, Pete. I'll tell her you're fine, and not to tell your dad... yet. You decide that when you're ready. How's that sound?'

'Good. Thanks, Elly. We'll be in touch,' said Peter.

'Yes, one hundred percent we will. Bye,' said Helen.

'Don't bloody forget, Pete Johnson!'

'No, I won't,' he said laughing at Elly's commanding voice.

'Bye,' she said. Then the phoned line went dead.

'See, that wasn't so bad, was it?' said Helen.

'No,' he said, smiling, wiping his eyes at the same time.

'Right, when's your mum's birthday? I'll make a note of it.'

'September the fifth. Elly's is on the twelfth, a few days later.'

'Good, so you can start in a couple of weeks. Excellent.'

'Yep, will do.'

That's what he did, sending a card to Elly for his mum on her birthday every year, without fail, and hers too. He didn't need prompting from Helen. But he couldn't tell them where he was, or go back. Not yet.

He carried on working in the club as Petra Juno. He learnt lots of other songs, and topical jokes every week, working two nights a week one week, and one night the next. Johnny said that'd keep him fresh. And he helped out Arthur in the bar for two evenings a week, though Johnny said he didn't have to. Peter did it because he loved it, picking up stories from the clients which he used in his act! The regulars realised who Petra Juno was, often buying him a drink after the show; especially the ones he'd taken the mickey out of!

Helen meantime, worked closely alongside her uncle, starting to take over the running of it all within a couple of years. Johnny was sixty-two in 1978, still working, but taking a back seat. He knew Helen missed her opportunity for university. She said this is what she always wanted to do; must've got the bug from her own mum who used to work in the club years ago with Johnny.

The club was booming, lots of celebrities came to watch not just Peter's show, but the comedian and the band; or other groups who'd had success in the pop music charts. Everything was going swimmingly until the April of 1978.

18
Bad News

On a late sunny morning, in early April that year, Peter woke up in his room above the club; Helen didn't always stay with him. Going down to the kitchen, Terry was already there.

'Drink, kid?' he asked.

'Yes, thanks,' he replied, knowing Terry and most everyone in the club still called him by that name.

As they sat drinking, Helen arrived. Peter knew something was wrong straight away; she always kissed him if they hadn't slept together the night before. This morning, she didn't.

'You look pale. What's the matter?' Peter asked.

'Drink?' asked Terry.

'No. I was going to call, Pete, but you've got to come with me. Went to pick up Uncle this morning, that's why I'm late,' she said, her voice quivering with emotion.

'What is it? What's wrong?' Peter asked again.

Terry sat staring, as Peter questioned her.

She could hardly get the words out. 'It's… it's Uncle. When I got to their house, Auntie let me in. I saw an ambulance outside. She grabbed me, dragging me into their kitchen. There were two guys over Uncle, as he lay on the floor.'

'What!' Terry shouted, jumping out of his chair.

'They saved his life. Said he'd had a heart attack. Pete, he might die! Auntie Ruth went with him in the ambulance. Come on, we've got to get to the hospital!' she said, crying.

'We're all going,' said Terry.

'Okay,' said Peter. 'Forget the club, we'll close if we have to.'

Helen nodded in agreement, as they left the kitchen, going to her car. When they arrived, finding Ruth, they had to wait for half an hour before a doctor came out to speak to them.

'Would you come with me please,' said the doctor, ushering them into a waiting room close by. 'I'm Dr Adams, been treating your husband, Mrs Fenton,' he said looking at Ruth.

'Is he alive?' Helen asked.

'Barely. Firstly, let me tell you what's happened. I'll make it brief.'

Ruth collapsed into Helen's arms, as the doctor continued. 'He's alive. The medical team at your house saved his life. If they hadn't used CPR, he wouldn't be with us now. Are you aware what CPR is?'

'Yes,' said Helen, calmer in her reply knowing that he was alive. 'I learned about it at school. Seen it on television. I've been trained in it, if that helps.'

Terry and Peter listened as Helen sat Ruth down in a chair, with the doctor continuing. 'It can be life-saving. It was for your husband,' he said looking again at Ruth. 'Right now, he's in intensive care. He's on oxygen and fluids. I don't know if he'll survive,' said Dr Adams before pausing to continue. 'We were told he was complaining of a dry throat – classic symptom of dehydration – when he arrived. Plus, Mrs Fenton told us he had severe chest pain before falling unconscious.'

Ruth nodded as he said this.

'Mrs Fenton, your quick action calling the ambulance and the team's intervention kept your husband alive. I can allow you to see him, but only you, I'm afraid,' he said glancing at them all, looking lastly at Ruth.

'Thank you, Doctor. But, can I take my niece to see him; she's like a daughter to him?' asked Ruth.

'No, I'm afraid not. You can go in afterwards on your own. Sorry, that's how it is when we have a patient who is critically ill.'

Helen nodded, saying, 'Thank you, Doctor. Go in, Auntie, I'll wait.'

It was a few minutes later when Ruth came out ashen-faced, with the doctor accompanying Helen to see Johnny.

When they returned, the doctor spoke again. 'As I said whilst we were with Mr Fenton, it's likely a circulation problem. We've got to wait and see how much of a fighter he is. I'm informed he owns a club in Soho, working late nights mostly running your club?'

'Yes,' said Helen.

'Quite frankly, the lifestyle he has led for many years wouldn't have helped his health. From what you've said,' added Dr Adams, looking over at Ruth, before continuing, 'he's been a smoker, as well as drinking regularly, with little exercise due to his heavy work schedule for some time. This all adds up to, I'm afraid to say, classic symptoms for a heart attack.'

'So, if he pulls through, what should we do?' asked Helen.

'Yes, Doc, what can we do?' Peter questioned him after listening intently.

'Well, he'll have to change his lifestyle completely, if he wants to live.'

'But, the club, it's his life!' said Ruth.

'We know that, Mrs Fenton,' said Terry, finally standing up after sitting with his head in his hands for a few minutes. 'He's been saying he wants to take a back seat. Now Helen knows pretty much how the club runs, it's got to happen.'

'You're right, Terry. He's been saying that for a year or so now. Okay all of you. He's retired as of now. I've decided. When, and not if, he pulls through, he is only going to be allowed into our club, accompanied by me. I'll sort him out. He's looked after me all my life. It's my turn to do it for him now,' said Ruth, full of confidence.

'That's a good starting point, Mrs Fenton. Let's see if he recovers; I cannot predict that. We have staff who can help, plus your own GP,' said Dr Adams.

'Good,' said Ruth. 'I'm staying here, until he comes round.'

Helen nodded.

'Can we go and see him one at a time?' asked Terry, putting his hand on Peter's shoulder.

'You can. I don't normally allow this, but under these circumstance, yes, one at a time,' answered the doctor.

Helen went first in again, followed by Peter, Terry going in shortly after. Johnny didn't move: he was still unconscious. They were all glad they had a chance to see him; just in case he didn't pull through.

By early afternoon, they left Ruth at the hospital, alone. She told them to close the club for two nights. Everyone would be paid as normal. If he knew, Johnny would've gone crazy, she told them. But as she said, he's not in charge now; she is, with Helen's support.

Going back to the club, Helen's parents were already there, not knowing which hospital Johnny was at. They drove straight to it when Helen told them he was in a room on his own, and they should ask for Dr Adams.

Everything was in limbo that evening and the next day. Peter and Terry made calls to the staff, all except Arthur, who was already driving, on his way to work. When he arrived, Peter told him the news. 'He's got to pull through, Pete. He's a tough old fella,' said Arthur, dismayed at the news.

'I know, Arthur. He didn't look good in that hospital bed. He's in the best place though.'

'Well, I might as well do some work while I'm here. You want me to sort out the cellar for a few hours?'

'No, you get off to your wife and kids. I'll sort that out; I'm here on site.'

'You sure, Pete?'

'Yes. Don't come in tomorrow evening. I'll call you if we hear anything.'

'Thanks, I'll go via the hospital, if that's okay?' he said shaking Peter's hand, putting his arm around him. 'Keep your chin up. He'll pull through.'

'Cheers, Arthur. They may not let you see him.'

'Yep, I know. But I'd still like to go.'

'That's good of you.'

'Hey, you guys have been great to me, it's the least I can do,' said Arthur, letting his hand slip from Peter's grasp.

'Thanks,' said Peter, as Arthur turned and left the club. Then he went into the kitchen where Terry was chatting to Helen, saying, 'Right, I'm going to sort out the cellar. Told Arthur to go home. We'll call him tomorrow, I said. He's going to the hospital on his way.'

'Knew we got one of the good guys when he was taken on,' said Terry.

'Just like you two,' said Helen, who burst into tears.

'Hey you, come on,' said Peter, hugging Helen as her head nestled on his shoulder, adding, 'he'll make it, you know he's a strong fella.' Then he turned to Terry, saying, 'You want to get off, go and spend some time with Alice. Don't come back tomorrow. We'll call you, okay with that?'

'Yeah, that's a good idea. You go, Terry,' said Helen, still embracing Peter.

'Okay, if you kids are sure?' asked Terry.

'We are,' said Helen.

'Crikey, you guys are so grown up for your age. Don't know what I'd have become if... if I'd not started working here all them years ago,' Terry said, his voice croaking with emotion.

'Me neither,' said Peter, smiling.

'And me as well,' said Helen, smiling at them both. 'Go on, get going to your lovely lady. We'll call you as soon as we know anything.'

'Okay, cheers,' he said, turning to leave the club.

They sat staring at one another, when Peter said, 'Right, I'm doing the cellar. Got to do something.'

'And I'm coming to help you,' said Helen.

'What, in them shoes and clothes?'

'Got some gear in your room upstairs. I'll get changed, be back down in ten minutes.'

'Okay,' he said, kissing her.

'Oh, hey. Forgot to tell you, Mr Johnson.'

'Tell me what?'

'I love you, that's all,' she said, smiling at him.

'Thanks. I love you too. Go on, get yourself sorted, let's cheer ourselves up in the cellar, keep us busy for a while; take our minds off it.'

He kissed her again, smiling at her as she left the kitchen. The club was locked up. The only person left other than themselves, was Big Dave. He'd put a notice on the doors, saying he'd stick around until nine o'clock to let the clients know what's happened.

They spent a few hours, sorting out the gas and the barrels in the cellar, generally tidying, before going back up. Helen phoned her parents who were back at their house. She was staying at the club tonight. No change with Johnny was the message.

Knowing the club would be closed the next night as well, they drove to the hospital in the morning. Ruth was nowhere to be seen in the waiting area, so Peter asked at reception if they could see a doctor. They waited.

'Hello again,' said Dr Adams, after they'd waited a short time. 'He's very weak, but he came round this morning. We're not out of the woods yet, so to speak, but he's back with us.'

'Thank you, Doctor,' said Helen.

'You know what needs to be done. Mrs Fenton is with him now. I'm allowing her ten minutes, that's all.'

'Can we go in as well?' said Peter.

'I'm afraid not. One person at a time until I say otherwise. We can discuss a plan of action for him, providing he makes a good recovery. It'll be a long road ahead for him. I've told his wife not to tell him what he's likely to go through, being a complete life change. That can wait until later.'

'Okay, Doctor, thank you. We'll wait until you let us see him, all day if necessary,' said Peter.

He nodded before replying, 'Hopefully that won't be the case. I'll be back shortly.'

As they waited patiently, Ruth came into the room, shortly after Dr Adams had left. 'He's awake, and talking. He remembers a pain in his chest, falling over, then nothing,' she said, with a wry smile.

'Good. It's a start. Small steps, Auntie,' said Helen, putting her arms around her.

'Thank you, Helen. I'd be lost without you, you know that, don't you?'

She smiled, hugging Ruth, saying, 'Same here.'

'The doctor said it's going to be a slow process. Probably take months and months before he's back to normality; if he ever is. Obviously, that's what we all want,' said Peter.

'Yes,' said Ruth. 'Now, listen. The first thing he said is, "what's happening at the club?" I told him to forget about it. It'll be run by you, Helen, with me around to help. There's nothing to worry about, I told him. Be like old times for me, getting back into the front line. Haven't told him about changing his lifestyle yet.'

'Well, we all know he's a larger than life character. Standing at the bar with a cigar, with his drink in his hand. That's got to stop, we know that,' said Helen.

'Right then, you two go in and see him when the doctor lets you. Don't say anything about the club, other than you'll be running it. Just say he's to take his time; you know almost everything there is to know about it now anyway, Helen?'

'Yes. Wait and see what the doctor says when he comes back and we'll go from there,' Helen replied.

For the rest of that year, it was recuperation for Johnny. He had to learn how to be told what to do. But, he listened.

When he came out of hospital a week after going in, he wanted to go straight to the club in the middle of the afternoon. Ruth and Helen took him there, knowing Peter was out collecting supplies. As they took him in sitting in his wheelchair, he could see it was just the same. 'Well, it looks good to me,' he said, as Ruth wheeled him into the kitchen from the restaurant and bar areas.

'Hey, boss, good to see you. These guys have got everything all under control, nothing to worry about,' said Terry, shaking Johnny's hand, looking at Ruth and Helen.

'That's what I've been told, Terry. Good to see you. How's your wife?'

'Great, boss, thanks. The kid told me you've got a long way to go health wise?'

'Yep, that's right. Okay, luv, take me home. No need for me to be here, like you said. See you soon, old friend,' he said to Terry, as Ruth turned him towards the swinging doors.

'Bye, Terry. See you this evening,' said Helen.

'Will do,' he replied, carrying on with his chores before continuing to prepare the food for the evening.

As they helped Johnny back into the car from his wheelchair, he said, 'Christ, that's absolutely knackered me.'

'The doctor told you to take it easy, you said you'd listen. I'll tell you again, you've got to rest. No more club for a long time,' said Ruth.

'Yes, Uncle. It IS all under control. I'll be in touch by phone all the time as well as coming to see you, with Pete. Don't worry about anything, okay?' added Helen.

'Point taken,' said Johnny, breathing heavily.

'Now, let's get you home, and have a drink; not one of those Long Island ones you always have at the club either!' said Helen, smiling at him, then Ruth.

'Yes, okay,' said Johnny, knowing that they were both right. 'You women. Why are you always bloody right!' he said, laughing at them.

'Because we've always been the fairer sex, isn't that right, Auntie?'

'Sure is. And we'll get you right too. Just keep listening to us and you'll be up and about in no time.'

'Come on, let's get going then,' said Johnny, still breathing heavily, but smiling at them.

Ruth knew it would be a long time before he could even walk. She'd been told by Dr Adams it could take a year for him to even cover a short distance. It all depended on his own powers of recovery. Johnny knew it as well. They all did. It was going to be a long road back for him...

19
Recovery and Beyond

Ruth spent every day with her husband from the moment he came out of hospital. Luckily the house had a downstairs toilet, he said to her the day he came home! For two months, he couldn't climb the stairs to their bedroom. It took that long for him to be able to walk out into the garden and back. But he was trying.

He had lots of visitors in that time; then Ruth put a stop to them all, other than Terry, Peter, Helen, her parents and Tommy. She could see how breathless he got just speaking. She banned him from talking on the phone for more than a minute, cutting him off even if he hadn't finished his conversation! It became a running joke with them all. They knew he was always abrupt, but Ruth became worse than Johnny!

By August, he was walking up and down the stairs, not getting out of breath. And, he could go to the corner shop, which was about a mile away, every other day. He didn't have the strength to walk back, so Ruth picked him up in their car.

November came and went. Ruth allowed him five minutes on the phone now. He was making his own drinks, non-alcoholic only! Ruth and Terry taught him to cook. He'd never had time before, being so busy running his club.

Then, in December, he asked Ruth to take him to the club one evening. She said yes. But, they didn't tell anyone. He wanted to surprise them all. Johnny had lost weight. None of his suits fitted him any more, so they went shopping to get a new one. He was feeling more energetic every day.

The only thing he ever got himself, was his suits, having them tailor made. It'd been many years since he visited Broad Ways, his tailor shop in Savile Row. The staff knew him instantly, commenting on his weight loss and how well he looked.

A week later, he went back with Ruth to collect his suit. He was walking two miles every other day now, only getting really tired in the evenings, going to bed before ten o'clock. That was unheard of less than a year ago; he was always up until two or three a.m.

It was Saturday the 23rd of December 1978. Johnny had an afternoon nap. He forced himself to stay awake in the daytime in recent months, knowing he would sleep well; which he did. But, he fell asleep, as did Ruth sitting next to him at their home. Waking up at seven p.m., he turned to see Ruth, who was still asleep. 'Hey there, you,' he said, giving her a little nudge.

She opened her eyes slowly. 'What time is it?'

'Just gone seven,' he said, leaning over, kissing her.

'What was that for?' she said.

'I just wanted to. For everything.'

'Ah, that's nice.'

'Right, I'll go and make us a cuppa, luv. Then we can get changed and go to the club. You still okay with that?' Johnny asked his wife, standing up.

'Yes. You've waited patiently until now. And, I'm saying you can go,' she said, smiling at him.

'Ruth, wouldn't be who I am without you. Just want you to know that. I know I don't usually do schmaltzy often, but hey…' he said with a croaky voice.

She stood up from the settee, kissing him, before replying, 'You've looked after me all my life. It's my turn, and my pleasure, to return the favour. You're the best, Johnny Fenton.'

They smiled at one another again.

'Okay,' he said. 'I'll stick the kettle on.'

'Yes, I'll go and get changed,' she said, going upstairs.

It was after eight o'clock by the time Johnny had got changed. He was feeling good, although everything he did nowadays, was slower than before his attack. Johnny had never smoked a cigarette or a cigar again, since it happened.

Ruth had allowed him the occasional alcoholic drink at home for the last couple of weeks, telling him that he could have one drink at the club. It was a cold, dry night, as she drove them there, chattering away. 'They'll be surprised, won't they?'

'I reckon so,' he replied, laughing.

'Take it easy when you arrive, no rushing around.'

'Okay, luv.'

'You've lost so much weight, some of the clients might not recognise you!' said Ruth, laughing.

'Don't know about that,' said Johnny, smiling back at her.

'Well, let's have a nice meal. I asked Helen to keep a spare table for us. She's the only one who knows we might be going tonight.'

'I thought you said nobody knows?'

'I had to tell her, so we've got somewhere to sit.'

'Fair enough.'

After a half hour drive from their home in Balham, South London, they parked around the corner near the club. Walking up to the entrance, the first person they saw was Big Dave.

'Boss! Great to see you. Bloody hell, you've lost weight since I saw you a few months ago. Think I'll have to have one of them heart attacks, see if I can lose weight too!' he said, patting his own big belly.

'Dave,' said Johnny, smiling at him, shaking his hand. 'You don't want to go through one, my friend. Good to see you've still got your sense of humour though.'

'Mrs Fenton, good to see you too. Didn't know you were coming tonight.'

'Thought we'd surprise you all. Johnny's been getting better over the last couple of months. So, I told him he could come.'

'So, you're wearing the trousers now, Mrs F?'

'You could say that, Dave,' she said, laughing with him and Johnny.

'Enjoy yourselves. Great to see you both.'

'Thank you,' said Johnny, before vanishing into the doors of the club behind Ruth.

As they went in, the band were playing. Johnny knew that Peter had been doing his act on some Saturday nights, as Helen kept him informed throughout his recuperation. As they walked up to the bar to order a drink, Helen was there. She gave Ruth a hug, and Johnny as well. Arthur leaned over the bar to shake his hand.

Then, all of the lights went out on the stage. 'What's going on?' Johnny asked Helen.

'Bit of a surprise, Uncle.'

Terry came through the double doors from the kitchen, thrusting his hand into Johnny's, with a beaming smile on his face.

Then, Peter came from behind the stage, microphone in hand, with the spotlight on him; he'd not changed into his costume as Petra Juno yet.

'Good evening, everyone, my apologies for the lights going out, there's nothing to worry about,' he said pausing. 'We've got a little announcement before we continue with the show tonight.' There was mumbling in the crowd, a full house on a very busy Christmas Saturday night.

'Hit the lights, boys,' said Peter, turning towards the curtains on the stage.

Immediately, the spotlight left Peter, shining straight at the bar area, illuminating the spot where Terry, Helen, Ruth and Johnny were standing. Terry and Helen backed away, leaving Johnny and Ruth alone in the spotlight.

'Ladies and gentlemen,' said Peter from the darkness of the stage. 'I'd like to introduce to you, the man and woman who've made your entertainment possible inside this club for many, many years. He looks a little different, don't you, Johnny, with all the weight you've lost?'

Johnny smiled. So did Ruth, before Peter continued, as laughter rippled around the club.

'Please, may I ask you to put your hands together, to welcome back to their home, the one and only, Mr and Mrs Johnny Fenton!'

Everyone stood up, clapping and cheering wildly. The lights went back on in the club as they whistled and shouted his name. Within seconds, he was surrounded by the crowd of his clients, many of them having become friends.

The cheering didn't stop for over a minute, as Peter said over the noise, 'Johnny, Ruth. Please, join me on stage.'

They walked past the tables, as he shook hands with lots of people he knew. When they reached the stage, the clapping and cheering got even louder. Peter hugged Ruth, then Johnny, handing him the microphone.

Johnny put his hands out in front of himself, waving them up and down to get everyone to sit down. They didn't. So, he waited until they stopped cheering and clapping, putting his arm around Ruth.

It was a few minutes before he could speak. 'Thank you, everyone. This is just incredible. We didn't want a fuss. Just came out for a quiet meal, that's all!' he said, as the crowd laughed, before he continued a few seconds later. 'You know what happened to me. I'm lucky to be here, and to be able to say thank you, to you all, for coming here to my club, sorry, our club. This is my family, right here. It wouldn't be what it is without you coming here to enjoy yourselves. Helen, Pete, "the kid as we know him", Terry, Big Dave, Arthur, all my waitress friends. We've known one another such a long time. What can I say, other than thank you one and all for supporting us. Long may it continue; enjoy the rest of your evening,' Johnny said, bowing, standing on stage for another minute while rapturous applause rang out in the club again.

When they left the stage, the hubbub quietened down, as he walked round to every table, saying thank you. Finally after almost half an hour, Helen came over to rescue them. 'Sorry,' she said, tapping him on the shoulder. 'Time for you to sit down, Uncle.'

'Oh,' he said. 'Sorry, folks,' to some old friends at their table. 'Got to listen to the ladies in my life now,' smiling at them.

'Come on, we've got a table put by for you over there,' said Helen, pointing in the direction of where Ruth had already gone. He followed her, sitting down, where a drink was already waiting for him.

'Long Island tea?' he asked Ruth.

'Yes, you can have one. And it's alcoholic.'

'All the usual ingredients in it?'

'Yes, made by Arthur. Vodka, tequila, triple sec, gin and your splash of coke, with a little ice.'

Johnny stood up, with glass in hand, looking towards the bar where Arthur was serving. He saw Johnny raising his glass, and waved back to him, smiling, giving a salute.

Sitting back down, Ruth said, 'Dinner, luv? I've ordered us both a steak.'

'Wonderful. Just bloody wonderful!' he replied, having a sip of his drink, before saying, 'Ah! Gorgeous. Forgot how nice this was.'

'Only one! That's all you're having.'

'That's all I need,' said Johnny, smiling at his wife, stretching his hand out to touch her face. She smiled back at him, knowing his scare had changed him. He would never have done that before the attack.

When they finished their dinner, Peter came on stage, going through his act. He sung his two songs, the first he'd sung a few times before. He told the audience this one was especially for Johnny Fenton. The band and pianist assisted him, as he belted out "We've Got Tonight", by Bob Seger.

His second, he dedicated to Helen and Ruth. It was "I'm Every Woman", by Chaka Khan. Everyone sang along with him for this one. When he finished, he said, still in character, 'Just had to sing that one, folks. Thanks for singing along. Mr and Mrs Fenton, over there in the corner, hope you enjoyed the show.

There wouldn't be a show without you. Don't think we'll ever have a night like this again!'

The spotlight shone on them both, as Peter started clapping on his own. Then Helen did, who was standing at the bar. Within seconds, the whole club erupted again, cheering wildly, as Peter led a chorus of 'There's only one Johnny Fenton, there's only one Johnny Fenton!'

He and Ruth stood at their table, clapping back themselves as the raucous noise died down. 'What a night,' Johnny shouted. 'Thank you, one and all, again. The kid is right. Don't think we'll have a night like this again. Cheers!' he shouted, raising his drink in the air.

Peter left the stage and as the audience quietening down, Johnny said to Ruth, 'This has been, probably, the most memorable night of my life. And I nearly wasn't here to see it. Thanks, luv, it's been beautiful.' Then he kissed her.

He rarely used to show affection in public, as she replied, 'I like the new Johnny Fenton. You can stay.'

They smiled at one another, sitting down, as Johnny yawned. 'Tired are we?' Ruth said, noticing it.

'Crikey, yes. Way past my bedtime of late!' he said, laughing.

'Right, come on then, let's get going shortly.'

'You're the boss now, Ruth. Sounds good to me. Just say a few goodbyes.'

'Of course.'

Walking round for almost another half an hour before reaching the bar, Johnny kissed all of the waitresses on the cheek, shaking hands with every member of staff, finally seeing Terry and Helen. Peter came round from the back stage passageway, as the band continued playing.

'Great show,' said Johnny as they shook hands, Peter pulling him into his body gently for a man hug.

'Cheers, boss. Wasn't planned until an hour before you arrived. We all just thought it'd be a nice gesture.'

'It was. Thank you again. Time to go, my wife knows it's past my bed time!' Johnny joked.

They turned to depart the club, leaving Helen, Terry and Peter laughing, as some of the customers were leaving as well.

'See you tomorrow, Uncle,' shouted Helen.

'You will. You will,' he called back, going through the big exit doors.

From then on, Johnny visited the club just once a week in the evening. Ruth allowed him one drink. They always left early by ten p.m. He really did get tired. Everything in his life had slowed down because of the heart attack. But, he got back to as much of a normal life as possible.

They had a big garden, so Johnny started working on it. They'd had a gardener for years looking after it, keeping him on, as Johnny got involved, giving himself a hobby he could work on.

All was going well with Johnny and the club until a spanner was thrown in the works in May 1981…

20
Spain Calling

One evening, when Peter had finished his act, he went to the bar to have a drink. Whilst there, he was met by a man he'd seen in the club a couple of times, but didn't know, who had jet black hair, a moustache and was dark skinned.

He introduced himself to Peter. 'Hello, I'm Randy Martinez. Watched your show a few times; you've got a great act. Can I buy you a drink, then may I have a word please?'

'Yes, of course. Let's sit at the table over there,' replied Peter, as they shook hands.

Once he'd ordered the drinks, Peter nodded in the direction of a table. Sitting down, he told Peter of his proposition. 'They call you the kid, I believe? Is that right?'

'Yes. As soon as I started working here years ago, I was given the name by Johnny Fenton. It stuck!' he said, smiling.

'So, what's your real name?' asked Martinez.

'Bit of a mystery there, I'm afraid. A story for another day,' Peter said, being rather suspicious.

'No problem. We'll stick with Petra Juno and "the kid", if that's okay?'

'Yes, that's fine. My real name's Peter Johnson, hence the P and J,' he replied, feeling instantly more comfortable about telling him his name.

'Oh, yes. I see. I'll get to it then,' said Martinez, sipping his drink before continuing. 'What it is, as I said, I've been watching your act and I think you're very good. Very good indeed. So good in fact, that I'd like to offer you a contract for three months' work. I've checked and apparently you only do one or two nights each week, is that right?'

'Oh? A contract? Well, there's no need to do more than a night or two, we've got a comedian, our band, occasional celebrities and pop groups, with their different acts.'

'Okay. Here's my pitch.' He paused to sip his drink again. 'I've got nightclubs in Spain. Two in Benidorm, one in Alicante, Torrevieja, Almeria and Marbella. In the last five years, there's been a massive influx of holidaymakers from the U.K. Millions of people who can afford the cheap flights over to the Costas, as we call it. We've got the weather, the hotels, bars and clubs.'

'So, why ask me?'

'You see, I've got comedians, bands, dance acts; all good. But, I've got no drag artists. There are rival clubs – no animosity between us – that have drag acts. They bring in the crowds, men and women. Even families. I want to cash in on it. That's why I'd like to offer you a job, just for three months, see how it goes.'

'Crikey. I've got a great job here, Mr Martinez, no need for me to go anywhere.'

'I can see that. A month ago, I asked Mister Fenton, your boss, where he got you from. He said you turned up one day years ago and you've been here ever since. Couldn't speak highly enough of you. You're dating his niece; said he thinks the world of you both.'

'Well, that works both ways. He's a great guy.'

'So, are you interested? I will pay very well. If you want to bring your young lady over, I'll pay for the flights if she wants to visit. It'll be six nights a week, like I said, for three months, from early June, covering the summer season.'

'I can't give you a decision. I'll have to talk to Helen. I'm very happy here. You've got to come up with something good to take me away from here.'

'I can do that. You can earn enough money to get a big deposit for a house if that's what you want? Please, talk to your young lady. Here's my card. I'm staying at the Savoy Hotel for the next two days before flying back. I've seen some other acts; none of them are as good as you.'

'Thank you, Mr Martinez. I'll let you know, one way or the other.'

They shook hands as they stood up, Martinez nodding before leaving the club.

Peter was in a quandary. He found Helen straight away, who'd been in the kitchen with Terry, sorting our menus. 'Need to talk to you.'

'What is it?' she said.

'You got a minute, come up to my room.'

'Ooh!' she whispered in Peter's ear. 'Sounds very inviting.'

'Huh, great idea,' he said, 'but it's not that. Mind you…' he said, winking at her, then smiling.

He grabbed her hand, taking her upstairs. When he got to his room, he told her all about it. 'Bloody hell, Pete! What do you think?'

'Well, I don't know. That's why I'm asking you?'

'To be honest, with what we're making at the club, we don't need the money. Not to say it wouldn't come in handy. You know we'd both like to get our own place, get married, have a family, don't you?' said Helen.

'Yes, I know we do. Shit! Everything's going well, then this guy comes in. He spoke to the boss about a month ago. Johnny never said anything to me, nor you, did he?'

'No, first I've heard of it.'

Peter put his hands on his head. Since they'd been going to Bognor occasionally and doing the trips to France for the booze, which stopped ages ago, he'd always fancied going to Spain. They'd never been. He had an idea.

'Right, sit down, please,' he asked Helen. 'Here's the thing. You know we've said we'd fancied going to Spain?'

'Never had time, have we?'

'No, I know.'

'What is it, Pete?'

'Let's speak to the boss, and Ruth. He's a lot better now. I know he's been taking a back seat. We've never had a long holiday, either of us, other than the odd week at Bognor. So, how about we talk to your aunt and uncle, see if they'll allow us both to go away to Spain; see what these clubs are like. I can't decide on my own, I want to know what you think.'

Helen took a deep breath. 'Okay, let's go see them now.'

'Right now?'

'Yep. This Martinez chap is only here for a few days, so come on,' she said grabbing his hand, as she got up from the bed.

'It's too late now. We'll go in the morning,' said Peter, adding, 'let's sleep on it, okay?' smiling at her, knowing they'd be sleeping in his room at the club later.

The next morning, they went to Johnny's house, telling him all about it. No way would they go to have a look if he said no. He didn't. Knowing it was a great opportunity, Johnny said it could lead to something else in the future, even if he only went for three months.

Peter told Johnny that's all he was going to do. Just one summer season. Then he called Randy Martinez; within an hour, Peter, Helen, Johnny and Ruth were in his room at the Savoy.

He had a contract set out already. Johnny looked it over; so did Helen. It was impressive. Peter would have a car to travel to all of the nightclubs. Six nights a week, he would be working in each one. All fuel would be paid. He'd have an allowance to buy food; which he likely wouldn't need, as the clubs all had restaurants, being similar in style to Johnny's. Flights would be paid for and accommodation each night. He had pictures of all the clubs, which were huge, open air venues.

When he flew out, if he did, with Helen, she could stay the whole duration if she wished. And he, Randy Martinez, would pay for flights back for her, up to three times. Half the money would be paid before Peter left the U.K. The remainder at the end.

Leaving the hotel, they all got into Johnny's car; Ruth was driving. 'Let's get back to the house, have another look at this contract, okay, kid?' said Johnny.

'Yes, boss. Good idea.'

On the way, Helen took the contract from Peter, studying every word. Once they arrived, she was the first to speak after they had driven in silence; all stunned by the contract and what it was worth.

'Pete,' said Helen, as Ruth went to make drinks, 'this is a no-brainer. It's a watertight contract as far as I can see. You have another look, Uncle.'

When Ruth came in with the drinks a few minutes later, Johnny spoke. 'She's right,' he said to Peter. 'It's up to you. I do NOT want to lose you! I know you're coming back to my – our – club. But, there's three big buts. One, you've got to come back to us in three months. Two, I want Helen to have a holiday with you over there to check it out. Three, it doesn't happen, if my wife says we are not up to running the club, while Helen is away. What do you say, luv?' he said, looking at Ruth.

'It's a great opportunity. Go and have a look, by all means. Don't sign the contract, until you see the places for yourselves. Helen, my God, you deserve a holiday! Yes, we can cope. We'll get your mother and father roped in as well. Terry will help out and I'll rule your uncle with an iron rod!' said Ruth, smiling at him, then bending down to kiss Johnny, while he sat in the chair.

'Pete, you up for this?' questioned Helen.

He breathed in, then exhaled, raising his eyebrows. 'Bloody hell! You all reckon I can handle it?'

'Too right you can,' said Johnny.

'Yes!' shouted Helen. 'I'll miss you, but I'd love a holiday!' she added, laughing, whilst putting her arms around his neck.

'That's it then. I'm going. We're going!'

'And we can keep in touch with the landline phone. Doesn't matter how much it costs, does it? with the money you'll be earning,' said Ruth, holding the phone in her hand, smiling.

'Settled then,' said Johnny.

And it was. At the end of May, Peter and Helen flew to Spain. Randy Martinez knew he'd not signed the contract yet. It didn't matter to him, he was confident Peter would. They spent the first week of their two week break, figuring out where the hotels were, visiting them all, signing the contract once they'd checked them out. In the next week, Peter polished his act. He had all his dresses, worked out routines already, before they left. Then, with the help of Mr Martinez, he started picking up Spanish phrases.

In these two weeks, Helen had never been so relaxed. She laid in bed in the mornings, swam at the hotels they stayed at. And, knowing they may not see one another for a month, had as much sex as they possibly could!

Time came for her to leave. A taxi took her to the airport, as she said goodbye to Peter at the hotel. He vowed to himself, he wasn't going to drink any alcohol, only on his one day off which would be every Monday. Randy Martinez could not have been more helpful.

They kept in touch via phone. Once he'd worked there for a month learning more Spanish phrases, even though the audiences were predominantly British, he knew Helen was coming over.

She flew out to surprise him a day early, knowing he'd be working at the club in Marbella. She had Randy Martinez's phone number, who picked her up from the airport personally. 'He's been fantastic,' he said. 'I knew he would be,' was the first thing he said to her, even before saying hello.

'Hello, Mr Martinez, that's good news,' said Helen.

'I'm so sorry. Where are my manners! Good evening, Miss Armstrong. Let me take your bag,' he said, kissing her on the cheek.

'Thank you. Please, call me Helen.'

'I will,' he said, smiling at her. 'And you call me Martinez, please.'

She nodded, saying, 'I will,' smiling at him, as they got into his car.

On the way to the club, Martinez told her that Peter was normally on stage at nine p.m. His act was about an hour, but it was always longer. He'd started getting members of the audience on stage with him, making up games like a Mr and Mrs Quiz, or with balloons, anything to get the crowd participating. And, he never swore, because of the children, he added.

'It's going well then?' Helen asked.

'Brilliant. I knew I'd got the right person in Peter; I mean, Petra Juno.'

'Yes, he's quite a guy. He's no idea how good he really is. Can't tell him that, though!' said Helen, laughing.

'You're right there, Helen. He's great with the kids too. Gets some on stage early like I said, does a numbers game with them. Always gives them prizes. Terrific fun.'

They arrived at the hotel at nine p.m. Martinez took her just in time to watch the start of the show, sitting at the back of the open air arena. She already knew rules were far more relaxed in Spain, allowing children into the shows.

Peter had no idea she was there; he thought she was arriving the next day. He was hilarious. She didn't stop laughing; except when he sang. He had a good voice, not the strongest, but she knew he could sing well.

When the show finished, she was yawning, tired from the journey. The whole audience were on their feet, shouting "more, more" when he went off stage. He came back to sing one more song. It was "Spanish Eyes". Then, he curtsied, just like she'd shown him. Martinez told her this song had become his signature tune.

Along with Martinez, she went to the bar. Not fancying alcohol, he got her a lemonade, telling her that because of Peter, his profits were already up at all his clubs. He told her that if he could stay, he'd keep Peter for longer; but, he knew the contract was only for three months.

When they finished their drinks, he took her backstage. Peter had already changed into shorts and T-shirt; that's all he wore in the Spanish heat.

'Hey, Pete Johnson,' Helen said at his doorway.

'Oh!' he shouted, jumping out of his seat surprised, as he finished wiping the make-up from his face. Turning round, he saw her, rushing over grabbing her, in full view of Martinez kissing her, holding her tightly at the same time.

'Must be love,' said Martinez, smiling, going outside, closing the door to give them privacy.

'Yes!' said Peter, loudly, with a beaming smile on his face.

'Correct,' said Helen, smiling back at him.

'You're a sight for sore eyes! Wasn't expecting you until tomorrow?'

'Thought I'd surprise you,' she said, kissing him again, before continuing, 'you were great out there. Loved the games you did.'

'Thanks, I'm really enjoying it. Missing you like mad, though. I love you, Helen Armstrong. Been waiting to tell you that in person for weeks.'

'Likewise, Mr Johnson. Or should I say Petra Juno?'

'Just the stage name. It's all an act, you know!' he replied, laughing, smiling at her, still holding her tightly in his arms.

'So, where are we staying?'

'Got a room at a hotel nearby, do you remember?'

'Yes, of course I do. We used the bed a lot,' said Helen laughing.

'Huh. Yep, we did. Missed you,' he said, still with a beaming smile.

'Missed you too. Come on, let's get going, we've lots of catching up to do,' she said.

'Course we have. I know what you've said in the calls, but that's small talk. Tell me all about the club and everyone.'

'Okay let's go,' she replied, as he led the way out of the club, which had disco music blaring out, saying goodbye to Martinez.

When they got there, she changed into her nightie, pulling him onto the bed, eager to have sex with him. She'd missed it, just as he had.

Afterwards, he made them a drink. He told her again he only drank alcohol on his day off – Monday – so they had coke.

'Right, come on then, tell me all about what's been going on at home then I'll tell you what's been happening here?'

She told him the club was doing fine. He already knew that Tommy had come back as the drag act, just for one night a week. He was good, everyone said, but not like Peter. Johnny had worked every night when she was in Spain with him last time. When she got back, he worked three nights, from nine p.m., admitting the two weeks she was away, exhausted him. Ruth worked with him every night, as well as Helen's parents helping out.

This time, she was only away for four days. Ruth said she'll keep a close eye on Johnny, as always.

Peter told her about all the different clubs, although she'd been before a month ago. He liked the heat, got used to it now. On his day off – Monday – he took himself off to the beach each time. Sunday he always finished in Benidorm, so that's the beach he went to; the one they went to together when she was last there. Nobody knew him, even though his picture was on billboards as "the kid/Petra Juno". It was nice to sit in a bar and have a quiet beer, go and watch other acts for a change. Martinez couldn't have been more accommodating, he added.

So, for the next few days, she went with him, watching him perform. He'd even started to sign autographs, which surprised her. As she arrived on a Friday, she planned to be with him on his day off, Monday, flying back on the Tuesday.

They spent the Monday at the beach together. 'This is great,' she said, as he came back to the sunbeds they were on, with a drink.

'Fancied a beer. I know it's early – well, midday – got you a coke, like you asked, that okay?'

'Yes, thanks. Don't feel like drinking alcohol at the moment, might be the heat.'

'Probably. It is hot today. Well, it's July so we're here at the hottest time of the year.'

'Hmm,' she said, nodding in agreement. 'One month down, two to go.'

'Yep. Meant to ask you, is Arthur still doing a good job behind the bar?'

'He is. Got the banter with the customers; not in your league though,' she said, smiling at him.

He lifted her sunglasses up from her eyes then smiled before kissing her, as he looked into her eyes.

'We were lucky meeting, weren't we?'

'Think it's fate, Mr Johnson.'

'Yep, maybe so.'

They smiled at one another as he moved onto his sunbed, picking up his paper. Helen read her book. Both of them fell asleep several times in the day.

In between nodding off, he told her that he didn't have much time to himself in the day. It was good he could lay in until late morning; in the afternoons, he drove to the different clubs. Monday was good, he got the chance to recharge his batteries. He did the same act for a week, working out a slightly different routine each Monday.

'Yes, I know you do the same act, you've done it for the three nights I've been here.'

'Tomorrow it changes. Then, I change it back a week later. That way, if people are at their hotel for a two week holiday, they'll see two different shows.'

'Makes sense.'

'Martinez suggested it. I was going to try and work out a different act each of the six nights; he said no need, just have two routines. Makes it easier for me.'

'Good,' she said.

They kept having snippets of conversation like that throughout the day; chatting about the weather at home, how well Johnny was doing.

Leaving the beach as the sun went down, they wandered to a restaurant, having an early meal before going back to the hotel. He had a beer, while she had a coke again. Going to bed early, he told Helen that's what he always does each Monday, tired from laying on the beach.

Waking the next day, she left in the early afternoon. He took her to the airport, before driving to the club, meeting Martinez early before his evening show. 'Has she gone?' he questioned Peter.

'Yep,' he said quietly.

'Think you've got a problem there, Peter.'

'What do you mean?'

'You two are crazy in love. Why are you not married?' questioned Martinez.

'Err, never thought about it really?'

'Well, you should. How long you been together?'

'Oh, about six or seven years.'

'What! Get yourself married. Take my advice. I only have to look at you both to know. When she comes back, ask her. You've got a month before she's back, work on a plan. Maybe propose on the beach, or the club?'

'You know, I think about it sometimes. It's scary.'

'No, it's not at all. Doesn't matter which side of the tracks you're from; you told me that. I had nothing when I married years ago. Even in this business, you need stability. I can see you've got that between you. Let me help. I know you've only got a couple of months here now, so what do you think?'

'I think yes!'

So, over the next few weeks, Martinez worked on a plan with Peter for when Helen returned. They kept in touch by phone. But before she was due to fly out, she called him.

21
Change of Plan

'Hey you, how's it going out there?' asked Helen.

'Great. Been terrific. Missing you, looking forward to seeing you in a few days.'

'Pete, there's a problem. I don't know how to tell you this... well, I'll just have to say it.'

'What?' he questioned her. His mind was racing. He thought he should've asked her to marry him a couple of years ago. He feared the worst.

'I've been feeling poorly for a few days, doubled up in pain. Spoke to my doctor, who advised me not to fly. It'll take too long by car, I'm sorry.'

He breathed a sigh of relief. 'Well,' he said, disappointment in his voice, 'can't be helped.'

'Should be okay in a week or so, though.'

'Wait until the end, in a month's time, then I'll be coming back with you, the three month stint will be finished then.'

'Okay. I miss you,' she said, before continuing. 'The other thing is, Auntie Ruth has had a fall. She fell down the stairs, broke her ankle.'

'What!'

'Yep, Johnny's fine, but he's got to look after her. Best I stay here until she's up and about again. I'm so sorry, Pete.'

He didn't speak for a few seconds. 'It's fine, honestly, Helen. I miss you like crazy. It'll only be a few more weeks anyway. Look, I love you. I won't ever do this again, no matter how much money is on the table. I'm not going anywhere without you again, okay?'

'Oh, Pete. And I miss you. I love you, too. Now you've made me cry,' she said, though he could hear her laugh.

'Don't set me off. You know what I'm like, it's me that cries at the drop of a hat!' he replied, laughing as well, before continuing. 'You stay there, keep the club in tiptop shape, and sort out your aunt and uncle. I'm fine here. Let's just look forward to the end of August, okay?'

'Okay. No more tears. Tell me one of your jokes, a silly one.' He did. They ended the conversation laughing. But they both kept a secret from one another.

Peter spoke to Martinez, telling him that she wasn't coming over until the end of the contract. His plan would have to wait until then, not knowing she had her own secret.

As it was a Monday, he went to the beach again, in Benidorm. The locals there and holidaymakers alike, knew that the beach had a name for a particular reason. When Helen visited, he explained it to her when they had their day together on the beach. He took her into the sea for a swim, but asked her to stand and turn around to face the hotels.

He remembered as he stood alone in the sea now, listening to it. It was a cacophony of noise. When she was there, he told her it's called "the wall of sound". The noise as he stood in the sea again, merged into one buzzing, screeching sound. He was glad that she'd heard it. Every time he came to the beach, he listened to it before having a swim.

Then, he dived into the water, swimming away from the noise. Being a strong swimmer, he usually swam out a couple of hundred metres, the water being warm. He floated in the sea before turning to swim back. But instead of the wall of sound, he heard something else, completely unexpected.

Looking up to the shoreline, he saw a crowd gathered, shouting, screaming at the top of their voices.

Seeing two men dive into the water, he looked left, seeing nothing. Turning right, he saw a small dinghy floating on its own about a hundred metres away; the two men were heading towards it. One of them he could see was a lifeguard.

Instinctively, he knew something was wrong. He was much closer than either of them. As quickly as he could, he swam over to the dinghy, as a speedboat drew up beside him. The man in it shouted at him, 'I saw a little girl in the dinghy as I went by a couple of minutes ago, she must've fallen in. It's really deep here, can you try and find her?'

'Yeah, I'll try!' shouted Peter, who could see the other swimmers were still a long way away.

No time to think. Taking a deep breath, he dived under the water, murky as it was, staying under as long as he could. There was nothing under the dinghy, just a grey darkness.

Coming up for breath, he shouted at the man in the boat. 'Can't see anything. Did you see what she was wearing at all, a colour for me to look for?'

'Pink! I think she was wearing pink!' he shouted back after a few seconds.

'Okay!' Peter shouted, taking a deep breath before diving back under. He scanned the darkness for a bright colour, knowing he had less than a minute to find her. He found the bottom of the sea, feeling sand in his hands and some rocks. As he looked around, he swam in a circle, directly under the dinghy, or so he thought.

He was deep, aware that there was little time left. So, he took a chance and swam to his left, realising that the tide was flowing that way, away from the dinghy.

Within seconds, he saw it! Something pink! He forced his arms forward, down onto the sea bed again. Grabbing at the body, he knew he was running out of breath. With one arm, he held the little body whilst pushing off the sea bed with his feet, racing as fast as he could to the surface.

He couldn't see anything other than the darkness around him, feeling his lungs were bursting, needing air!

Closing his eyes, kicking his legs and feet, he held on tightly to her for what seemed forever. The salt water stung his eyes, so he closed them. He had to get air. He thought of Helen. Then his mother. This can't be the end, not like this. He had too much to live for. So did this little girl.

Opening his eyes, he could see clearer blue sea. He gulped, swallowing some salt water. Pushing his legs with all his strength, he burst through the surface of the sea, holding tightly onto her. He gasped, panting heavily, spitting water out from his lungs. Dizziness overtook him as he pulled the little girl up next to him, getting her head above water.

The guy in the boat saw him, shouting at him, 'Hey fella! Hey fella!'

Peter turned round, but couldn't speak, still coughing water out of his body.

'Over there! Over there! Take her to shore, they got equipment there. Go on, swim, it'll be quicker than me taking her from you!'

Coming to his senses, he realised he was much closer to shore, only about a hundred metres. She must've drifted away from the dinghy, which was a long way away from him now. The other men were with the dinghy, but could see Peter had the girl.

Keeping her head above water, he squeezed her body, as he swam backstroke, trying to get to the beach as quickly as possible, whilst trying to get water out of her body. She must've been about five or six years old, he thought.

He could hear people shouting again, screaming at him. Then a splash of water. It was impossible for him to see, trying to keep her head out of the sea as he swam.

Thrashing his feet as fast as he could, he managed to get more air into his own body, going as fast as he could. Then he felt a hand under his body. Still holding the girl in his arms, he put his feet down onto the sandy sea bed, taking the girl the final few feet onto the beach. Two men helped him, as he laid her down. A lifeguard was there, then he heard a man shout through the crowd, 'I'm a doctor, let me through!'

Peter collapsed onto the sand, down on his hands and knees, gasping for air. Having swallowed some water, he coughed it up, being physically sick as well.

Moments after being sick, he felt better. Glancing at the crowd, he saw the little girl being given mouth to mouth resuscitation by the guy who said he was a doctor. Nothing happened for over a minute. Everyone around the girl was silent. Peter got up and walked away, thinking he'd failed. As he did, he heard a cry. It was the little girl. The doctor had brought her back to life. Peter turned back to see the crowd staring at him. Then he collapsed himself.

Next thing he knew, the doctor was bending over him, pressing down on his stomach. Peter felt water and bile coming out of his mouth, as he shouted, 'Argh!'

In a split second, two men helped him to his feet, as the doctor spoke to him. 'You okay, young fella?'

'Yeah, yeah. Thanks. Feel a bit sick. Dizzy too.'

'Not surprised after what you've been through.'

Peter nodded at him, as the crowd, stayed around him.

'You saved that little girl's life, young man!' said the doctor.

Then, one of the two men who helped him up said, 'I don't know how you did that, buddy. She was miles away from the dinghy. Incredible!'

'How can I ever thank you?' said another man, who was cradling the girl in his arms, crying when he spoke.

'I... I... err. Well, just tried to help.'

He thrust out his hand as he held the girl in his arms, who was breathing now. Peter shook his hand, asking, 'She okay? Doctor, will she be all right?'

'Ambulance is here already. You go too, young man. They'll take you both to hospital, get you checked over,' said the doctor.

Peter nodded. He didn't want any fuss, but knew he felt queasy. It made sense to get checked over.

'What's your name? You saved my daughter's life. What you did was miraculous, my friend,' said the man holding the girl.

'Peter. Peter Johnson. Not sure how I did it to be honest with you. Trying to help, that's all.'

'Anything you ever want, you let me know. My name's Frank Watson. Do I know you?'

'That's really kind, just glad I could help.'

'You look familiar? Can't place it?' questioned Frank again.

'Have you seen a drag artist show here in Spain? An act named Petra Juno?' said Peter.

'Yes, took the kids and my wife a few nights ago.'

Peter leaned to whisper in his ear. 'That's me,' he said smiling.

'No!' he said. 'You're bloody good! We had a great night. Wow!'

'Got to earn a living somehow,' Peter said, smiling.

'Well I never. Again, can't thank you enough,' he said, still holding onto Peter's hand.

As the crowd began dispersing, they walked up to the end of the beach where the ambulance was waiting, the doctor walked up with them, explaining everything to the ambulance crew. Peter went off to collect his belongings, returning, still feeling dizzy.

'When's your next show?'

'Not tonight, I have Monday's off. Back on stage tomorrow night, here in Benidorm.'

They climbed into the ambulance as Frank said, 'Let me know where. Like to come to the show, say thank you properly.'

'There's no need, honestly. Thanks enough is seeing your little girl alive.'

Frank hugged him then, crying. Peter smiled at him as the doors were closed.

When he was released from hospital early that evening, he'd had an X-ray. All was well. The little girl, named Claire, was kept in overnight, he was told. She was expected to make a full recovery. She'd fallen out of the dinghy after paddling out, not being noticed by her parents at all, who were watching their young son at the time.

He had his usual early night that Monday, with a drink in the bar around the corner from his hotel, not telling anyone of his experience that day; being the centre of attention on stage was enough. It was different when he was Petra Juno; that was a character he could hide behind. He thought of his mum and the little girl he'd saved. And the baby his mother lost. But not for long. Going home in a few weeks, he thought. 'Big question to ask before I go,' he said to himself.

That Tuesday night, he went to work, finishing the act again to rapturous applause. Afterwards, Frank Watson and his family found Randy Martinez, telling him the story. He knew exactly what to do. They went back stage together, Frank giving Peter his address in England; whether he wanted to keep in touch or not, they would be eternally grateful.

Martinez had the story splashed all over the papers in Spain; it was headline news in Benidorm. The rest of his shows were attended by Spanish celebrities and dignitaries who wanted to meet him. Martinez said it would be good for business. It was. Peter felt embarrassed by all the publicity, but went along with it. Fortunately, by the time his contract was almost over, his heroic act had faded from people's minds.

22
End of the Contract

As the pair continued their chats on the phone, neither of them hinted at what they were going to say or do when Helen flew out. Peter had one night left, the last Sunday in August when she arrived. Martinez picked Helen up from the airport in the evening, taking her to the show.

Peter was on great form. Martinez had gone on stage telling the crowd that this was the last night of the season for Petra Juno. There was loud applause, which seemed to go on for ages. At the end, as Helen watched with Martinez, she told him it felt like déjà vu from a few years ago, explaining what had happened when her uncle returned to his club in London a few Christmas's ago, after recovering from his heart attack. 'You will both always be welcome here anytime, Helen,' he said, 'as my guests.'

'That's very kind. Thank you,' she said, kissing him on the cheek, as he hugged her.

The applause finally died down, as they made their way back stage. Martinez did not tell Helen about the plan Peter had for his last Monday, nor did he tell her about him saving a little girl's life. Peter hadn't told her either.

Back stage once again, with Peter changed into his shorts and T-shirt, Martinez knew they would be flying back to England the next day. He had a surprise, before they had their own surprise for one another.

Taking them to the hotel, for what Peter thought would be a quiet drink, Martinez had other plans. Helen had only planned to stay the one night, wanting to see Peter, to travel back with him.

When they walked into the hotel lobby, Martinez went in first. All of his other clubs had closed this Sunday night; he didn't tell Peter. Walking in behind Martinez, they saw all of the familiar faces he'd worked with over the last three months.

Martinez turned and smiled at him, before speaking. 'Peter, this is to say thank you from all of us, to you. And to your young lady, Helen, who we've all met briefly. I – we – want to show you our appreciation. We've so far had our best summer season ever; that is partly because of you and your act.' He stopped, turning around to orchestrate his staff in a chorus of a song Peter had made his own.

They sang a rendition of "Blue Spanish Eyes". All of them knew he and Helen both had blue eyes; Martinez had told everyone.

It was a wonderful moment. When the song finished, a little girl came up to Peter, with a box. Martinez had arranged it. She was Claire Watson. Martinez had flown her and her family back, to say goodbye and thank Peter, again. Frank Watson shook Peter's hand, then hugged him, unable to speak, with tears in his eyes.

Martinez took the box from Peter, asking Helen to open it. There were pictures of him on stage and newspaper cuttings in English and Spanish showing photographs of Peter with the headlines: *Lifesaver; actor saves English girl.*

As she looked at Peter, Helen shook her head. 'You never said?'

'Don't like to make a fuss,' he replied.

She hugged him, kissing him. 'You are the one for me, Mr Johnson.'

'Ditto,' said Peter.

Applause rang out, as over one hundred people clapped, chanting his name. That name was who they knew: Petra Juno.

When the applause died down, it was Peter's turn to walk among his colleagues and friends, just like Johnny had some time ago. Different circumstances here, though. He made a point of speaking to Frank Watson, his wife, their little boy and Claire, who said, 'Who's this man, Daddy?'

'He saved your life, Claire, don't you remember?' said Frank, holding his daughter in his arms.

'When I was in the dinghy in the sea?'

'Yes,' said Frank. Peter smiled, as did Helen. For once he was speechless.

Claire put her arms out towards him, as her father passed her towards Peter. 'Thank you,' she whispered into Peter's ear. He just nodded at her, then her parents, tears in his eyes, holding her tightly for a few seconds, before handing her back to her mother.

They wandered around, talking to all the people he'd got to know, as he had a couple of drinks, before Helen finally said to him, 'Home tomorrow. You can become "the kid" again. Can't wait to show them all what you've done. But first, we need to go upstairs to our room. Got a bit of news for you as well.'

'Oh, everything okay?'

'Yes,' she said. 'Tell you in a while.'

Going to their room an hour or so later after saying their goodbyes, Helen said he'd better sit down, with what she'd got to tell him.

'Okay, come on then. What's up?'

'Told you a little white lie a few weeks ago. Well, not completely.'

'Helen? What's wrong?' he asked her.

'Sit down, Pete, please,' she said, quietly.

He did, on the bed, rubbing his face with his hands, before saying, 'Think you'd better tell me. Is it Johnny, the club, what's the matter?'

'Nothing like that,' she said, sitting next to him, before continuing. 'I didn't come over four weeks ago, because I felt unwell, you know that. And Auntie broke her ankle.'

'Yes, you said when you called a few days ago, she'll be having the cast off soon. And, what else?'

'So, here's the thing. I know we've not talked about this much, being so busy in the club and you working here. I didn't tell you a month ago, because I wasn't hundred percent sure. But now I am, my reason being that I wanted to tell you in person. So...'

'So...?'

Bending down, she kissed him, saying, 'You're going to be a father. I'm pregnant!'

He jumped off the bed before shouting, 'No! Really! But how? I mean, well, not how, but when, and... fuck... it's brilliant!'

He stood in front of her, holding her head in his hands, then stared at her with a beaming smile.

'When I came over for the holiday. That's when, three months ago. You knew I was on the pill, but I forgot to bring them with me. I didn't plan it to happen. You're happy, then?'

'Happy! Happy? I'm absolutely... absolutely over the bloody moon!'

They kissed, then held one another, before he said, 'A baby!'

'Yes,' she said. 'I've not told anyone yet, though Mum and Auntie suspect already. I wanted to tell you first, Pete, before my parents.'

'Wow! I'm stunned. This is just amazing. You're... you're going to be a mum! I'm going to be a dad!'

'Yep,' she said nodding, with a massive grin on her face.

'So, err. How long then?'

'Been to see my doctor, he says end of February or early March next year. Couldn't be more specific, needs to give me a thorough examination for that; and I want you with me when that happens.'

He continued smiling, saying, 'Blimey, just doing... you know... creates this,' he said pointing at her belly. 'You okay now? Still feeling sick? I should've known, what an idiot!'

'I didn't want you to know; you had this job to think of, as well as being on your own.'

'Well, I'm glad you told me yourself. I love you to pieces, you know that, don't you?'

'Course I do, silly,' she said, hugging him tightly, pausing before continuing. 'Now,' she said, 'have you got everything packed? No rush as the flight isn't until six p.m. tomorrow.'

'Yep, pretty much all done,' he said, remembering his plan Martinez had helped him with. It'd been forgotten with the sending off party and now this wonderful news. 'All done, almost. Thought we'd have a last walk on the beach in the morning. That okay with you?'

'Sounds good. Right, you, I want to cuddle up and shag you now. Don't worry, I checked with the doctor and we're fine doing it still,' she said, smiling at him.

'Oh. Well, I was going to ask you about that. If you're sure?'

'Oh yes!' she said, smiling. Then she pulled him onto the bed, where they eventually fell asleep in one another's arms. Peter woke first, suggesting again they go to a beach side bar or café for a final breakfast. She agreed. He'd planned to get to the beach at eleven o'clock, where Martinez would be waiting.

When they arrived, walking hand in hand onto the sand, Peter said, 'Hey, what's going on over there?' In the distance away from the crowds on the beach was an area cordoned off. As they walked closer, he could see Martinez, along with a giant umbrella covering a table and two chairs. 'Let's have a look,' he said.

Helen didn't notice it was Martinez. He was dressed in all white, with a chef's hat on his head. But, Peter knew.

'No, come on,' she said, 'let's go and have breakfast before getting sorted to go home.'

'Just a little peek, come on,' he replied.

As they got closer, paddling through the sea, walking up to the table which they could see was laid for breakfast, she saw it was Martinez.

'Welcome!' he exclaimed. 'Please sit! We have breakfast for you. Sir, please take your seat. Madam,' he said, pulling out a seat for her to sit down on.'

'What's going on here?' Helen questioned Peter.

'I'll pour your drinks, sir, madam. I will be back when you are finished,' said Martinez smiling, bowing, then walking away outside of the cordon, to sit on a seat he had left there himself.

A crowd had gathered near where he was seated, Peter and Helen couldn't hear what he was saying, as they were out of earshot. But, within a few seconds, the crowd dispersed.

'Pete?'

'Okay, got you here under false pretences. You had a massive surprise for me last night. I've never been happier after you told me. Bloody marvellous!' he said pausing. 'But, when you couldn't get here a few weeks ago, I missed you like crazy. Now, I know exactly why,' he said, smiling at her.

'So, this is a final breakfast. On the beach. Romantic gesture?'

'You could call it that.'

'It's lovely, thank you.'

'Just one more thing before you tuck in,' he said, pausing again, lifting up a handkerchief in the middle of the table, revealing a small pink box. Picking it up, he got out of his chair, walked round to her, getting down on one knee, opening the box to reveal a ring. She put her hands to her mouth, gasping for air, saying nothing.

'When you couldn't get here, I knew I should've done this a long time ago. I love you, Helen Armstrong. Just one thing I'd like to know?' he said, stopping for a deep breath. 'Will you marry me?'

'What! What! Yes! Yes!' she shouted, leaning forward to kiss him. As they stood up together hugging, he took the ring from the box, placing it on her finger. Then he picked her up in his arms, swinging her around, as they kissed again.

'Oh, Pete Johnson. You're the best,' she whispered into his ear.

'Likewise, with you,' he replied.

As he held her, Martinez walked over. 'Well?' he asked, 'looks like it worked, Peter?'

'Yes!' he shouted.

'You in on this?' she asked Martinez.

'Sort of, yes,' he replied.

'Bit more than that,' said Peter. 'He made me realise what I had with you. Being away from you hit home, so to speak.'

Martinez smiled, clapping. Then he hugged them both, as Peter still held Helen in his arms. 'Come on, you two, eat your breakfast. Then I'll take you to the airport.'

When they left the beach, Martinez picked them up later from their hotel with his wife Mina, taking them to the airport. Peter had met her a few times, although Helen had only seen her briefly on her visit back in June.

'You two have got your whole lives in front of you. Have a great time. And remember, anytime you want to come back – work or holiday – you let me know. You have my number,' Martinez said, shaking Peter's hand.

'Thank you. Got a bit more news before we go,' Peter said, putting his arm around Helen, nodding at her.

'Only told him last night,' Helen said looking at Peter, before turning back to Martinez, telling him, 'I couldn't come over until now, because... I'm pregnant!'

Mina grabbed Helen, hugging her, then did the same to Peter, saying, 'This is beautiful. Congratulations!'

Martinez kissed her on both cheeks, before shouting, 'Yes! Bambino!' throwing his arms up in the air before shaking Peter's hand again. 'Now you must come back. Keep in touch, let me know all is okay.'

'We will,' said Peter. 'Thank you for everything.'

'You deserve all the good luck in the world, my friends. I'm, sorry to lose you, but I understand. I will look out for you in the famous pages of the newspapers, okay?' said Martinez.

Peter laughed, before replying, 'Don't know about that. But we'll be back. That's a promise.'

'Yes, we will,' said Helen.

'Goodbye. Take care, all of you,' Martinez said, smiling, pointing at Helen's stomach, before turning away from the airport entrance, leaving them to get their flight home, as he and Mina walked arm in arm.

'We'll see them again, won't we?' Peter questioned Helen, as they boarded the plane.

'Oh yes. Most definitely,' said Helen.

By the time they'd got out of the airport and in a taxi, she phoned her parents. There was no answer, so, she phoned the club. Ruth answered, telling Helen her parents were having an evening at the club.

She told Peter, 'We're going to the club. Mum and Dad are there.'

'Usually closes on a Monday?'

'You're out of touch, must be the heat. It's August bank holiday today. We always open on most bank holidays, you know that.'

'Oh, is it? I am out of touch.'

'Won't take long to get you back in the groove,' she said smiling at him.

23
All Change

It was ten p.m. by the time they arrived at the club. Getting out of the taxi, coming back home, Peter said, 'Blimey, it may be August, but it's not as warm here.'

'That's because you've still got shorts and T-shirt on!' said Helen.

'Right, let's give them the news then,' he said, rubbing his arms.

'You tell them about getting married. Still can't believe this,' she said, smiling at him, 'then I'll tell them about having a BABY!' out of earshot of the taxi as it drove away.

'Okay,' he said, smiling at her.

'I've been trying to hide it from them all, but like I said back in Spain, I think my mum and aunt might suspect. Mum heard me a couple of times at home when I've been sick; but that was a few weeks ago now, when I couldn't come over.

Big Dave was on the door as they walked into the club, Peter pulling his cases.

'Welcome back, kid!' said Dave, grabbing his hand, shaking it, as he stood alongside another guy nearly as big.

'Good to be back, Dave. Nice to see you.'

'And you. Both of you,' Dave replied, nodding as they walked in, adding, 'see you're still dressed for the Spanish weather then?'

'Yes, bit chillier here though,' said Peter, turning to smile at Big Dave, looking down at his shorts.

Going through the double doors, they saw Johnny at the bar. He didn't see them, as they crept up behind him. 'Hello, stranger!' said Peter.

Johnny turned round to face him. 'Kid! Pete! Great to have you back!' he said, putting his arms around him.

'It's good to be back. Had a great time. Missed you all though.'

'That's good to hear. Now listen, get yourself a drink, no need to be here for a few days, take some time off the pair of you.'

'Thanks, Uncle,' said Helen, as Johnny hugged her as well.

'How you feeling?' Peter asked him.

'Fine. Good. Look, your parents are over there, Helen. Go and join them, I'll stick your cases behind the bar, save you lugging them about. Arthur, stick these in the store room for a while, please,' he shouted over everyone at the bar.

Arthur came straight over, shaking Peter's hand. 'Good to see you, Pete, great to have you back,' he said, as they smiled at one another.

'Go on, off you go. I'll be over with some drinks in a minute, just going to find my boss!' Johnny said, laughing.

A few minutes later, after greeting Helen's parents, shaking her father's hand, and kissing her mother on the cheek as she hugged him, Peter sat at the table. Some of the customers had seen him arrive, so they gathered around, greeting him fondly.

'Missed your act, kid! Good to see you back in one piece,' said one of the crowd.

'Thanks. Good to be home,' he said, turning to shake his hand.

'See you're dressed for summer. Surprised Big Dave let you in, we all know what he's like for smart dress!' said the same man, as the small crowd of half a dozen laughed.

'Have to get used to this after a season in the sun,' Peter replied, smiling. 'Really appreciate your kindness, guys. Just going to have a drink with the boss. Think you'll likely know Miss Armstrong's parents,' he added, looking in their direction.

They all said good evening to Helen's parents, nodding politely, before Peter spoke again. 'How's Mr Fenton been, not been coming in too early?' he questioned the group, before one spoke.

'No, he and Mrs Fenton haven't been coming in until at least nine p.m., Miss Armstrong's seen to that,' said one of the other men, nodding in Helen's direction.

She smiled, then said, 'Yes, someone has to keep an eye on him as well as his wife! Enjoy the rest of your evening, gentleman, here comes our drinks,' she said, seeing Johnny walk over with a tray.

The group laughed, then two of them shook Peter's hand, whilst another patted his shoulder saying, 'Really good to see you back, young man.' Must be at least eighty years old, Peter thought, as he turned to say thank you to him.

Walking away to their respective tables, they all said, good evening, sir, or good evening, boss, to Johnny, who nodded at them winking at the really old guy before saying, 'Enjoy the entertainment, all of you, this one will be back on stage in a few days,' he said, looking over at Peter.

Johnny sat down to join them, as Ruth came over a few seconds later, hobbling on her crutches. 'Just been in the kitchen,' she said.

Right behind her, was Terry. He walked right round the table following Ruth, as she hugged Peter.

Then Terry kissed him on the cheek, hugging him as well before saying, 'Missed you, fella, good to see you.'

'Great to be back, Terry. Good to see you too.'

'Can't stop, full house tonight, got to keep on top of the kitchen, you know the one!'

'Yes, I do. Catch up with you later, or tomorrow.'

'Sure thing, kid!' said Terry, letting him out of their embrace, going back to work.

'Who was the old guy in the group here a moment ago, boss, who you winked at?' questioned Peter.

'Used to be my teacher. Lovely chap. What teachers should all be like; encouraged me to try and do whatever I wanted when I grew up,' Johnny said, sitting down, nodding to Helen's parents, as he handed out the drinks, before continuing. 'I was a bit of a bloody rogue back then. He took me aside many a time, knew I was good at English, just like my sister,' he said, nodding at Joyce.

'Yes,' said Joyce. 'Great teacher, dear old Mr Twyman.'

'He was that,' said Johnny. 'Told me to reach for the stars when I left. That's what I did and here I am.'

'Yes,' said Ruth, 'and you met me at school as well, didn't you?'

'I did. Lucky me!' he said, laughing, sitting down, then sipping his drink.

'Now,' said Joyce, holding her daughter's hand sitting next to her. It was her right hand. Helen had been trying to hide her left hand so that nobody could see her ring. 'We know you two missed one another. Glad to have him back?'

'Yes, Mum,' said Helen, turning to smile at Peter.

'How's your ankle?' Peter asked Ruth.

'Plaster coming off in a week's time. Feeling much better now. Sorry it ruined Helen's visit, I was a mess for a few weeks or so, all battered and bruised after my fall.'

'She told me all about it. Good to know you're on the mend,' Peter replied.

'It was tough going at the time. Couldn't have got through it without Helen and her parents,' said Johnny, being unusually serious.

Helen took a deep breath before saying, 'So, it's great having my man back. Bloody marvellous.' She turned and kissed Peter in front of them all, nodding at him, whispering to him, 'Tell them now.'

'Okay. Here's the thing,' he said. 'Really pleased to have you all around the table. Mr and Mrs Armstrong, Mr and Mrs Fenton,' nodding at them all. 'Got a little announcement and we wanted you to be the first ones to know.' He glanced at Helen as she smiled, then he said, 'I asked Helen to get married this morning in Spain. She said yes! Don't know where or when, but... we're getting married!'

Helen finally put her left hand out over the table, flashing her ring.

'Oh, that's wonderful,' said Joyce, hugging her daughter.

Her father Brian got up, walked round to Peter who'd already got out of his chair. 'Welcome to the family, son. Sorry about years ago, wasn't sure about you. I know you're a good 'un,' he said, as Peter hugged him. Her father was not an emotional man; this was the first time he'd ever held Peter in his arms.

Peter saw tears in his eyes, as he replied, 'Thank you. Didn't have a chance to ask for your permission, sir.'

'No problem. Please, call me Brian. Congratulations.'

Brian went back to his seat with Peter following him, as Helen's mother rose to hold him in her arms, kissing him on the cheek. She too had tearstained eyes, he could see.

He walked round the table to Ruth, leaning down to hug her, telling her not to get up because of her ankle. She had a beaming smile all over her face as he kissed her cheek.

Johnny had already gone round to Helen. Peter was walking round the table towards him as he let go of his bear-hug on Helen, turning to Peter, saying, 'I knew you we're a good 'un too, when you started here. Doesn't matter about the past. That'll work out when you're ready. Like a son to me, you are, kid,'

Johnny said, hugging him, as Helen went over to Ruth, who was still sitting in her chair.

Peter and Johnny finally let one another go, going back to their chairs. The people around them knew something was happening, but kept away.

Then, as they all quietened down for a moment Helen said, 'That's not all.' Her mother raised her eyebrows, smiling at her, squeezing her hand. Before anyone could ask the question, Helen said, 'I'm... we're... having a baby!'

Her mother said, 'Bloody thought so! Fantastic!' she shouted.

'Wow!' said her father.

'This just keeps getting better and better,' said Johnny.

'Oh, congratulations,' said Ruth, with a beaming smile again.

'Had to tell Pete first. As well as your ankle, Auntie Ruth, I felt too ill to fly a few weeks ago. Lots better now, though,' she said, turning to Peter again, smiling at him.

'Right, champagne it is. I'm having more than my one drink tonight, luv,' said Johnny.

'Exceptional circumstances. Yes, I think so,' said Ruth, still smiling.

'This is just amazing,' said Brian, puffing out air from his cheeks, as he rocked back on his chair.

'You okay, Dad?' asked Helen.

'Yes!' he replied. 'Bloody marvellous!' having a big grin on his face. Helen laughed out loud. It was the catchphrase she'd picked up from her father.

Johnny got up from his chair, going to the bar, telling Arthur the news, who got one of the waitresses to go straight over with two bottles of champagne and six glasses. 'A toast!' said Johnny. 'To the happy couple, Helen and the kid. Another Mr and Mrs to be. Congratulations times two!'

'Cheers everyone,' said Brian.

They all clinked their glasses together in the middle of the table, taking sips from their drinks; even Helen had a little taste.

'Phew!' said Peter. 'What a day!' sitting back in his chair.

'Best day ever?' asked Helen.

'By far.' Then his mind wandered for some inexplicable reason to the day his dad taught him to ride his bike. He knew this was better. 'Yes, the best day ever, so far, for both of us,' he said, leaning over to kiss her.

They all had another glass of champagne, except Helen. She'd already told Peter it must be the pregnancy that'd put her off alcohol.

Some of the regular customers who knew Helen and Peter came over to offer their congratulations.

They both went into the kitchen to tell Terry the news. He told them it was about bloody time they got married! And he was elated they were having a baby.

The waitresses came round to their table, encircling them all, singing "we're getting married in the morning", giving them a round of applause afterwards. In the meantime, the band played on, for another hour or so, until the club closed.

Peter had already asked Helen not to mention the incident with the little girl he saved. Keep that story for another day, he said, not wanting any fuss. They did tell them about Martinez's generosity; he even paid Peter an extra month's pay. And, they would go back one day, but only for a holiday.

Her parents said they'd help finance a house; so did Johnny and Ruth. Helen told them they'd saved quite a bit, and with the money from the season Peter worked in Spain, they had enough for a big deposit.

They were paid well by Johnny, enough to cover a big mortgage. But, they all insisted they wanted to help. They weren't allowed to say no, her mother and Ruth said.

That night, they stayed in Peter's room. They were both exhausted, falling asleep in one another's arms.

24
Time Flies By

Over the next few months, Peter got back to his job on stage and his act as Petra Juno. Helen's bump grew bigger, as Johnny took over running the club at Christmas time with Ruth, her parents helping out too.

The wedding hadn't been planned; they were so busy, there'd been no time to organise it. They'd bought a house near her parents in Balham, South London, not far from Johnny's home, moving into it, in early 1982. Knowing her parents, uncle and aunt lived nearby reassured Peter and Helen, who were concerned about the Brixton riots in April 1981. It was no more than a half hour drive to the club.

Before they knew it, she was going into labour in the middle of March. It was a time when it was becoming popular for fathers to attend the birth of their children, if the mother wanted them there. Helen wanted Peter with her.

They had a little girl, naming her Tammy. Helen sailed through the birth, Peter told them all. Her parents, then Uncle and Aunt visited the hospital, as did Terry and his wife, along with Helen's best friend, Kate.

Peter wanted to mark the occasion, so a few days after she was born, he went into an antique shop in London. He'd looked in the windows of a couple of them before Tammy was born, thinking he should get a gift to mark the arrival. Going into one named Leonard's Antiques, he strolled round the shop, not really knowing what to get. 'Can I help you, sir?' asked the man.

'Well, yes,' replied Peter. 'Not really sure what to get. Just become a dad for the first time.'

'Firstly, let me offer my congratulations,' said the man. He was tall, like Peter, with long blond hair in a ponytail. 'And is mother and baby well?'

'Yes, fine thank you. Had a little girl, named her Tammy.'

'Great news. Sorry, I should have introduced myself, I'm Richard Leonard. This is my shop. Well, I should say, it's been handed down through generations of us Leonards; I've inherited it from my father,' he said, pausing for a moment to shake Peter's hand. 'Now, what can we find for a new-born baby girl?'

'Been looking at your antique spoons, and pots. But, I'd like to get something a bit different.'

'Might have something for you. Do you like cars?'

'Yes, of course. Helen – my other half – loves them more than me.'

'Give me a moment, could have just the thing,' said Richard, going out of a door at the back of the shop.

When he came back a couple of minutes later, he was carrying three small boxes on a tray. 'Before I show you these, may I ask you a question?'

'Sure, please do,' Peter replied.

'You look familiar to me. Do you live or work here in London. Can't quite place where I may have seen you?'

'Are you a Londoner yourself?' asked Peter.

'Yes, I live above my shop now, since my father passed away last year.'

'Sorry to hear that. Do you visit any clubs, nightclubs around here?'

'Yes, started going to a couple of places. One not too far away, called Johnny's.'

Peter smiled, saying, 'That's where I work. Sometimes I'm behind the bar helping out. But, a few nights a week, I'm on stage.'

'Got it! You're the drag artist. Bloody hell, you're good! Seen you two or three times, with some friends. Can't remember your stage name; think it's, err, possibly… Petal James, or something like that?'

'Close. Very close,' said Peter, laughing. 'It's actually Petra Juno.'

'Oh, I'll remember that. So, what's your actual name?'

'Well, they all call me "the kid" at the club.'

'I see. Sort of a stage name cover-up, a man of mystery, so to speak?'

'No, not at all,' Peter said. 'Peter Johnson, nice to meet you. But please, call me "the kid", almost everyone does. I was given the name years ago when I started working at Johnny's by the owner, Johnny Fenton,' he added, shaking Richard's hand again.

'It's a pleasure to meet you,' Richard said, as their handshake ended. 'You'll have to let me know when your act is on stage again, so I can come along with the lady in my life. It's a great venue, we've had a meal there, of course. Great service. Think I've seen the owner, always used to have a cigar in his hand, but not recently. Has slicked back hair I believe?'

'That's Johnny all right. So, what've you got for me there?' Peter asked, waiting to see inside the boxes.

'Ah! Yes. Sorry,' he said, proceeding to open all three, gesturing to Peter to come forward. 'Come on, have a look inside.'

In each box, was a small ceramic car, about six inches in length; one was green, one blue and the last one he looked at was red. The make of each one was a Rolls Royce. The details of them impressed Peter, they were ceramic, but looked like the real thing.

'These are collector items. They are expensive. Rolls Royce make them. Very difficult getting hold of them, you know. I only ever get three each year. Well I have for the last four years; sell them all within a few days of receiving them. They have the trademark underneath, dated as well,' he said, showing Peter.

'That doesn't surprise me,' said Peter. He knew he had to get one as a keepsake for Tammy. 'No pink one then?' he asked.

'Afraid not. Only these three colours.'

'I'll take the red one please, not even going to haggle over the price with you!'

'Good. They were only delivered last week. I don't put them on display, too expensive you see.'

'The price is immaterial. It's a gift for our baby girl; a memento of the year she arrived. She can keep it, I hope, forever.'

'You came in at the right time. I'll wrap it up for you,' he said, putting the other two under the counter, placing it in the box with bubble wrap, then in a bag with the shop name on it.

'Cash, cheque or card, sir,' he asked, smiling.

'Card, thanks,' Peter replied, making the payment shortly after.

'Now, is there anything else I can interest you in?'

'Not today, Mr Leonard. Maybe another day.'

'Please, call me Richard. And you'd prefer me to call you "the kid" or Peter?'

'Yes, either's fine. Thank you again. I'll be back, you can be sure of it,' Peter said, turning to leave.

'Oh! One thing, could you tell me what nights next week you're on stage please?'

'Err, next week. Don't think I'm working for a couple of weeks, well not the act, I'm afraid. Promised I'd stay at home, help out with the baby, especially in the evenings.'

'Sorry, my apologies. Be going there soon, I'll ask when I go.'

'No problem,' Peter said, having turned back to shake Richard's hand again. 'Goodbye.'

'Yes, cheerio for now,' he replied, closing the door behind Peter.

Decent chap, Peter thought to himself. He'd told Richard his real name, thinking there'd be no chance of his father coming looking for him here. It was only Helen, her parents, Terry, Johnny and Ruth who knew his real identity. They'd all urged him to at least contact his mother, if not his father. Only those people knew why he came to London. Then he remembered Spain; they all knew his real name too.

He pondered over it now, walking back to the car, to drive to the hospital. Tammy was only three days old, Helen would be in hospital for another few days recovering. Every now and then she asked him to contact his family; he always said no, other than his mother's card on her birthday, the odd letter and calls to Elly. Helen always told him it was never too late.

When he got to the hospital he saw the curtains were drawn around her bed. His eyes shot around looking for a nurse or doctor, thinking something was wrong. He thought of his mother as he pulled them open, panic setting in his mind. The emotion of seeing Helen give birth; their baby; not seeing his family; Richard in the shop telling him he'd lost his father last year, all rushed into his brain. He started to cry, as he looked at Helen.

'Hey, you okay?' she asked him, as he stood over them.

'Yep. I thought something was wrong when I saw the curtains closed around your bed.'

'Silly. Just breastfeeding, that's all.'

'Can see that now.'

'Pete, what is it?'

'Nothing. I just went to get a gift for Tammy. See what you think when you open it in a while,' he said, sitting down on the bed, kissing her, as she continued to breastfeed Tammy.

'Open it, I'll have a look now.'

'Okay,' he said, taking the box out of the bag, opening it to show her.

'That's lovely. And it's a red Rolls Royce, same colour as the first car I had.'

'That's why I got it. The colour. No pink ones I'm afraid. A collector's item the guy in the shop said. Nice fella, had a good chat with him,' he said, repeating the conversation he had with Richard Leonard.

'You know I've got a few more days here, just want to come home now.'

'Rules are rules. Won't be long.'

'What else is it, Pete? What's wrong?'

'Nothing. Well, not nothing,' he said, pausing as she carried on feeding Tammy. 'Everything rushed into my mind when these curtains were closed. As well as you and Tammy, because we had a girl, I thought about my mum.'

'You know what you've got to do. I haven't mentioned it to you for ages now, but you know what I think. It's about time you went to see her; not your dad, I know you can't handle that; don't know if you ever can.'

'I know. I'll think about it. I really will.'

Three days later, when Helen came home with Tammy, he told her what he was going to do. 'It's been eating away at me. I'm going to call Elly. Then I'm going to see Mum. On my own.'

'Oh, Pete! Do you mean it?'

'Yes, I do.'

Helen smiled at him. She started crying. 'I've waited for you to say that since I met you. It's been a long time coming.'

'I know,' he said pausing. 'Having Tammy, being with you, our own home, great job. Most people would think I had everything I ever wanted. Well, I have, you know that.'

'But something's always been missing, hasn't it?'

'You know it has. I've hidden away from doing this for too many years. I almost lied to Richard in his antique shop about my name. That plus everything else made me realise... well... you know,' he said, as Helen cuddled him, while Tammy was asleep in her crib.

'Oh, Pete Johnson. Pete Johnson. What are we going to do with you?' she said, smiling.

'Don't know really. Silly sod, aren't I?'

'Yes, you are. Elly said your dad will look for you forever. He will. Now you're a dad, even though Tammy's a baby, you know how he feels, losing you – his child.'

'Yep, I understand it now.'

'Okay. Uncle said he doesn't want to see us at the club for two weeks. My mum and dad are helping out like they used to. Get on that phone this evening and call Elly. Set it up. Go and see her. And your mum.'

'I will,' he said, still cuddling into her.

That evening, he called Elly. He was crying on the phone, hardly able to speak. Helen took over from him, telling Elly they'd just had their baby. Peter took the phone when he'd stopped crying, telling Elly himself he was coming up.

They arranged the day. He knew she'd moved out of her parents' house because of her different phone number, living with her partner Jenny for a few years now. She couldn't take time off work; she was a teacher just like his mum, in a different school.

He asked Elly not to tell his mum. She didn't. Helen said she'd be fine without him for a night; two if he wanted.

In late March, 1982, with Tammy just a couple of weeks old, he drove up to Manchester. It would be the first time he'd gone back since 1968. Fourteen years was a long time. He was twenty-seven now, his mum would be just over fifty years old. There was no plan, he would see how it went...

25
Been a Long Time

Driving up, he'd get there for about four o'clock in the afternoon. Elly gave him directions to her house; Jenny would be there if she wasn't home from school.

He was there by three thirty, so decided to drive to the area where they grew up. It had hardly changed at all. Elly told him that his parents never moved; just in case he came back.

Finding Elly's house, he parked round the corner, waiting until it was four o'clock. Then, he drove to her house, parking directly outside.

Walking up the path to the door, he didn't need to knock on it; it was opened as he approached. At the door, was his oldest friend, Elly, smiling. 'Well, get your arse in here!' she said, grabbing him, closing the door, then hugging him with all of her strength. 'You've been away too bloody long. I'm not going to have a go at you. It's just great to see you, Pete,' she said, as he saw tears rolling down her cheeks.

'Must be a first, never seen you cry before,' he replied, kissing her cheek, still hugging her.

'Well, I've good reason. You're my oldest friend, Pete Johnson.'

'And you're mine too,' he said, with a croaky voice.

'Come on, meet Jenny. She's got the kettle on already. You can tell me everything; where you're living and working. You'd better have pictures of Helen and your baby, Tammy. If you haven't, I'll beat the shit out of you!' she said, laughing at him.

'I have. Got a set for you to keep in here,' he said smiling, pointing at the bag he had with him.

They went down a hallway, into the kitchen. 'Looks like a nice house?' he questioned.

'Yes, Jenny's a teacher as well; got a mortgage between us. Had a bit of trouble getting it; been here three years now.'

'Good,' he said, seeing Jenny making tea for them all.

'Jenny, this is the mystery man you thought a few years ago was a figment of my imagination. Pete Johnson, meet Jenny.'

'Hi, Pete. I really did think she'd made you up!' said Jenny, kissing him on the cheek.

'Happy to prove you wrong, Jenny. Nice to meet you. Think I've got a bit of explaining to do.'

'Too bloody right you have!' said Elly, smiling.

'Yes, I know,' he said, pausing. 'Went round the roads where we grew up; looks just the same.'

'It is. You know your mum and dad never left; could've done when your mum became a teacher,' Elly said, sipping her drink before continuing. 'Right, come on then, start at the beginning, Mr Johnson,' she said, raising her eyebrows.

Peter told her all about what happened, from the night he left, going to London. Sleeping rough, getting the job at the club, meeting Terry, Johnny and then later, Helen. Moving onto Spain, he told her about his job over there. He didn't mention Claire Watson, the little girl he saved. But, he told her about his proposal, moving into their house, and now becoming a dad. He asked her not to tell his mum, nor his dad, where he was. He wasn't ready for them to know that yet; if he told his mum, she'd tell his father. He still couldn't face him, he told Elly.

And, he told her that he'd landed on his feet, though he'd had to work really hard for everything.

When he'd finished, Elly said, 'Right then, I'm not going to tell your parents where you are. You decide that. Keep sending your mum's card to me with mine, I'll hand deliver it like always. Your dad won't know; she's told me he doesn't know. But I'll tell you this,' she paused, 'I've spoken to him many times, and he regrets what he did, Pete. He'd do anything to know you're okay. Please, tell your mum when you go and see her, to let your dad know you're safe. And well. Let her tell him; she'll want to. Just tell her you're not ready to see him yet. Okay?'

He nodded. 'I will. Look, I'm going round now. You said he works away as a football scout in the week, is that right?'

'Yes, he travels all over the country in the week, comes home at the weekends.'

'Right, I'm going. I'll tell her I've seen you. I'll be in touch. I will ring. Promise, okay?'

'Okay, Pete. Make sure you do,' she said, with teacher-like authority in her voice.

He got up, hugging Jenny. Walking to the front door, he opened it, turning as Elly spoke to him. 'Listen, Pete, I know I'm a bit in your face, but all I've ever wanted is what's best for you. You know you're my oldest, best friend, don't you? Apart from Jenny, that is.'

'I know. Always felt the same about you, Elly. I'll be in touch. Oh! Here, the photos. Got two sets, one for you and Mum,' he said, handing an envelope to her that had photos of them all inside.

'Your baby is beautiful, Pete. And Helen looks lovely,' said Elly, as she looked at the pictures.

'They're great,' he said, smiling, hugging her.

'Get going, see your mum. She doesn't know you're here, I never told her. Let me know how it goes.'

'I will. Bye for now,' he said, walking to his car, as he turned to wave to her. Jenny came to the door, waving as well.

'Seems like a lovely guy,' said Jenny.

'Yep, I know. I've always loved him. Not… you know… like me and you. But, always loved him, sort of like my big brother.'

'Did you tell him that?'

'No.'

'Well, go after him now, just tell him!'

'He knows I'm not like that.'

'Well, be different for a change… go on,' said Jenny pushing her out of the door as Peter got into his car.

She got to him as he turned the engine on. 'Pete, got one other thing to say.'

'What?'

'You know I'm not one for the lovey-dovey stuff, but it's been a long time. Just want to tell you that I love you. Always thought you were a…'

She couldn't finish what she was going to say, as he got out of his car, hugged her, and said, 'Always loved you as well. I knew you weren't into boys when we were kids. I couldn't care less. You're a great person. Thanks for putting up with me.'

'Go on,' she said, wiping her eyes again, 'bugger off and see your mum!' laughing at him before turning away.

He tooted his horn as he drove past their house, Jenny joining her outside, both waving goodbye.

Now it was off to his mum's house. He hoped it would go well.

26
Mum

He went via the road Elly used to live in, where they played hopscotch, before going under that railway bridge, where his jumping saved his own life and where he knocked over his mother. He'd never driven on these roads, but he knew them well. Still having doubts, he parked down the road, next to the letterbox; the one he and his brothers used to jump on, remembering playing football – him being the referee mostly – and playing chase with the other kids in their street.

Walking up the front path, he noticed there were new windows, all double glazed. The green front door looked the same. Seeing the doorbell, it triggered another memory for him; he was the one who used to hold his finger on it, to annoy his mum, just for fun.

Peter decided to hold his finger on it, hopefully waiting for his mother to answer it. He held his finger on it for ages; must've been about thirty seconds he thought to himself.

Then, the door opened. As it did, he took his finger off it. He couldn't speak, smiling at his mother, wiping his eyes as he did, trying to hold back his tears.

Brenda burst into tears, hugging him, crying her eyes out. She didn't let him go for a long time, both of them crying, uncontrollably. She knew it was her son.

Finally, looking at his face, she said, 'My handsome son. You're a sight for sore eyes. I've missed you so, so much. You're even taller than your father! This is the most wonderful surprise! I thought I'd lost you forever, until Elly gave me the birthday cards. Come on in!'

He followed her down the hallway, into their old living room, then into the kitchen. Brenda hugged him again saying, 'I love you. You'll always be my little baby boy, even though you're bigger than me!' she said, laughing at him.

'Mum, I'm sorry,' he said, as she let him out of their embrace.

'It's okay. It's up to you if you want to tell me about your life. Elly told me you're safe and well. She didn't tell me you were coming here though.'

'I wanted to surprise you,' he said quietly.

'You did that all right!' she said, smiling at him, turning to put the kettle on.

He laughed, then sat down, saying, 'Came straight from Elly's just now. I'll tell you everything, Mum. I can't stay though, there's a reason why. Well, a couple of reasons.'

'Oh? Are you okay. Do you need money, or help?'

'No. Nothing like that, far from it. I just can't see Dad; no way can I handle it. Sorry.'

She bent down, hugging him, then said, 'Did Elly tell you about him being a football scout?'

'Yep. Stan and Joe still play for Middlesbrough, I always check their scores. Jimmy's the boss at the accountants still, and he's got a little boy; well, must be about nine now?'

'Yes, they named him Charlie. He's eleven now. Lovely lad. Your dad dotes on him, as does your brother, Jimmy.'

'Good. So, Jimmy doing well then?'

'Yes, he was the manager, but two years ago, became a director.'

'Brilliant! You know that's thanks to you, Mum, don't you?'

'No, not really. Do you remember Mr Crawford, the headmaster? It's because of the extra tuition he arranged at school, as well as getting Jimmy the job.'

'Well, you helped, started him off in that winter years ago, when most of the schools closed.'

'Maybe. Now, tell me what you've been doing. If you want to.'

'Mum, I can't stay, just in case he turns up. I'm sorry; it's not just that.'

'I know, I know. He won't be home; stays away all week in the football season, comes home on a Friday evening.'

Peter gave a sigh of relief before continuing. 'After what he did and said I don't think I can ever see him. He obviously hates me.'

'Nothing could be further from the truth. He loves you more than ever. You know he travels around the country for his job. I know what he does. Checks all of the phone books wherever he goes looking for the name Johnson. Uses phone boxes, calling all the ones with the initial P for Peter, of course.'

'Tell him to stop. Look, Mum,' he said, getting angry, 'I'm not ready... yet... to see him. Maybe one day. Please, tell him to stop looking. I'm here now!'

She hugged him again, before speaking. 'Okay. Okay. Calm down, please. I'll make him stop looking. But, can you tell me where you are?'

'If I tell you, you'll tell him. Then he'll want to come and find me. I said, I'm not ready!' he shouted at her, before continuing, in a quieter voice. 'Mum,

I'm sorry. Listen. I'll be in touch. You must've shown him the birthday cards, haven't you?'

'Yes, of course I have.'

'I can't say where I am. I just can't, not yet, other than I'm down south.'

'All right, When he's home on Friday, I'll tell him you visited. And I will make him stop looking.'

'Thanks. I promise I'll stay in touch. Been in contact with Elly now and again, I'll carry on doing that. Maybe send the odd letter to her for you. Is that okay?'

'Yes. I'm sorry too. That'll be great,' she said, pausing. 'Now, can you tell me what you do? Have you met anyone?'

He told her all about how he got a job as a washer up, then working in the kitchen and bar. Now, he's on stage; nothing important. But it pays the bills. He never mentioned Spain. Then he told her about Helen.

'So, while this was all happening, I met someone, Mum. Her name's Helen. She's great. Just the best person I've ever known; well, apart from you!' he said, smiling at her.

'Oh, son. I'm so pleased.'

'That's not all. Got a photo of her here,' he said, handing it to her.

'Oh, she's beautiful,' she said, smiling again.

Then, he handed her another picture. It was the one with Tammy in it.

'No! You're a dad?'

He nodded.

She cried again, with the words stumbling out of her mouth, 'A little girl.'

'Yes, Mum. I kept that till the end, wasn't sure how you'd react.'

'How I'd react? I know what you're thinking. Put that out of your mind, right now. You were not to blame! Remember that,' she said, grabbing him out of his chair, hugging him again, harder than she had when he arrived.

When she let him free, he said, 'Okay, okay,' quietly.

'Never think that. It was an accident, that's a fact. Do not ever dwell on it.'

'Right,' he said, wiping his eyes.

They sat back down, before he spoke again. 'Hey, Elly told me you're a teacher?'

'Yes. Finally took up the offer after you'd... gone. Had to have something to occupy my mind. Best thing I could do, was to try and help teach other kids.'

'You did that training then, for a couple of years?'

'Aha. Stan and Joe had gone off to Middlesbrough, Jimmy moved out. So, I had time on my hands.'

'You must enjoy it?'

'Yes, I do. Keeps me busy. Thanks to Mr. Crawford, there was only one school I could teach at, after all he did to help. I teach maths to those under fourteen. Haven't got the qualification for the older ones. Quite happy with that.'

'Blimey! I'm really proud of you, Mum.'

'Well, I'm more proud of you. A dad!' He smiled at her, before she spoke again. 'My handsome young man.'

They sat, holding hands for a few moments, before Peter said, 'Right. Never told you our baby's name. She's Tammy. Only a couple of weeks old. It's because of her I came. Mum, Helen has more or less begged me to see you for years. I really am sorry it's been so long. Not going to repeat why, let's draw a line under it, okay?'

She nodded, then said, 'Okay. You're here now. I know you're well. A family. You've made me a grandma again. Can't wait to tell your dad.'

'Yes, tell him. Show him the pictures.'

'I will,' she said, smiling again.

'Now listen,' he said. 'I have to go. Want to get back to Helen and Tammy.'

'I understand,' she replied, nodding. 'You will keep in touch? Please? Via Elly? I'll tell your father. Make him stop looking for you. I promise. When you're ready, maybe you'll see him. He's a different man now. Not touched alcohol since that night.'

'Yes, Mum. I'll keep in touch. Give me time, okay?'

'Okay,' Brenda said, hugging him again. 'Thank you for these,' she said, holding the pictures up.

'I'll send some more as she grows.'

'Lovely,' she said, with tears rolling down her cheeks.

'Same old house. New windows though. You still got the metal bucket we used to bath in as kids?'

'Yes. Your father put a shed up, wanted to keep it.'

'I see you've extended the kitchen, noticed it earlier. An inside toilet down here,' he said, pointing to the doors at the back of the kitchen.

'Could've moved. Did the extension instead. Put a bathroom in upstairs too. Told your dad we're not moving... not until we knew you were alive,' she said, stroking his face gently.

As he smiled, he said, 'Time to go, Mum. Sorry. Want to get back to Helen. And Tammy. Tell Dad I've been, he's a right to know, it'll put his mind at rest.'

She nodded again, as he picked his keys off the table.

They hugged again, saying nothing when they walked to the front door. Peter turned, saying, 'Have you got a photo of you and Dad? So, I can show Helen.'

She dashed back to the living room, coming back with a glass framed picture he recognised. It was the one of his parents, his brothers and himself, taken when he was ten years old.

'Mum, I can't take this. It's the one you had taken specially, of us all. It's the only one you've got, isn't it?'

'Yes, it's the only one. I want you to have it. Keep it safe. One day… when you're ready, you can bring it back. Meet your brothers too, okay?' Then she hugged him again, as he held the photo. 'I love you. And your father does too. Just remember that,' she said, letting him ease out of her arms.

'Thanks, Mum. Love you too. Thanks for this,' he replied, showing her the picture.

'When you're ready, let me know where you are, please. Just in case anything happens, through Elly. That okay with you?'

He nodded, before leaving the house, going to the car, with tears welling up in his eyes. As he drove away, he could see in his rear mirror, his mum went to the end of the front garden, waving at him. He saw she had one hand over her mouth, stifling tears, he thought.

When he got round the corner out of sight, he pulled over, turning the engine off. He cried his eyes out, looking at the photo of his family. His brothers. His parents. After a minute or so, he composed himself. Then he went to the phone box at the end of the road and called Helen.

She was fine. Tammy was fine. He told her everything. Told her he loved them both. Starting the engine as he ended his conversation with her, he took a couple of deep breaths. Feeling a sense of relief, he said to himself, 'About bloody time, Pete Johnson,' quietly.

It was a good drive home. He felt like a weight had lifted from his shoulders. He knew he had to deal with his dad one day, and his brothers. But, the shadow that had followed him for fourteen years was lifted. Driving on into the night, to his home and Helen and Tammy, he knew he'd finally done the right thing...

27
Keeping in Touch

When he arrived back at their home that night after leaving his mum, Helen was up, feeding Tammy. She told him Kate had been round.

He showed her the picture. She said they were all handsome; him more so, of course, telling him he looked more like his mother than any of his brothers.

The picture stayed in their bedroom. When he was ready, he would meet his father and brothers, he told Helen.

Continuing to work at the club, doing his act as Petra Juno, he saw Richard Leonard a few times, the owner of the antique shop. They became good friends.

Almost three years later, with Helen now juggling being back at work with looking after Tammy, she became pregnant again. Nine months later, in February 1986, she had their second child. A boy. They named him Ronnie. Peter was with her again for the birth.

He sent two sets of pictures to Elly; one each for her and his mother, after Ronnie was born.

A week after he arrived, Peter went to Leonard's antique shop; he'd popped in buying some small items now and again.

'Morning to you,' said Richard, shaking his hand as soon as he walked into the shop. 'Has your baby arrived yet?' he asked, having seen Helen at the club, knowing she was pregnant.

'Yes, last week. A little boy, we named him Ronnie.'

'Wonderful. Mother and baby doing well?'

'Yes thanks. She's at home after a few days in hospital.'

'May I visit, if that's okay in a couple of weeks?'

Peter knew Richard had been trying to have a child. He'd married the year Tammy was born; so far, it hadn't happened for them. 'Yes, of course. Give me a call next week, pop round with Grace. Where is she by the way?'

'More tests today,' Richard said quietly.

Peter knew exactly what he meant. He'd confided in him and Helen about the fact they'd not conceived a child yet. It seemed it was Grace who likely had a problem. 'Oh, I see,' replied Peter.

'So, baby boy, eh!'

'Yep. Big too. Weighed in at eight pounds and half an ounce.'

'Good. Excellent. Now, when was it, about three or four years ago, when you came in after your little girl was born?'

'And you helped me out with a great gift,' said Peter, as the door to the shop opened.

Turning to greet the man who walked in, Richard said, 'Hello, Arthur. How are you? Have you got anything for me today?'

'No, just a flying visit again, Richard,' Arthur replied, shaking Richard's hand.

'Sorry,' said Richard. 'Please excuse my rudeness. Arthur, this is a good friend of mine, Peter Johnson. Otherwise known as "the kid"!'

'Nice to meet you, Arthur,' said Peter, as they shook hands, seeing he was shorter than himself, with a moustache and glasses.

'Arthur Dempsey at your service, sir. Please, call me Dempsey, everyone does. Well, except Richard here, still trying to get him to do that. Maybe he will one day, eh Richard?'

'All because of that Lovejoy character on television,' said Richard, smiling.

'I'm in the antiques business myself as well,' said Dempsey, releasing Peter's hand.

'Oh, I see,' said Peter. 'Seen that on the telly: good show.'

'Well,' said Dempsey, 'thought it might help drum up trade, be good for business. Hasn't made a blind bit of difference; but I'm stuck with it now!' he laughed.

'Arthur's got a shop on the Kent coast. Popped in there a few years ago, didn't I?' questioned Richard.

'Yes. Hit it off as soon as you walked into the shop. Mine's called The Old Curiosity Shop. If you ever make it down to Broadstairs, on the Kent coast, Peter, come in.'

'Okay. Not for a while though, I'm afraid. Just came in to see Richard. He helped me with a gift, when my daughter was born.'

'Oh, nice,' said Dempsey.

'Back again today, after another something special; just had our second child, a baby boy.'

'Congratulations!' said Dempsey, loudly. 'Let me buy you a drink, at least. Maybe we could go to a bar nearby, I'm staying in London overnight, got an antiques trade fair to go to later this afternoon.'

'That's very kind, I'd love to, but I need to get back to Helen, that's my better half, to help her for a couple of weeks. All hands to the pumps when you have a baby, you know?'

'No problem. Another day, perhaps?' asked Dempsey.

'Got an idea!' said Richard. 'How about when you're up next, Arthur, I take you to a club. I know just the place. Not far from here. It's called *Johnny's*.

They've got great evening entertainment. You can stay overnight here in the spare room above the shop, if that's okay with you?'

'Sounds good. Might be a few months; think I'll have to get myself a young lady to accompany me. I've got someone in mind,' replied Dempsey.

'Good, that's settled then,' said Richard. 'Now, seeing as it's my shop, I'm closing up for half an hour. Owner's prerogative! Let's go and have a drink in my office, then I've got a surprise for you, Peter!'

Richard flipped the sign around on the shop door window, locking it as they all went to his office. 'When your little girl was born, I'm sure you recall the Rolls Royce car you purchased?' asked Richard.

'Yes, I do. Got it in the box still, in a cabinet, for Tammy. That's my little girl's name,' he said, turning to Dempsey, who nodded in return.

'Rolls Royce stopped making them that year. You had one of the last ones. Don't know why, but I kept the other two.'

'You've still got them then?' asked Peter.

'I have,' said Richard.

'And are you willing to sell? Have to be the blue one, for a boy?'

'Certainly. I'll wrap it and pack it for you. Think I'll keep the other one for myself,' replied Richard.

'Great!' said Peter, revealing a beaming smile.

'A good deal, indeed!' said Dempsey.

'Sure is,' replied Peter, as Richard went to collect it for him.

'So, the Kent coast, Dempsey? Is it a thriving, busy place down there?' asked Peter.

'Can be,' he replied. 'Especially in the summer season. Got a fantastic beach. Lovely place, I've always liked it there since moving from Ireland when I was younger.'

'Worked in London all my life so far,' Peter replied.

'So, what line of work are you in?' asked Dempsey, as Richard came back in with his gift boxed and wrapped.

'Ah!' said Richard, interrupting. 'Told you about that club, didn't I?'

'Yes, *Johnny's* wasn't it?'

'Correct, Arthur. That's where this young man works, isn't that right?' said Richard, turning towards Peter.

'It is,' replied Peter. 'Started as a washer-up, then the bar. Met Helen there. More recently for the last few years, I've been on the stage.'

'Are you a singer?' questioned Dempsey.

'No. Well, yes,' said Richard, excitedly. 'Bit of everything really. And something different,' he continued, smiling at Peter. 'You'll be really entertained when we go.'

'What do you do then?' asked Dempsey.

'On the stage, I play Petra Juno. I'm a drag artist,' said Peter.

'Really?' asked Dempsey.

'Yes, really. And I have to say, I enjoy it.'

'Wow!' said Dempsey, raising his eyebrows.

'Yes, wow!' said Richard. 'When you're coming up next, we'll go and watch the show. Be prepared to be picked on, Arthur!' he said, and all three of them laughed.

'I wouldn't do that,' said Peter.

'Yes you can,' said Richard, still laughing.

'When you can finally make it, Dempsey, get in touch with Richard; I'd like you to be my guests for the night. I promise I won't pick on you! When the show is over, the band usually plays for an hour or two; sometimes we have a disco. I'll come over and join you, along with Helen. We'll arrange for a babysitter. But, I'm afraid it'll have to be put on ice for a few months, she's not going to be working for a while.'

'Fully understand,' said Dempsey, 'that's very generous of you. Very generous indeed,' he said, shaking Peter's hand as he spoke.

'Any friend of Richard's is a friend of mine. It's my pleasure,' said Peter.

'You're a very kind man. That's not the first time you've done that. Thank you,' said Richard, also shaking Peter's hand.

'Gentlemen, I like to think I've been fortunate. My mother said that to me when I was younger,' said Peter, smiling. 'Now, I need to pay you for this, Richard, please,' holding up the gift box.

'Yes, of course,' said Richard.

All three of them finished their drinks, then Richard led them into the shop, taking payment from Peter. Dempsey asked why he had the name of "the kid". Richard intervened, explaining that it was a nickname given to Peter when he first worked at the club, and it stuck.

'Ideal gift, thank you again,' repeated Peter, shaking Richard's hand once again, then Dempsey's, before bidding them goodbye, after the owner had unlocked the door, turning the sign around to open again.

As Peter left, Dempsey turned to Richard, saying, 'What a lovely fella.'

'He is. Great guy. Met him by chance a few years ago, like he said, when he was after a gift for his little girl.'

'Good looking chap, as well,' added Dempsey.

'I agree. Not the sort of fellow that even realises it. I've met his partner Helen, lovely woman. Think they're a bit older than us, Arthur, early thirties I'd guess. And the club has to be the best around in my humble opinion. Be great if you came up for the evening, see Grace again. Try and get yourself fixed up, bring someone with you.'

'Working on that, Richard. There is a certain someone. Been out of the game since my divorce. Should never have married that girl. Only lasted three bloody months!'

'Well, we live and learn, Arthur.'

'I never told you she buggered off to Australia, did I?'

'No. Well, at least you got divorced, so you're free to marry again.'

'Thank goodness,' said Arthur, raising his eyebrows.

'Well, good that you've got your eye on someone new.'

'Have to see how that goes. Well, I'd best be off to my antiques fair, see what I can find. I'll be in touch, let you know if I find anything of interest,' he said. 'Bye for now,' he added, shaking Richard's hand as he left the shop.

'Yes. Keep in touch, Arthur. Cheerio.'

When Peter got home, he showed Helen the blue ceramic Rolls Royce car. She was just as pleased as him.

He told her about Richard asking to visit with Grace; not a problem, she replied. And about Arthur Dempsey, offering them to be his guests for the night when they could make it to the club.

Then he made her a promise. He said he still couldn't see his father yet. But he wanted to go and see his mum, with her and their children.

They kept in touch via Elly. It was a further seven months later, before they were in the car driving up to Manchester, on Thursday the 5th of September 1986 – his mother's birthday. Elly knew, he'd called her. But Peter wanted to surprise his mum again…

28
Reunion

Throughout the time Peter was in contact with Elly, his mother told her that his dad had stopped looking for him. It'd been nearly four years since he'd first visited his mum, although Peter had been to see her several times since then. The club kept him busy, along with helping bring up the two children, with Helen.

Driving to Manchester on that morning, with Helen and their children this time, Peter was excited. Helen sensed it in his voice. 'Can't wait for you to see Mum,' he said.

'Well, you know what I think. It's about time. Just glad you've come to your senses.'

'You know why. I've got you and the kids now. Have to live my own life, that's what I'm doing. We're settled in our house, it's going great at the club. Life's sweet, don't you think?'

'Of course it is. Just that missing piece of the jigsaw. Your brothers and your dad.'

'I know, I know. I will see him, just don't know when.'

'Okay. Enough of that,' said Helen. 'Change of subject.'

'Eh?'

'When we get back, you can take me on holiday. I want to go abroad, take the kids. They'll be fine on a plane. To Spain.'

'You think so? Ronnie's not even a year old yet. Bit young for going on a plane, isn't he?'

'I've seen on the telly loads of people – well celebrities – taking babies on planes. He'll be fine.'

'Well, if you're sure. Let's have a look when we get back, okay?'

'Yes. Be great. Uncle and Auntie will be fine, I know he's in his mid-sixties now, but Mum and Dad have helped out a few times recently. Don't forget Mum used to work there herself years ago, before she had me.'

'Oh yer, right. Then we can go and see Randy Martinez. I've still got his number and you know he came over to the club last year,' said Peter.

'Yes, I know. Good, that's sorted then. Just a week away before the end of September.'

'Sorted!' said Peter, excitedly, smiling as he drove.

'You're really happy, aren't you?' asked Helen.

'Yes, very. Just remembered something.'

'Which is?' Helen questioned.

'Silly thing really. When I was a boy, and when I've been up to see Mum I did what I used to do.'

'And what was that?'

'I always keep my finger on the doorbell, until the door's answered. Mum knew it was me then.'

'Yes, very silly, Peter,' she said, smiling at him, 'and I suppose your plan is to do just that when we get to your mum's?'

'Of course.'

'If you must, Mr Johnson,' said Helen, stroking the back of his head as he drove, then turned the radio on in the car, as both Tammy and Ronnie had already fallen asleep, turning to him, adding, 'and, I think it's time to tell your mum where we live and what we do for a living, okay?'

'Yes. You're right,' he said, nodding in agreement.

A few hours later, they'd arrived at Elly's house. She'd already told Peter that she was going to book the day off school; difficult when you're a teacher, she told him, especially at the beginning of the term after the summer holidays.

When they got out of the car, Elly came out, hugging Peter straight away. She ran round to Helen as she got out of the car, pulling her in towards her body saying, 'I've wanted to meet you for years, Helen. Wonderful that you came.'

'It's his fault I've not been up yet. Keeps getting me pregnant!' said Helen, pointing to the back seat of the car.

'Ah! You never said you were bringing up your children, Pete: crafty bastard!' said Elly, smiling at Helen, easing her grip, before laughing, looking at Peter.

'A little surprise for you as well, Elly,' he said, as they embraced again.

'Brilliant!' she replied, before saying, 'Now listen, are you coming into my place first, or are we all going to your mum's? You know she always treated me as the daughter... you know, Pete... she never had. Look, sorry, I don't mean to upset you, but she does.'

'Elly, it's fine, I know that. Where would I be if you hadn't been a straight talker when we were kids? Took me a while to suss you out, my little best friend!'

'Pete, you're such a twat!' said Elly, laughing.

'Hey, no swearing in front of the children,' said Helen, laughing at them both, adding, 'you two are like little kids. You've both regressed to being teenagers again,' she added, laughing out loud at them both.

Helen was right. Peter looked at Elly, as she stared at him. They both nodded their heads, laughing, before Peter said, 'Well, yes. Right. It's only three thirty, let's have a drink, stretch our legs, then go to my mum's for four thirty, you know she'll be home by then, right Elly?'

'Yes, she will. I'll go round first, then you knock on the door just after. I won't breathe a word about you being here.'

'Sounds good to me,' said Helen.

'Helen, I'm sorry if I appear brash. I won't go into it, but when I met Jenny teaching, we took a lot of stick because we're lesbians. Even now in the 1980s some people don't understand it.'

Helen said, 'I don't care. Neither does Pete. You're his best friend from when you were kids. It's great you're back in touch; honestly, I think it's wonderful. I know all about him, just like you do.'

Elly smiled and said, 'Come on in, meet Jenny. She's put the kettle on. Well she better had!'

'Think I know who wears the trousers in your house, Elly!' said Helen, as they both broke out into laughter.

Peter got Ronnie out of the car, as Helen took Tammy. They'd both just woken up.

'Elly, would you like to hold Tammy?' asked Helen, handing her daughter to her.

'Thought you'd never ask,' she replied as they went into the house, the front door being wide open, shouting, 'You made that tea, Jenny?'

'Yes, of course,' came the voice back.

Going into the kitchen, they all said hello to Jenny, with Helen feeding Ronnie, who'd now progressed to small mashed up meals.

When they'd had a drink and a sandwich, Elly asked if she could take Tammy out into the garden; it was all enclosed, mostly laid to lawn.

Helen had fed Ronnie, passing him to Peter, who was still eating a sandwich. 'I'll come out with you,' said Helen, as she went outside with Elly, who was still carrying Tammy.

As she put Tammy down, she said to Helen, 'I'm sorry again about being a bit in your face with my manner. I'm harmless really.'

'Elly, it's fine. I can see already how much you care for Pete.'

'Did he tell you about the night he left?'

'Yes, he did, when we started our relationship. Told me everything,' said Helen.

'Never seen him scared of anything, ever, when we were kids. He was different to the other boys; softer. No, not softer, caring. I love him, Helen, like a brother.'

'I can see that, Elly,' she said, hugging her again. 'He's safe with me. I won't let anything happen to him, okay?'

'I know that. He's a jammy sod! Weird that, he fell on his feet meeting you.'

'Got to agree with you there. He was lucky getting me!' said Helen, letting her go, both of them laughing, before adding, 'You've got a nice house here, Elly: it's lovely.'

It'll do us until we both retire. Can't see us adopting kids. Maybe... well... if it's okay... if you visit more often, we can look after Tammy and Ronnie when they're older?'

'I think we can arrange that,' Helen said.

'Okay. Now listen, I don't mean to pry, but, well, Pete's never said where you live exactly. I know he calls now and again, and sends the cards to me for his mum. Now you're here, can you let us know what you do and where you actually live? He's not told us properly what he does for a living,' asked Elly.

'Well, I think it's about time we did. Let's go inside, I'll make sure he tells you. All of you. But wait until we get to his mum's, okay? She needs to know as well. And I think you all need to be told together. In my head it's a way of saying thank you for putting up with, and helping, both of us. I think you'll be really surprised!' she said, smiling at Elly.

As they turned to go back into the house, Tammy ran up the garden, to hold Elly's hand. Shortly after, they got in their cars, going to Peter's mother's house, where they parked a short distance away.

Elly and Jenny went in first as they planned.

A minute later, Peter, Helen and their children, carrying one each, were at the front door. Peter held his finger on the doorbell. Helen smiled at him, waiting while the incessant ringing continued; until the door was opened. It was Elly who answered the door, putting her finger to her mouth, quietly saying, 'Shush,' whilst waving them into the house, adding, 'Your mum's in the garden.'

Closing the door behind her, Helen followed Peter and Elly as they walked into the living room, then down the few steps into the kitchen.

Jenny was making drinks, as Brenda came into the house from the back door, with her arms full of washing in a basket. When her eyes set upon Peter and the others with him, she dropped everything, putting her hands to her mouth, shouting, 'No! I don't believe it!' pausing, then putting her hand on her chest, taking a big sigh, saying, 'Helen! Peter? Is it really you? And the children!' putting her hand over her mouth again.

'Yes. It's all of us. Happy birthday! Tried telling him loads of times to bring us here before, but you know your son!' said Helen, stepping towards Brenda.

'Stubborn, just like his dad!' said Elly.

Brenda stepped over the basket, grabbing Helen. 'I've waited so long to meet you. And your babies! On my birthday!' she said, with tears in her eyes.

'This is Tammy, grown a bit since the last photo you saw,' said Helen, as Brenda held her arms around her and Tammy, smiling at them.

'And this is your grandson, Mum, little Ronnie,' said Peter.

Brenda reached out to Peter, who passed Ronnie to her. 'Seven months now?' she asked.

'Yes,' said Helen, 'nearly eight.'

'Oh, he's gorgeous,' she said, kissing his head gently, before saying to Helen, 'and you're beautiful too, little Tammy,' kissing her on the cheek.

'Wanted to surprise you again, Mum,' said Peter.

'Well, you certainly did that!' she said, almost shouting at him.

'Hmm, sorry. Thought you'd guess by the doorbell ring.'

'I was in the garden getting the washing in, as you can see,' she said, pointing to it, now all over the floor, having fallen out of the basket. 'Never heard it.'

'No matter,' said Helen. 'We're all here now. Finally. Nice to meet you,' Helen said, thrusting her hand out towards Brenda. 'I'm Helen Armstrong, one day, when he gets his arse in gear, to be Mrs Johnson!' she added, smiling at Brenda.

Brenda laughed out loud, smiled, still holding Helen's hand saying, 'Thank you for coming, you've made an old woman very, very happy,' before letting go of her hand, putting her arms around Helen and Tammy again, kissing Helen on the cheek this time.

As they embraced, Elly said, 'And don't you ever leave it so long before you visit again, Pete! You'll have me to deal with!'

'Okay. Okay!' he said, nodding at Elly.

'That's right, you tell him, Elly,' said Helen, laughing.

'Now, now,' said Brenda, smiling at all of them in turn. 'This is the happiest day of my life. It's a wonderful surprise, truly it is.'

Jenny put her arm around Elly, while at the same time, Peter put his arm around his mother, saying, 'Won't be as long in future, Mum. It's about time I told you where we live and what we do.'

'Been waiting for you to tell me for so long,' his mum replied, stroking his face, then cuddling him.

'Go on then,' said Elly. 'Helen told me it'd be really interesting; what you do that is. Spill the beans, Pete!'

'You know what we said on the way up. Everything. It's time,' said Helen, raising her eyebrows, with a stern look on her face.

'Yes, I know,' said Peter. 'Let's all go into the living room, quite a lot to tell you.'

When they'd sat down, Brenda now holding Tammy and Helen holding Ronnie, Peter began. 'Right, here's the story – all of it, up to today…'

He told them about the night he left, about getting the coach to London, sleeping rough for a few nights, before going to the club in Soho, meeting Johnny, working in the club with different jobs.

'So, you really are lucky then?' questioned Elly.

'You could say that,' he said, adding, as he glanced at her, 'it was at the club I met Helen.'

She smiled at him, before he continued. 'And, I had a season in Spain working at some nightclubs, for three months a few years ago,' he continued, 'and that's where I asked Helen to marry me.'

'And we still haven't got around to that yet, have we, Mr Johnson?'

'No, Helen, not yet, but we will,' he replied, smiling.

'And when we do, you'll all be coming to the wedding,' Helen said.

'Lovely,' said Brenda, as she smiled looking down at Tammy.

'So, that's the job. We've got two kids, and our own house, a big three bedroom place about half an hour away from the club in London.'

'And when he's ready,' Helen shot a look at Peter, 'you will be welcome – all of you.'

Brenda put her hands to her mouth again, before saying, 'That's two weddings, then. Stan's getting married, he told me last week. Not seen you to tell you, Elly; and now you two,' she said, going over to Helen, hugging her.

'We've got to sort it all out first, Mum,' said Peter.

'Oh, Pete! I'll organise it. Leave it to me. I'll keep you all informed. Elly, I've got your phone number. It's about time I had yours, my future mother-in-law?' said Helen.

'That would be wonderful, thank you,' said Brenda, wiping tears from her eyes again.

'And you... your dad WILL be coming to the wedding! Okay?' said Helen, looking at Peter.

He nodded, saying, 'Okay. Yes.'

'That's all settled then,' said Elly. 'Great!'

They spent the rest of that afternoon and early evening chatting away. Helen told them all about her family: being an only child; her involvement in the club herself; her own parents being involved in running *Johnny's* in the early years it opened; her uncle's heart attack and of course, becoming a mum herself.

It was late in the evening before they left, to drive back to London.

Brenda told them it was her best birthday ever. She asked them not to leave it so long before getting in touch, phoning or visiting.

Helen told her they'd call every week. Now they were in touch, she'd make sure her son stayed in touch, for good. Peter agreed, promising his mum he would call himself; but he still refused to speak to or see his father, saying he would eventually.

Brenda said she'd tell his father everything; making him promise not to visit or turn up out of the blue.

Driving back to London, with the kids asleep, Helen said, 'Well, that's two weddings in the family. Your twin brothers are still playing football for a living, aren't they?'

'Yep, Elly told me they've both got their own houses in Middlesbrough. Mum mentioned it earlier when you nipped off to the toilet; forgot to tell you, sorry.'

'That's all right. Can't wait to meet them all.'

'You will now. I'm glad. You know I wouldn't be anything if it wasn't for you, don't you?' said Peter.

'Yes, I'm obviously the best thing that ever happened to you!' she said, smiling at him. 'Just your dad to sort out now. And your brothers to see. I reckon he'll be as happy as your mum. She said he regrets it. Quite a thing him looking all these years for you, Pete?'

'I suppose so. Just got this nagging doubt he'll go ballistic at me. I know now that's unlikely after what Elly and Mum have said. But still I know I'm a grown man, but my dad… he attacked me.'

'Yes, I know the story. Put it behind you. Keep talking to me about it, you know I'm always going to be here for you.'

'I know. Thanks,' he said, reaching his hand over to hold hers.

They drove on quietly, before Helen broke the silence. 'So, holiday. We'll talk to Uncle tomorrow about us going away. The kids will be fine on the plane, don't worry about them.'

'Okay, sounds good. I know we can afford a bit of luxury if we want, but I'd love to go back to Benidorm: see Randy Martinez and a few of the others.'

'That's fine by me. Exactly where I want to go.'

'And, I'd like him to see our little family. Told you ages ago he's the one who prompted me to ask you to get married, didn't I?'

'Yes, you did. Still haven't done it yet though, have we?' said Helen, raising her eyebrows.

'No. Had a thought on that. Think there's only one place for that.'

'The club?' questioned Helen.

'Of course. That's something else we can ask your uncle; I reckon he'd love it, especially as you sort of co-run it with him now.'

'Let's ask him that as well.'

He turned briefly, seeing her smiling at him. Driving on, they got home in the early hours of the morning. That didn't matter, they'd both become night owls due to the hours they worked at the club.

The next afternoon, when her parents arrived to babysit, they told them about their visit to Manchester, the holiday and wedding plans, before going to Johnny and Ruth's house to ask them.

29
A Holiday First

Welcoming them in, Ruth said, 'This is a nice surprise. How did it go up north?'

'Great,' said Helen. 'Pete's mother is lovely; doted on the kids.'

'Good,' Ruth replied. 'Come on through, your uncle's in the garden.'

'Got something to discuss with you both,' said Peter, as they made their way through the house.

'Oh?' asked Ruth, turning as she reached the door to the garden.

'Let's go and see Uncle, want to ask you both together,' said Helen.

'Okay,' nodded Ruth, as they walked to the end of the garden, where Johnny was tending some flowers and bushes.

'Hi, Uncle,' said Helen.

He pushed himself off the ground slowly saying, 'Old age! Bloody knees and back!' laughing.

'Something for us to look forward to then?' Peter said.

'Yes, it is,' Ruth said, smiling at him.

Stretching his body, arms up in the air, Johnny said, 'So, what brings you round here before work later?'

'Got a couple of things to ask you,' said Helen.

'Fire away,' said Johnny.

'Firstly, so you know, it went really well at my mother's yesterday. Finally told her what we do for a living and where we live,' Peter said.

'Good,' said Ruth, 'about time too.'

'Exactly what I said, Auntie,' said Helen, adding, 'well, anyway, couple of other things, one being, we'd like to take a holiday abroad if that's okay with you?'

'Sure, no problem,' said Johnny. 'I'm feeling fine, aren't I, luv?'

'Yes, it'll be fine. He is feeling well. I'd know if he wasn't, I keep a beady eye on him, as you know,' said Ruth.

'So, the plan is to go to Benidorm, where Pete worked,' said Helen.

'Fine by us,' said Ruth.

'Next week though,' added Helen.

'No problem, whenever you want. I've got Tommy who can help out if needed, there's me and Ruth, and your parents as well,' said Johnny.

'Great, we'll book it up for next week then, mid-September weather is nice and sunny, I've already checked,' said Helen.

'Good, you kids deserve a break. When's the last time you went abroad, or to your parents' flat in Bognor?' asked Ruth.

'Blimey, before the kids were born. Must be about four years since we've been down there,' said Helen.

'How long you going for?' asked Johnny.

'Just a week,' said Peter.

'Well, that's settled. Anything else?' asked Ruth.

There was a pause before Helen spoke. 'Yes... it's about time we got married, just haven't got round to it. One of those things.'

'So?' asked Johnny.

'If it's possible, and it's a big if, we'd like to use the club for the wedding day; all of it, from the vows, to the meal and reception afterwards. It'll mean closing the club though. Is that okay?' asked Helen.

Johnny smiled. So did Ruth, before he spoke. 'Too bloody right it's okay!' he shouted, putting his arm around Ruth.

'We've been waiting years for you two to sort this out, since the day you came back from Spain!' said Ruth, smiling, then hugging Helen.

'Five, actually!' said Helen, flashing her engagement ring at Peter, putting her arm around his shoulder saying, 'and it's not going to be another five years, is it, mister?' raising her eyebrows, smiling at him.

'No, it's not. But, we need to get it organised, isn't that right, Johnny?' said Peter.

'We'll need to get a special marriage licence for the club, never been done before. Don't know how long it'll take or if it's possible. Catering we can do, got all the staff to cover that. Entertainment is covered, and you are not doing that, okay, kid!' Johnny said, looking at Peter.

'No, boss, course not,' he replied, smiling.

'Right then,' said Ruth. 'You organise your holiday, we'll look into the wedding plans with your parents, see what we can find out.'

'Thanks, Auntie,' said Helen. 'Told them we were coming over to see you about it already.'

'Good. So, anytime of year you'd like to get married?'

'Only thing we'd like is for it to be a nice warm day. We don't need to worry about that really if it can be done in the club, but that'd be nice for some pictures maybe,' said Helen.

'I know a fella who can video it for you,' said Johnny.

'Ooh, yes please,' said Helen.

'We'll work on all that, with your parents. You two think of a date when you're away, okay?' asked Ruth.

'Sorted then!' said Johnny.

'Sorted!' said Peter, nodding his head, smiling.

'How about May next year?' said Helen.

'We'll add that to the list. Any particular day of the week?'

'Traditionally, weddings are on a Saturday,' said Ruth. 'But, you do what you want to. Have a chat when you're in Benidorm; you'll need to work out a guest list as well.'

'We will,' said Helen. 'Leave it to us.'

Peter nodded before adding, 'Okay then. Action stations. Let's get down to the travel agents, get our holiday booked.'

Ruth and Helen hugged one another again, whilst Peter and Johnny shook hands, saying their goodbyes.

At the travel agent, they booked up a hotel name Peter knew, along with the flights, where he stayed a few years ago when he worked there.

Helen called her parents with the news about the wedding date, possibly in May 1987, telling them they wouldn't be long as they were going directly to the travel agents from Johnny and Ruth's house.

When they got back to their house, they told her parents they were flying out in four days. The travel agent advised them, they'd only need to get an Identity Card for the children. They didn't need that Helen told them, she'd already arranged for their children to be named on her passport after Ronnie was born.

Four days later, they arrived in Benidorm. Randy Martinez picked them up from the airport; they called him the night they booked the holiday.

He took them to their hotel, telling them he would be back in two days to pick them up, giving them time to settle in. When he returned, he would take them to his home, after a tour of the clubs Peter worked at.

For those next two days, they became normal tourists, playing on the beach, with Tammy and Ronnie, going in the sea, building sandcastles and eating ice creams.

When Martinez picked them up, he made a real fuss of the kids. Peter had met his wife a few times; knowing that they had three children of their own.

They toured all the clubs Peter worked at; it took all day, as they were spread all along the Costa del Sol, seeing some faces of staff he worked with. Driving to Martinez's house inland afterwards, Helen said to him, 'We've got news for you.'

'Oh,' he said, 'which is?'

'We're planning on getting married, we've never got around to it,' she said.

'Wonderful!' shouted Martinez.

'It's hopefully in May next year. And,' said Peter pausing, 'we'd like your wife and your family to come over if you can?'

'Try and stop us! Fantastic!' he shouted.

'Brilliant,' said Helen. 'It's been a while since we've seen you. We both wanted you to come, to say thank you.'

'It will be our pleasure. Thank you,' said Martinez, driving up a steep hill, which led to an enormous white house. Getting out of the car, he said, 'Come, come, meet my wife and children. You are our guests. We have enough bedrooms for you to sleep, if you want to? And everything you may need for your children.'

'That's so kind,' said Helen. 'Thank you again.'

Following him into their house, Helen said to Peter, 'Shall we stay?'

He nodded saying, 'Don't see why not, do you?' She nodded back at him, as they went into an enormous hallway, with a circular staircase.

Coming from a downstairs doorway, was Mina, his wife. 'So good to see you, Mr Petra Juno!' she shouted, smiling at, then hugging Peter.

'Good to see you too,' he said, embracing her whilst holding Ronnie.

'And Helen too, and your children,' said Martinez.

Mina went straight over to Helen after kissing Peter on the cheek, embracing her, saying, 'Nice to meet you again after all this time,' she said as she stroked Helen's face, then kissed her on the cheek.

'Good to see you too,' said Helen, smiling.

'Come on, into the house. I've dinner for you. Randy said you may stay overnight; is that okay with you?' Mina asked, excitedly.

'Yes,' said Helen, looking at Peter.

He nodded, holding up a holdall bag saying, 'We've got all we need for the kids, nappies and all that stuff, so… it's a yes!'

'Great!' shouted Martinez. 'Wonderful, we shall celebrate tonight.'

'Sounds good to me,' said Peter, as they all followed Mina into the doorway she'd appeared from.

Martinez introduced Peter and Helen to their three sons. All of them spoke very good English, just like Martinez and Mina; the older two were already teenagers, with the youngest seven years old.

As they were now all in the kitchen, Mina asked Helen, 'You like my kitchen?'

'I love it,' said Helen. 'It's enormous. It's bigger than the kitchen at the club back home.'

'Dinner is ready. The boys will serve us out on the veranda,' she said pointing out through patio doors in the kitchen. 'Come,' said Mina, taking Helen by the hand, leading her outside.

'This is amazing,' said Helen, taking in the beautiful undisturbed countryside view from the veranda and garden, where she saw a swimming pool as well.

'We like it,' said Mina. 'My husband works very hard, for all of us.'

'He's a good man, knew that the first time I met him with Pete all those years ago,' replied Helen.

'Yes, all that time. Now you have two babies. And after Peter's proposal, you got married?'

'Well, that's something we'd like to talk to you both about, Mina.'

'Oh! You have no wedding ring? What happened?'

Helen laughed before replying. 'We've been so busy, had our children, lots of other things going on in our lives; never got round to it.'

'The boys will organise dinner, then we can all sit and talk over a glass of wine before we eat, okay, Helen?'

'Okay,' she replied, following Mina into the giant hallway where Peter, holding Ronnie, was still chatting to Martinez and his three sons.

'Peter has met our children years ago,' said Martinez to Helen. 'Our oldest is Raul, Carlos is a year younger, and Franco is our youngest; he turned up a few years later than his brothers!' added Martinez, laughing.

The boys said their hellos to Helen, having already spoken to Peter.

'Come with me,' Mina said, taking Peter's hand leading him towards the kitchen doorway. 'Boys, you prepare dinner for us all. We're going outside. You get it organised please, Raul?'

The tallest one answered, 'Yes, Mama. We'll sort it out.'

Helen looked at Mina, before she spoke again, 'Good boy. Your brothers will help. Get the wine please, Raul, you two older boys can have a drink, but not you, Franco,' she said, looking at their youngest son, who nodded in reply.

Smiling at Mina, Helen said, 'Wow, you've got them organised.'

'In this house, I'm the boss. Outside, the boys and my husband are the bosses. It works. I teach them all to cook and to have good manners. That includes my husband!' she said, smiling herself.

Going out onto the veranda, the two men followed the ladies, sitting around a massive old wooden table, with chairs around it.

'We have many visitors,' said Mina. 'My two oldest sons have girlfriends, we know their families. Because we live here in our big house, they are popular with the girls at school and of course, because of the nightclubs we own and run. They are like mini-celebrities here in Benidorm,' she said, laughing.

'Well, it's a very big house,' said Helen.

'Oh yes, it was smaller when we moved in, but we made it bigger when we started having our babies. Our plan is to retire in a few years, let our sons take over the business. We will be in our fifties soon and have worked hard all our lives to get where we are now.'

'I can see that,' said Helen, admiring the house, as they sat on the veranda.

'Mama,' shouted Raul, 'when do you want dinner, now, or in half an hour after a glass of wine?'

'Wine first please. Not for you boys yet, wait until after dinner is served.'

'Okay, Mama,' Raul shouted back.

'Moments later, one of her other sons – Carlos – came out of the kitchen, saying, 'Would you like red or white wine, ladies?' flashing them a smile.

'White for me,' said Helen.

'And me too,' said Mina.

'The same for us,' said Martinez, looking at Peter, who nodded. Shortly after, Raul came out with a bottle of wine and glasses, followed by his brothers.

Sitting down, Martinez said, 'I… sorry, we shall give you a tour of our house after dinner. There is a spare room for your children, or they can sleep in your room, it's up to you.'

'Thank you,' said Peter. 'Your generosity is... is—'

'Wonderful is the world you're looking for,' interrupted Helen, smiling at him.

'Yes,' Peter agreed.

'For what you did for us years ago, I will be forever in your debt, Peter Johnson,' said Martinez.

'I only worked for three months, surely it didn't make that much difference to you?'

'Peter, you gave us the best summer season we'd ever had back then. Because of that, I have many people who come back again. They are not always here for the entertainment. They come back for the hospitality and kindness of my staff; you showed them all how to be friendly to everyone. That, and of course, they come for the sun,' said Martinez, smiling, pointing to the evening sky.

'Which is why we came,' said Helen. 'We needed a holiday.'

'You've been busy at your club and making babies,' Mina said, laughing.

'Yes, and we're here for another reason,' said Peter.

'Oh,' said Martinez, 'and what is this?' he added, winking at Peter, thinking that Mina wasn't aware of the impending wedding.

Peter nodded at Helen, as she shifted Tammy from one arm to the other, before she spoke. 'It's like this. We haven't got married yet. But we're going to next year.'

'Wonderful!' shouted Mina.

'And we've got a question for you – all of you,' said Peter.

'Spill the beans!' said Martinez, laughing.

'We'd like you all,' Helen said, waving her arm from left to right, 'to come to our wedding, as our guests. It wouldn't be the same if you weren't there.'

Martinez jumped to his feet, shouting whoops of delight. 'I knew it. I knew it! Yes, yes, yes!'

'So, you'll come then?' asked Peter, looking at Mina.

'Of course, yes! Nothing would make us happier,' she said, going over to Peter and Helen who were sitting next to one another, hugging them as one.

'Raul, champagne, for all of us please,' shouted Martinez.

'Yes, Papa,' he replied, going into the house.

Martinez bounded over from his seat, shaking Peter's hand, who'd stood up, then kissed him on both cheeks, followed by Mina who did the same, as all three of them hugged together, with Ronnie still in Peter's arms, looking at them all.

'May I?' asked Mina, outstretching her arms towards Ronnie.

'Yes, of course,' replied Peter, handing his son over.

'Baby bambino,' she said, kissing him on his forehead, as Martinez stroked his hair.

'This is fantastic news, but when is your wedding?' asked Martinez.

'Not sorted out yet, but we're hoping it'll be May next year,' said Peter.

'We shall be there! Just let us know exactly when and where. It'll be our pleasure!' said Martinez.

'At the moment,' said Helen looking up at Mina, 'we've asked Uncle if we can use the club.'

'Ah! Johnny. You run it with him now, Peter told me?' Martinez said, looking at Helen.

'Well, yes, sort of. He's taken a backseat, but still helps when we need a break, like now and when we had the babies,' said Helen, looking down at Tammy, who was almost asleep in her arms.

Raul came out with two bottles of champagne and glasses for all of them, pouring it out, as they sat around the table.

'Can you go and sort out dinner, please?' asked Mina, looking at her other two sons.

'Okay, Mama,' said Carlos, as he and Franco left their chairs to go into the kitchen.

As Peter watched Raul go to the kitchen as well, he wiped his eyes. Helen saw him. 'What's the matter?' she said.

He gave a deep breath before saying, 'Just remembered a similar thing I did with my brothers years ago.'

'Which was?' asked Helen.

Martinez and Mina were staring at Peter, seeing he was upset about something.

'We all cooked a meal for my mum and dad the day we all got our school reports. It was when Mum home-schooled us for a few weeks because of a bad winter. Made me realise I should go and see my brothers. And my dad,' he said with a trembling voice.

Helen put her arm around him. As Peter wiped his eyes, she said, 'Do you want to tell them?' looking over at Mina and Martinez.

Peter nodded. He tried to speak, but the words wouldn't come out.

'It's okay, I'll tell them,' said Helen.

The three boys came out with the dinner, an enormous bowl of paella and rice, as Helen started to tell them about Peter's life. She told them it all, from when he ran away, to now. But she didn't mention why he left Manchester.

'What a story,' said Martinez quietly, before asking, 'Why did you leave Manchester, Peter?'

Helen kissed Peter, wiping tears from his cheeks, then he smiled at her, before speaking.

'When I was fourteen, my father attacked me. I thought he was going to kill me. So, I ran away, terrified. It was a long time before I had the courage to go back, as Helen told you,' said Peter, pausing to sip his champagne. 'When we all went to see my mother and friend last week, Helen made me realise it's about time I saw him. So, I will. And my brothers.'

'So, that's good then?' questioned Mina.

'His father has been looking for him ever since he left. He changed his job so that he could travel the country to find Pete,' said Helen, glancing at him.

'Now I've got my own children, Helen helped me realise I have to face him,' said Peter.

'Good!' said Martinez. 'Anything we can do to help, you just ask us, okay?'

'Thank you,' said Helen, as Peter smiled at Martinez, nodding.

'So, all will be well, yes?' replied Martinez.

'Yes, I hope so, eventually,' said Peter, smiling.

'Come on, let's eat!' said Mina.

They all tucked into the paella, drank their champagne, then some more wine. Martinez's sons cleared everything up, as darkness crept into their garden.

Going into the kitchen, Mina put some music on. The men and boys all sat down in their living room, putting the giant television on. Raul told Peter they all liked and played football, which was on the television now. He told them about his twin brothers, saying he'd never watched them play. But he was going to now, before they'd likely retire, explaining they were older than himself.

Ronnie was fast asleep, so Helen took him up to their bedroom, placing him in the carrycot Mina had kept in their loft. She told Helen they kept everything from their children's childhood up there. When she laid him down, checking on his breathing, Helen said to her, 'Thank you for your hospitality, Mina. This is quite overwhelming for me and I'm sure Pete too.'

'No need for thanks,' she replied. 'When my husband came back from England a few years ago, he went to see several people like Peter, doing their jobs. But, he went back to watch Peter four times. He was the only one he would have ever asked to come here to work in Spain. He watched Peter's act and saw him behind the bar.'

'I suppose he had to check that he was good enough?'

'No. He knew the first time he saw him. But he wanted to see what he was like as a person. When he saw how Peter was with the customers, his friendly manner, his jokes and his attitude, he called me.'

'Oh, I see,' said Helen.

'He told me, he'd seen a star in the making. He knows talent when he sees it, Helen. Peter has a way about him. He is a special man, I'm sure you know that. And you are the same. We think you are just…just, great people,' said Mina, hugging Helen again, as they stood over Ronnie, who was fast asleep.

'Thank you. Thank you,' said Helen.

'Now, come on, let's join the men for a while, I can have a talk with your daughter before she falls asleep, if that's okay?'

'Yes, of course it is.'

Joining the men, they spent the rest of the evening chattering away about their families and football, before going up to bed.

After putting Tammy – who was already asleep – into the bed in their room, next to Ronnie, Helen said, 'Lovely people, Pete, really lovely.'

'I know, can't thank them enough for their kindness.'

'Mina told me when we put Ronnie to bed, that Martinez told her he could see something special in you, and me, when he saw you working, before getting you to come to work over here.'

'Well, I just do the job. I love it, that's all.'

She leaned across, kissing him, saying, 'I love you, Pete. Really, really love you to pieces.'

'The feeling's mutual,' he replied, smiling at her after they'd kissed, 'because I sure as hell love you too.'

They'd had a long, lovely day. Peter kept his arms wrapped around Helen, as they fell fast asleep, until Ronnie woke them up with a few of his noises in the morning.

Helen told Peter to stay in bed, while she went downstairs to get them a drink. Martinez and Mina were already up, as was Raul. Mina told her breakfast would be ready in half an hour; there was nothing they needed to do but get themselves washed and dressed, then come down and join them.

When breakfast was finished, Martinez took them back to their hotel. Mina said her goodbyes at the house, telling them she was looking forward to their wedding, thanking them for their invitation.

For the remainder of the holiday, they spent time on the beach, relaxing with the children. On the day before they went home, Mina came down with their sons, spending the day on the beach with them; Franco and Tammy built sandcastles, chatting away together.

Martinez came along later in the afternoon, having work to do at a couple of the clubs.

On their last day, they were taken to the airport by Martinez. They couldn't thank him and his family enough, telling him when they come over for the wedding, they must stay at one of their houses, as their guests, not a hotel. He agreed.

On the plane home, Peter told Helen he was going to get in touch with his mum soon. He would go and see his dad, then his brothers. He knew it'd been too long. She was happy, delighted, that he'd finally made the decision.

When they got back home, they called Helen's parents, then her aunt and uncle, asking them to come round to their house the next day, so they could tell them about the holiday and see how the wedding plans had been going.

Peter phoned his mum, telling her he would be up soon and would finally see his father, asking her if she could arrange for his brothers to meet him as well, if possible. Then he called Elly, telling her he'd decided to go and see his family: all of them. He didn't know when, but it would be soon. She was delighted. And he said the wedding was hopefully going to be in May, a few months away yet, and he'd keep her informed.

30
Wedding Plans

The next day Helen's parents arrived first, so they told them all about the holiday.

A few minutes later, Johnny and Ruth came in with some news. It wasn't all good. 'So, how was the holiday? Did you meet up with Martinez?' asked Johnny.

'Yes, had a wonderful time. Stayed at his house for a night, met his wife and kids. It was really relaxing,' said Helen.

'Good. Did you work on your guest list?' asked Helen's mother.

'Yes, pretty much got that all sorted, we think,' said Helen, looking at Peter.

'What is it?' asked Johnny.

'I've decided – told Helen's parents just now – I'm going to see my father. I want all my family there; if they'll come,' Peter replied.

'Good. Excellent!' said Ruth.

'He knows it's long overdue, don't you, Pete?' questioned Helen.

'Yep, it is. I've been thinking about it since we've had the kids. He's a right to see his grandchildren, as well as me, I hope. And Helen, of course.'

'Okay,' said Johnny, shaking Peter's hand. 'Think we're all aware how tough it's been for you. You sort it out when you can, just let us know – if you want to.'

'I will, thank you, Johnny. I know you're all my family here, always will be. But, I need to get you all to meet my other family. It's about time now, I know that.'

'Say no more about it,' said Johnny, as Helen's father Brian came up to Peter, putting his arm around his shoulder.

'As Johnny said, you just let us know, son, okay?' said Brian, who had really warmed to Peter in the last few years.

'Right, wedding stuff,' said Johnny, as Ruth put her hand up to stop him in mid-sentence.

'Yes, we've got some news,' said Ruth. 'Firstly, we've been to the local council authority. The wedding can be at the club, but we've a few things to sort out; luckily, we know some councillors, which should help.'

'So, what has to be sorted out?' asked Helen.

'There are conditions that have to be met, which we have to comply with,' said Ruth.

'Which are?' questioned Helen.

Ruth took a piece of paper out of her pocket, and started reading the conditions. 'One, we've to appoint a suitable or responsible person to make sure the conditions are met. Two, give that person's details to the council after we get a licence. Three, tell the council if there are any changes to the premises. Four, make sure a superintendent registrar or local registration authority has approved the wedding arrangements before it takes place. Five, make sure the premises can be inspected at reasonable times and it is dignified. Six, display a notice that the premises are approved one hour before and during the proceedings.'

'Bloody hell!' said Peter, as they all looked at him.

'Wait, there's more, shush,' said Ruth. 'Seven, no food or alcohol to be sold or consumed in the specified area an hour before or after the proceedings. Eight, no religious content, meaning music or readings. Nine, the premises must be freely open to the public. Ten, the premises must have all fire and safety regulations and precautions in place.

'Flipping heck!' shouted Peter.

'It's okay, kid,' said Johnny.

'Yes, Peter, it is okay,' said Ruth, continuing, 'we've been to the council, got this list. We know what to do. As I said, we've a couple of customers who are councillors, they've already said it can be sorted out, legally as well.'

'Yes, but there's a lot of sorting out to do,' Peter said, more calmly.

'Ruth has answered nearly all of the questions and conditions already. Just leave it to us. Once we've got the approval, you know what, the licence lasts for three years. This could be the start of a great money making idea,' said Johnny, smiling at him.

'So, we can do it at the club then?' asked Helen.

'Yes. Just have to sort this all out. It'll take about three months we were told. We waited to tell you when we're all together,' said Ruth.

'September now, so we've got eight months,' said Helen.

'Yes, more than enough time,' said Brian.

'What about a priest?' Helen asked.

'No, we have to use a registrar, because it's called a civil ceremony. Still a marriage, but not in a church or registry office,' said Ruth.

'So, it's up to you both if you want to go ahead,' said Joyce.

'To me, it's a no-brainer,' said Peter. 'Wanted to get married for ages, not bothered about a priest. What do you say?' he added, looking at Helen.

There was a pause before she spoke. 'The club's been our life so far. YES!' she said throwing her arms around Peter, kissing him.

'Great,' shouted, Johnny, putting his arm around Brian.

'Lots to do then,' said Ruth. 'Leave it to us.'

'Okay, we will! Thank you,' said Helen, still holding Peter in her arms.

'Yes, we'll get it all sorted,' said Joyce, looking at Ruth.

'Course we will. Could be the first of many, you never know,' Johnny replied.

As they were in the living room of the house, Tammy woke from her sleep laying on their settee. Ronnie was fast asleep in his playpen. Helen's mother Joyce picked her up saying,' We've got a wedding to go to you know.'

Tammy, being only four, had no idea what she was talking about, as she smiled at her grandmother.

'Right, work tonight, folks, no celebrating this time. Organising to do. As Joyce said, we'll get it sorted,' said Johnny.

'Yes, we will,' added Ruth, 'but there's one thing we need.'

'Oh yes,' said Joyce, nodding in agreement.

'What?' Helen asked.

'A date,' said her father.

'Oh yes,' said Peter, laughing. 'Better have a look at next year's calendar to fix a day and date.

'Any particular date for you?' Helen asked.

'No, any day will do,' said Peter.

They worked out the days for May 1987 and chose a Sunday. Helen said the club would be closed, and it would be easy, she hoped, for everyone to travel there. And the next day was a bank holiday, so Johnny decided the club would be closed the day after the wedding.

So, Sunday the third of May it was. Now all Peter had to do was see his father, get his brothers to come and let his mother know all about it. And Elly. A trip back to Manchester had to be made, and soon...

31
Been a Long Time

The next few weeks sailed by. Helen was heavily involved in organising the wedding, with her mother's and Ruth's help. The catering was easy, Terry said it'd be his pleasure to organise it all, no need for any of them to be worried or concerned. Knowing he was a great chef, everyone trusted him.

Getting the licence proved easier than expected. All of the requirements were met, with council members visiting to inspect it was up to standard. Johnny knew one of the gentlemen who made the official visit; he was an old client and friend of his.

Helen organised the flowers; she told Peter it was her job. He didn't argue. She found the dress she wanted, while he sorted out the morning suits, going with Johnny and Helen's father, plus Terry to get measured up, whom Peter had asked to be his best man.

They'd not been to Manchester since his mum's birthday in September. He'd contacted his mother and Elly, telling them he'd be coming up, which is what he did in late November. He went with Helen; her parents were staying at their house, looking after the children. They planned to stay overnight; if it went well. He'd asked his mum to make sure his father was there.

Peter drove that day as they left late morning, arriving about four p.m.; his mum would have finished school by then. He was quiet on the journey, Helen noticed.

'You okay?' she asked as they reached the motorway turn off to Manchester, adding. 'Ooh, looks like an accident over there?'

'Blimey,' he replied, 'ambulances and everything. No, not really, in answer to your question.'

'Yes, looks like a bad one over there,' replied Helen, before continuing, 'Pete, it'll be fine. Your mum said your dad was looking forward to seeing you. He'll probably be more nervous than you,' she said, smiling at him.

'Don't think so, I'm shitting a brick!' he said, trying to laugh.

'Now listen you,' she said, 'you've done nothing wrong. You left because you were terrified. You're a man now, it's time to deal with this once and for all, okay?'

'Fair enough,' he said, quietly.

Not long afterwards, they arrived at Elly's. She knew he was going to see his father for the first time in almost twenty years. She hugged them, wishing Peter good luck.

It wasn't far to his parents' house. They drove in silence, with Helen putting her hand on his shoulder.

Getting out of the car, he knocked on the door, not placing his finger on the doorbell to annoy his mum.

His mother answered the door, instantly hugging him as he walked in. 'Your dad's on his way, should be here within the hour, been down to Birmingham to see a couple of young footballers.'

'Okay,' said Peter, as she released her embrace, immediately hugging Helen.

'Big accident at the turn off earlier, Mum. Looked really bad,' said Peter.

'Oh really. Well, come on in, I've just put the kettle on,' said Brenda.

Helen told her all about the children, giving her more photos. They discussed the wedding plans, telling her all about their holiday back in September, although they'd phoned and mentioned it already. Time flew by to almost six thirty. His brothers were all going to turn up later in the evening. There was still no sign of his father.

'I'll call his mobile; they gave him one a while ago at the football club,' said Brenda.

There was no answer, so she left a message.

A few minutes later there was a knock at the door. When Brenda opened it, there were two police officers standing there. 'May we come in please?' asked the shorter one, showing her his ID card. 'Be better if we speak, inside. You are Mrs Johnson?' he asked.

'Yes. Yes, I am. What's the problem, Officer?'

'Please, may we come in?' said the taller of the two policemen.

'Sorry, err… yes.' They followed her through to the living room, where Peter and Helen were sitting.

'So, what's this about, Officer?' questioned Brenda.

'It'd be best if you sat down, Mrs Johnson, if you don't mind,' asked the shorter officer.

Peter looked at Helen, then he got up, sitting his mum down on the settee he'd just got off.

The shorter policeman said to them, 'I'm Detective Inspector Dawkins, We've got some news for you. It's not good, Mrs Johnson.'

'Which is?' questioned Peter.

'And who are you, sir?' asked the taller officer.

'This is my mum,' he replied, putting his hand on his mum's shoulder.

'Sorry, we have to ask. And you are?' he questioned Helen, looking at her.

'This lady will be my mother-in-law shortly,' said Helen, looking at Brenda.

'Okay, my apologies,' said the taller officer, nodding to the shorter one.

Then, Dawkins said, 'The news is bad, I'm afraid. It's your husband. There's been an accident just off the motorway, in which he's been involved. It's very serious; he's in hospital being operated on as we speak. He had identification with him.'

'No!' shouted Brenda.

'So, so, he's still alive?' asked Peter.

'Yes, sir. We think it best that you come with us immediately. To the hospital,' said Dawkins.

'Come on, let's go,' said Helen, realising the gravity of the situation.

'We can go in our car, if you wish?' asked the taller officer.

'No, thanks, we'll follow you if that's okay,' said Peter.

Dawkins nodded, saying, 'That's fine, sir. We have to break protocol here. Follow us, closely.'

'We will,' said Peter.

Brenda grabbed her coat, staring at Peter, who said, 'Mum, it'll be okay, won't it, Helen?'

'Yes,' replied Helen. 'Come on, let's get there as quick as we can.'

The journey was silent. Helen sat in the back of the car with her arm around Brenda. After ten minutes they arrived. The two police officers escorted them through the hospital, Dawkins telling them he'd explain everything when they got to the waiting room.

Once there, Dawkins left to go and find a doctor, returning a couple of minutes later.

'I'm Dr Radcliffe,' said the man in the white coat who'd just entered the room before Dawkins. 'I'll come straight to the point. You are Mrs Johnson, I've been informed?'

'Yes,' replied Brenda.

Dr Radcliffe glanced at Peter and Helen, before speaking. 'I'm sorry to have to tell you this, but your husband has been in an accident. I can tell you no more about that; the officers here can do that,' he said looking at Dawkins and his colleague, before continuing. 'He has suffered some terrible injuries. A broken leg in several places, a broken arm, lacerations and cuts to his back, and a head trauma. This head trauma has led to a haemorrhage, which means there is a bleed to his brain.'

Brenda collapsed into Peter's arms, sobbing.

'So… will he live?' asked Peter, holding his mother in his arms.

'Right now, one of my colleagues is operating on him to stop this bleed to his brain, trying to stop the swelling. If he pulls through, he will be put into an induced coma.'

Sitting his mother on a chair, with Helen supporting her, Peter said, 'And what about the rest of his body?'

'There are two teams working on him. I've done everything I can for his body, limbs and back. My colleague Dr Spencer, a neurosurgeon, is working on his brain as we speak.'

'I don't believe this!' shouted Peter.

Helen jumped up from her chair, putting her arms around him. He started to cry. 'Come on, sit down,' she said.

'I'll tell you more when I know myself,' said Dr Radcliffe. 'I'm going back to assist Dr Spencer. It may be some time before I can give you an update,' he added, turning and leaving the room.

'Mrs Johnson,' said Dawkins, 'I know this is a difficult time and a shock. Whenever you want, I can inform you about the accident.'

'Can you tell us now; I'd like to know?' asked Peter.

Dawkins nodded, then sat down next to them, whilst his colleague waited at the door. 'He'd just turned off the M61, coming towards Manchester,' said Dawkins in a soft, quiet and calm voice. 'From witness accounts already, we know that a vehicle, an articulated lorry, crushed his car. Our investigation has only just started, but the extent of damage to the car shows it's possible the lorry driver didn't see the car. Equipment was used to cut your husband out of the vehicle,' he said, looking at Brenda.

'This is a bloody nightmare,' said Peter, shaking his head. 'That's the accident we saw!'

'We'll keep you informed of developments, if you would like to know,' said Dawkins.

'Yes I would, thank you,' replied Peter.

'I've to get back to the scene myself, so please excuse us for now,' Dawkins said, reaching out to shake Peter's hand.

'Thank you again,' said Peter, quietly.

Brenda hadn't stopped crying throughout the ordeal. Helen rose, telling Peter she needed the toilet.

Brenda wiped her eyes, mumbling 'Thank you,' to Dawkins, as he left the room with his colleague.

Peter said, 'Listen, he's a tough guy, always was, you know that, Mum.'

She sniffed before saying, 'I know. I know. It's just awful that you've come here to see him. When I called him this morning, he was so excited.'

'Come on, he'll make it, Mum. He has to. I want my family back, all of you. I've waited too long to see him, and my brothers.'

'Okay,' she said. 'Positive thinking. Let me phone Jimmy, Joe and Stan. They all need to be here. I'll tell them all you're finally here. They were all coming to the house this evening.'

'When Helen's back, we'll go and call them, okay?'

She nodded saying, 'Yes, be wonderful to have all my boys together,' as she continued sobbing.

Helen returned, telling them a nurse who saw them arrive would try and keep them informed of Jim's condition. Peter told her they were going to call his brothers; they had to know.

When they came back, Dr Radcliffe was in the waiting room with Helen. 'I've just got here,' he said. 'Dr Spencer has managed to stop the bleeding to the brain and he's now in an induced coma. It may be some time before we awaken him.'

'So, you don't know if he's going to make it or not?' asked Peter.

'I can't answer that I'm afraid. Dr Spencer has told me that there is a possibility, if he comes round, of brain damage.'

Brenda shook her head saying, 'This was supposed to be a wonderful day. Now it's just... awful.'

'Mum, he's going to make it. We know he is, don't we?'

She nodded.

'He's in recovery at the moment, we're putting your husband in an isolated room on his own; we've to monitor him twenty-four hours a day. In a couple of hours, you can see him, if you wish,' said Dr Radcliffe.

'Yes please,' said Brenda.

Helen and Peter both nodded.

'I'll be back later,' said Dr Radcliffe, leaving the room.

'Did you speak to your brothers, Pete?' asked Helen.

'Only Jimmy. He couldn't believe it was me, knew we were coming up though. He'll be here soon. Stan and Joe are out training. I spoke to Stan's fiancée, Janice. She said he and Joe have got those mobile phones like Dad; footballers' wages are good,' he added, smiling.

'So, is she going to get hold of them?' asked Helen.

'Yes,' said Brenda. 'It'll take about three hours for them to drive down from Middlesbrough. Because of the circumstances, Janice said it was likely the manager will let them leave as soon as they can; he knows their father's a scout for the club.'

'Nothing more to do other than wait then,' said Helen, adding, 'I'll go and phone my parents, you stay with your mum, okay?'

'Yep. Looks like we'll be staying for a night or two, maybe more. Have to sort out the kids, speak to Johnny as well,' he replied.

'Leave it to me,' said Helen, stroking his hair, going out of the door, smiling at Peter.

'Got a wonderful woman there,' said Brenda.

'I know, Mum. Means the world to me.'

'Just like your dad does to me.'

They smiled at one another, Peter putting his arm around his mother again, saying, 'Mum, I know I should've been in touch more; you know the whole story. I'm sorry for putting you through everything for all these years.'

'Look, you're here now, that's all that matters. We know why, don't we? Your dad regretted what he did. Your brothers know all about it. We told them together a few days after you… you left. They know he's always been looking for you,' she said, stroking his face.

'Here now. Yes,' he replied, kissing her on the cheek, tears in his eyes again.

He stood up to stretch, giving a sigh, as Helen came back into the room. 'So, spoken to Mum and Dad,' she said. 'They're staying at our place for as long as we need. Uncle said he'd cover the club for me – us – as long as we want. So, looks like you've got lodgers for a while, Mrs Johnson, if that's okay with you?'

'Of course it is,' said Brenda.

'But the kids?' said Peter.

'All under control. Don't forget, my parents are... well, parents. Mum's looking forward to looking after them,' she said. 'And I called Kate, she's going to go round every day after work.'

Peter nodded towards Helen, before his mum spoke. 'Let's just see how your father is. I'm not going anywhere until all you boys are here, then with any luck we can go and see him,' said Brenda.

The door opened. Standing in the doorway was a man slightly taller than Peter. 'Hello, Mum,' said Jimmy, adding, 'Christ! It's been too long since I've seen you, little bro, far too long,' as he saw Peter.

Peter strode over to him, hugging him. 'Sorry, Jimmy,' he said.

'No need to be sorry. Hey, when we found out years ago from Elly you were okay, that was good enough for us. Always knew you'd come home one day,' said Jimmy, cupping his hands around Peter's face, smiling at him, tears in his own eyes.

They continued hugging, until Peter said, 'Got someone for you to meet. This is Helen.'

Walking over to her, Jimmy said, smiling, 'Great to meet you. Heard all about you from Elly, and Mum,' hugging her as he said the words.

'Likewise,' said Helen, smiling back at Jimmy.

Then Jimmy went to his mum, cuddling her, saying, 'We know he's a fighter, don't we?'

'Yes, we do,' said Brenda. 'Now, let me tell you what we know so far.' Brenda sat down and told him more details about the accident. Then between her, Helen and Peter, they explained the operations that had taken place.

'So, he's in a coma for a while then?' said Jimmy.

'Induced,' said Peter.

Jimmy stood up, hugging Peter again, before saying, 'Right, you. No talking about what happened all those years ago. We know the story. We're here for Dad now, right?'

'Yes,' said Peter. 'Yes, we are.'

'Good. Right. Be a couple of hours before Stan and Joe get here I reckon. So, I'll go and get us some food. Guess you're hungry, seeing as you've driven up from London?'

'That'd be nice, thank you, Jimmy,' said Helen.

Jimmy went to ask a nurse if it was okay to bring food into the hospital; she said it was under the circumstances. About half an hour later, he came back with fish and chips for all of them, having suggested it before he left. Brenda ate hardly anything, just some fish.

For the next two hours, Jimmy asked them all about their life in London, asking if he could visit now Peter had finally returned. He showed them pictures of his wife Dotty and son, Charlie. Peter said it felt like he'd never been away, with Helen showing him photos of Tammy and Ronnie. As they chatted, Brenda smiled at them all, crying at the same time.

Then at ten o'clock that evening, Dr Radcliffe came into the room, saying they could go and see Jim. They knew he was still in a coma and were only allowed to go in two at a time. Brenda went in with Jimmy. Then Peter went in with Helen.

'You okay, Pete?' asked Helen as they went into the room, where he was about to see his father for the first time in almost twenty years.

'Yes. Didn't expect to see him like this, but... I want to see him,' he replied, walking up to the side of his father's bed. There were tubes in his arm, and his head had been partly-shaved. But he could see it was his father. Peter held his hand, then stroked his face with his hand, adding, 'Sorry, Dad,' before sobbing.

Helen held him in her arms. 'It's not your fault, I've told you that. He's alive, you've seen him. Be strong for him, Pete, okay?'

Wiping his eyes, he nodded. 'I will,' he said. Taking a deep breath he added, 'You've got two weddings to wake up and go to, Dad. And you've got two more grandchildren to meet, so you'd better wake up. I know you can hear me. I know you can,' he said, his voice trembling as he spoke.

Helen looked at him. 'Come on. He heard you. The doctor said we can only stay a minute or so,' taking his hand, about to lead him out of the room.

But, before they did, Peter kissed his dad gently on the head. Helen smiled at him holding his hand as they left the room.

Walking down the corridor, they saw Jimmy and their mum. 'Back to the waiting room then, we've told a couple of nurses to look out for Stan and Joe. One of them knows who they are, she's a football nut! Wants their autographs,' said Jimmy.

A nurse made them some tea as they waited for the twins to arrive. Peter went out to use the toilet. When he returned, he got another shock. Standing in the waiting room were his twin brothers, still in their tracksuits. 'Baby boy!' said Stan, smiling, putting his arms out as he walked over to Peter. 'You're a sight for sore eyes,' he added.

'My turn!' said Joe, taking the few steps over to Peter, who'd just been crushed by Stan. Joe did the same. 'Let's have a look at you. Yep, you're my little brother all right. Fucking great to see you!' he said, squeezing him as hard as he could.

'What can I say? Good to be back, shame about it being in here, guys.'

Jimmy walked over to the three of them as Stan and Joe had an arm each around Peter's shoulders. 'You're not leaving me out of this. Family group hug, boys, been waiting a long time for this,' said Jimmy, smiling.

All four of them embraced as one, whilst Helen put her arm around Brenda. Stan had already told his mum, brother and Helen they were having a late training session until Janice called them; that's why they were here later than expected.

As their group hug ended, Stan said, 'We've met your future wife, Pete, you've already been invited to my wedding, and we're all coming to yours. You knew that anyway, didn't you?' he said, looking over at Helen.

'You've quite a family here, Pete Johnson,' Helen said, crying again.

'I know. I know,' he said, wiping his eyes yet again.

'Right, listen,' said Brenda. 'I'm staying here. Already asked a nurse and she said they'll find somewhere for me to rest and sleep. You all get going soon, there's nothing you can do while your dad is… well, like he is.'

'Mum, the boss has given us a couple of days off, we don't need to be back until Friday; there's no midweek game, so we're not playing until Saturday,' said Joe.

'Can we see him, Mum?' added Stan.

'I'll go and see the doctor, they let us go in, in pairs, be back in a minute,' said Jimmy.

'We'll stay at the house tonight, Mum, if that's okay, no point in driving back up to Middlesbrough,' said Joe.

'And we're staying there as well,' said Helen.

'You stay here tonight then, Mum, we'll be back in the morning after we see Dad in a minute, hopefully,' said Stan.

Jimmy came back in with a nurse. It was the one who knew the twins, the football fan nurse. 'Let me take you to see your father. You can only stay for a minute,' she said.

They left, returning a few minutes later, ashen faced. They hadn't realised how gravely ill their father was. They all sat down, telling the twins exactly what had happened and why their father was in a coma. All of the boys were jokers, one way or another. But, this wasn't a time for laughter.

After discussing it, Brenda ordered them all to go and get some sleep. None of them knew or realised how tired their mother had been in recent months. They always did whatever their mother said. If anything changed she would call them.

32
The Next Six Months

Arriving at the house, the twins told them all about their lives as footballers. Both of them had bought their own house in Middlesbrough, having settled there since they were seventeen. Stan was living with his fiancée, while Joe lived on his own; though he had a girlfriend. They had mobile phones, courtesy of the club; their manager said they were in case he needed to get hold of them, at any time. Stan said today was a prime example why they had to have them: an emergency situation.

'So, you two are both, what, thirty-four now?' asked Peter, as they sat in the living room.

'Yep, thirty-five in May, couple of weeks after your wedding,' said Stan.

'You must be fit then, guys, still playing top flight football?' Helen asked.

'We get paid very well, you know that. Both been lucky with injuries over the years; managed to pay off this place for Mum and Dad, and clear

Jimmy's mortgage off as well. He didn't want us to, but we did anyway,' said Joe, smiling.

'Seems you're not the only lucky one in the family, Pete?' said Helen, smiling at him.

'Hmmm,' he replied, smiling back at her.

'What's that mean then?' asked Joe.

'Well, you know when he ran away, he could've gone anywhere but he went to London. He got a job at *Johnny's*, the nightclub, changed jobs to be on the stage, and… wait for it… met me!' said Helen, laughing.

'I worked hard though,' Peter replied, grinning at her like a Cheshire cat.

Stan and Joe smiled, before Helen said, 'So when's the wedding, Stan?'

'Not until July. The boss tries to make sure anything we do is out of season, whenever possible. Thing is, we're both on rolling one year contracts which end in June. Because of our age, we don't know if we'll get another season. I mean, we're not old but we are for footballers.'

'And you're both losing your hair a bit,' said Peter, smiling at them.

'Don't rub it in, baby boy, just because you've still got all of yours,' said Stan, rubbing his own and Joe's hair.

'So, what'll you do if you don't get contracts?' asked Peter.

'We've both done our coaching badges in the last three years, our last boss suggested we do it; told us we could be coaches, trainers or managers because of our experience at this level,' said Joe.

'That's good, you can stay in the game then?' Helen asked.

'That's the plan. Might not be at the same team, but we have to wait and see,' said Stan.

'And, the other thing is, we've both saved loads of money, thanks to Jimmy's help. If we don't get a chance to play or coach, we don't have to work any more if either of us don't want to,' added Joe.

'Brilliant. That's great,' said Peter.

'Well, we're not doing too bad, are we Pete?' Helen said.

'You know about the club, guys, makes a really good profit. Got our house, not much left on our mortgage. Helen's uncle offered to pay it all off for us, but we said no, we wanted to do it ourselves,' said Peter.

'Look, we can do that for you, you only have to ask,' said Stan, looking at Joe, who nodded in agreement with him.

'Yep, too right,' added Joe.

'Thanks, but no thanks,' said Helen, glancing at Peter.

'Guys, we don't need it, honestly. But hey, that's a wonderful gesture. Mum brought us up well, didn't she?' Peter said.

'Sure did. Well, if you ever need it, we've got it,' said Stan.

'Thank you. So,' Helen said, after a few silent seconds, 'think it's time for bed. Are we sleeping in your old room, Pete?'

'Yes,' he said.

'Mum always kept the bedroom the same after you left,' said Joe.

'You know, I've never been up there, not since... well, you know,' said Peter.

Helen put her arm around him, saying, 'Come on, let's go and have a look together.'

'Right, our bedroom's much the same as well, bit smaller since they added the bathroom upstairs though. She never wanted to change any of the beds. We come and stay now and again,' said Stan, continuing, 'well. I do with my fiancée, Janice.'

'Came down with my girlfriend once, to meet Mum. She'd already met Dad at the club, about two months ago. Her name's Bernice... I call her Berny,' said Joe, adding, 'she'll do for me,' smiling at them all.

'Right, Mum's not called so let's hope there's been no change with Dad,' said Stan.

'Yep, she said she'd call,' said Peter.

'I'll tidy up,' said Helen, as the twins wished them goodnight, hugging Helen, then Peter, telling him he has to come up and watch them play football, and soon; to which he replied they would.

After clearing up, they went upstairs, Peter showing Helen his old bedroom. It was indeed, just the same as when he'd left all those years ago. Laid out on his bed, were his old pyjamas. When he saw them, he cried.

'It's okay,' said Helen, holding him while he sobbed, quietly. 'I've got ours in my bag, don't think they'll fit you now,' she added, smiling at him.

He laughed, saying, 'I know. Just didn't expect to see them.'

Helen nodded. They undressed, Peter seeing the time was almost one a.m. He was tired, it had been a draining day for all of them. They cuddled up close in his old single bed, wrapping their bodies around one another, falling asleep within minutes.

The next two days, they visited the hospital. No change. Stan and Joe stayed until the Friday, when their boss called them, asking if they could come back for training ahead of the match on Saturday. Their mother told them to go. She had their mobile phone numbers, and would call anytime. Life has to go on, she told them.

The day the twins went back, Jimmy invited Peter and Helen to his house along with their mother, for dinner, finally meeting his wife Dotty and their son Charlie.

Driving back later, with Helen and his mum sitting in the back seat, she said, 'I'll go back tomorrow, that okay with you, Pete?'

'I can't leave,' he replied.

She understood. 'Never a problem, Pete Johnson,' she told him. 'We can beat anything you and me, can't we?'

'Sure can,' he said.

'Sorry,' said Helen, looking at Brenda.

'Don't be silly you've got your own family now. Jim's in the best place, we've just got to wait and see – see when, not if he comes round,' replied Brenda.

Helen went back to London the next day, asking Peter to keep an eye on his mum; she thought she looked pale. He said he would speak to her.

For the next two weeks, Peter stayed in Manchester, at his parents' house. Back in London, Helen worked at the club for a few nights, giving Johnny and Ruth a break before going back to Manchester with the children, all of them staying at Peter's parents' house.

He told Helen he'd visited his dad every day, talking to him, about all the things they'd done when he was a boy, and his life now. It didn't matter that he couldn't hear him. His mum told him all about her job teaching; she'd been given a leave of absence for as long as she wanted. And, he told Helen he'd had a word with his mum about looking pale and tired; she said it was probably everything going on, she'd be fine.

The family all visited Jim as much as possible, as did Elly, Jenny, Jim's mother and Brenda's parents. Members of the football team came, and the manager; they all knew Jim from his work as a scout.

Three weeks after the accident, Peter was sitting by his father's bedside, Helen was with their children visiting Dotty while Jimmy was at work. As he sat talking to his father, his mum having gone to lay down in the rest room nearby, he saw his dad open his eyes, glancing at him for a split second. It happened so quickly, Peter wasn't sure of what he'd seen.

'Dad! Dad, can you hear me?' asked Peter, after seeing his father's eyes for the first time in years. 'Nurse, nurse!' shouted Pete, rushing out of the room.

The football fan nurse was on duty, running up to him, saying, 'Mr Johnson, what is it?'

'Dad opened his eyes for a moment!'

'He did?'

'Yes, honestly, come on!' Peter said, grabbing her arm, taking her over to look at his dad. 'Sorry,' he said, more calmly to the nurse.

'That's all right. Just let me have a look,' she said, lifting his dad's eyelids. 'I'll call a doctor right away, you're right, he moved his eyes left and right.'

Hearing Peter shouting, Brenda raced into the room as the nurse flew out of the door past her. 'What's happened?'

'Mum, he opened his eyes!' Peter said, sobbing. 'He saw me!' She stared at him open-mouthed.

It was Dr Radcliffe who arrived. He checked his eyes, then asked Brenda to hold her husband's hand.

She did, telling the doctor, 'He moved his fingers!'

'May I?' said Dr Radcliffe, taking Jim's hand. After a few seconds, he said, 'There is movement. Leave this to me, I'll call Dr Spencer to confirm. Please don't get too excited, it's possible we can take him out of the coma. Remember, we're in the unknown here, because of the trauma to your husband's head, there could be... could, I say, be brain damage.'

Brenda smiled at Jim, as she hugged Peter, holding her husband's hand again, saying, 'He's squeezing it again.'

Taking her hand away, she pointed to Peter to take his father's hand. He knelt beside the bed, then looked up at his mum, smiling, then nodded. 'He's really squeezing hard.'

Dr Radcliffe returned. He explained that it would be a slow process and would take a few hours, but they were going to reverse the coma. Asking them to leave the room for a few minutes, he and the nurse adjusted the drips before allowing them to return. 'Now, I need you to be quiet, please. It may be possible, if his brain is functioning that he could speak,' said Dr Radcliffe as the nurse ushered them back into the room.

They waited in silence. For two hours. Then Peter whispered to his mother he was going to call Helen. She and Dotty could let the others know. No, Brenda said. Wait a little longer. So he did.

Half an hour later, with the nurse on one side, Peter and his mother on the other, Jim opened his eyes, squeezed Brenda's hand tight, turned his head to his left and said slowly and quietly, 'Is it you, son?'

'Yes, Dad, it's me,' Peter replied, smiling at him.

'I'm sorry, son,' he said.

'Doesn't matter, Dad,' he replied, hardly able to utter the words.

There was an attempt of a smile on his father's lips, as they both leant over him. He'd come round for about ten seconds, looking and speaking, before he closed his eyes again.

'Wait with him, please,' said the nurse, leaving the room.

She returned moments later with Dr Radcliffe. 'Did he speak?' asked the doctor.

'Yes. Yes he did, and moved his head,' said Brenda.

'Good. Very good. Now, we'll need to monitor him. It's likely he'll keep waking like this, saying a few words, then falling asleep again. That's normal for a patient coming out of a coma. The nurse will stay with you both for the next two hours. Shift change time then, so another nurse will take over.'

'So, what do you think, Doctor, about the brain damage?' asked Peter.

'Too early to say. But, as he's spoke and recognised you, that is a good sign. Remember, he's got lots of other injuries, so it'll be a while before he's up and about from his bed.'

'Thank you, Doctor,' said Brenda.

'I'll be back in an hour or so, to check on him again,' said Dr Radcliffe, nodding, then turning to the door.

'Thank you, Doctor,' said Peter, as he walked away.

'Just doing my job, Mr Johnson,' said Dr Radcliffe, waving his hand in the air as he left the room.

'Great doctor,' said the nurse. 'Always been my favourite one.'

'Agree with you there,' said Peter.

They sat quietly then, as instructed by the doctor, waiting for Jim to wake up again. He did, four more times. Each time, it was longer and longer. The fourth time, Dr Radcliffe had returned. 'How are you, Mr Johnson,' Dr Radcliffe said, leaning over him when he opened his eyes.

'Feel like I've been hit by a truck,' Jim said slowly, smiling.

'Always the joker, you,' said Brenda, smiling.

'That's exactly what happened, Mr Johnson,' said Dr Radcliffe, smiling, saying, 'Good to see you've still got your sense of humour.' Jim smiled, before the doctor continued. 'Now, can you follow my pen with your eyes please. Just your eyes, don't try and move your head.'

Jim followed the pen with his eyes, as they all watched him. 'Good. Please don't try to move your head, Mr Johnson, we'll leave that for a couple of days. Now, you've got severe injuries to contend with; broken arm and leg, lacerations and cuts to your back.'

'How long have I been here?'

'Three weeks,' said the doctor.

'Bloody hell,' Jim whispered.

'We had to place you in a coma because you had a bleed on the brain. It'll be a while before you leave, due to the extent of your injuries. I won't discharge you until I'm satisfied, plus the specialist neurosurgeon who worked on you, and have seen X-ray results first.'

'Okay, Doctor. Thank you,' said Jim, sombrely.

'It's likely you will keep falling asleep for a few days yet. Just try and squeeze my hand, will you?' asked the doctor. 'Good. Can you raise this arm?'

Jim moved his left arm off the bed two inches.

'That's good too. Well done, Mr Johnson,' turning to look at Brenda. 'Now as I said, we'll continue monitoring his progress. I'm afraid that from now on we can only allow two people in the room at a time, in case we need access; it's safer all round that way.'

Jim closed his eyes again, falling back asleep. 'Don't worry, he'll continue to do that, it's normal,' said the doctor, looking at Jim.

Brenda nodded, as did Peter, before he spoke. 'Mum, I'll go and call Helen and Dotty; they can let everyone else know.'

'Right. I'll stay here,' said Brenda.

Peter followed the doctor out of the room, calling Dotty, knowing Helen was still at Jimmy's house. Dotty told him she'd contact his brothers and the rest of the family. Helen told him she'd contact the family down in London.

It was a further six months from the day of Jim's accident, until Peter and Helen's wedding in May. All that time, Peter journeyed from London to

Manchester, sometimes with Helen and the children, sometimes on his own. He fitted in a couple of games of football watching his brothers' team with Helen, saw Jimmy, his mum, grandparents and Elly as often as he could.

Finally, after spending two months in hospital, his dad was allowed home, Peter driving his parents to their house. They cried. He and his father talked. And talked, just like they had in the hospital. Brenda said they could both talk the hind legs off a donkey! Then she said, no, not just those two, all of the Johnson men could!

Peter and his father made their peace with one another. Knowing they couldn't turn the clock back, they had a future as a complete family now.

With his dad getting better slowly, with no brain damage, they all joked that each of the Johnson men were very lucky indeed.

A few weeks before their wedding, after he'd finished his act one evening, Peter was approached by a man who introduced himself as Grant Devlin. He said he worked for ITV. If he ever wanted to try his hand at television, he should get in touch. Peter took his card, telling Helen about it. With visiting Manchester regularly, being busy at the club and their impending wedding, he dismissed the idea. Helen said she'd keep the card, just in case.

By the time it reached May the 3rd 1987, Jim could walk with a stick. The football club told him they would pay him off. When the accident happened, he was technically working for them, the manager and chairman told him. So, if he wanted it, they had a golden handshake for him. When he was ready, all he had to do was sign the papers; there was no need for him to work again.

Whilst Jim was recovering slowly, Brenda began to feel unwell. She didn't tell Jim, or any of the boys. In March, before the wedding, she visited her doctor, telling him she had indigestion, stomach cramps, was tired, and had back pain. He knew her family history and what had happened to her, so suggested some blood tests for her. He thought it might be IBS – Irritable Bowel Syndrome – so prescribed painkillers.

She had the blood tests. A week later she called her doctor's surgery for the results. It wasn't IBS she was told by her doctor when she went for the appointment the next day; it was very likely a virus and could be the stress of all she'd been through recently, leaving her run down.

The Easter break gave her a chance to rest and she began to feel less tired. Going back to school, she struggled through the next few weeks, as the symptoms returned; she was still looking after Jim, who was recovering well from his injuries.

It came to the weekend of the wedding. The twins had a fixture backlog. They had a game on the Saturday before the wedding, which they won against Chester, securing promotion. A new manager at the end of the last season, had turned their fortunes around at the club. He allowed them to go to the wedding, straight after their game on the Saturday, insisting they make it to the match on Bank Holiday Monday, May the 4th, against Mansfield.

Stan's fiancée Janice drove down from Middlesbrough with Joe's girlfriend Berny on the Saturday, as did Jimmy, travelling down with Dotty and their son, taking his parents. Elly and Jenny had already gone down the night before to see the sights of London.

Elly and Jenny were going to stay at Peter's house for the three nights. Jimmy, Dotty and Charlie were going to Helen's Uncle Johnny's house, along with Stan, Joe, Janice and Berny, when they all arrived.

Peter had contacted Randy Martinez a couple of times. He was coming over from Spain with his family; they'd arranged for them to stay at Johnny's house too, which was much bigger, with lots more room for them all.

Jim and Brenda were staying at Helen's parents' house.

On one of Helen's visits to Manchester with Peter, she'd taken her parents, so that they could meet his family. They knew all about Jim's accident. And, they took her aunt and uncle up as well, a month before the wedding.

By the time it got to the Saturday evening before the wedding, they'd all arrived in London, except the twins, who would be there later after their match. And the Martinez family who were due to arrive via their flight by seven p.m. Helen's parents were at her home. No seeing the bride before the wedding day. Peter was staying in his old room above the club for one night.

33
Night Before the Big Day

The twins didn't arrive until nine thirty, after having directions to Johnny's house. Janice and Berny were already there when they arrived. Johnny and Ruth were waiting for them. As soon as they got out of Joe's car, Johnny ushered them into a waiting limousine, taking them all to the club.

Randy Martinez and his wife Mina arrived later than expected. There'd been a delay on their flight. When they arrived, they called Helen, taking a taxi directly from the airport to her house. She welcomed them with open arms, putting all their luggage into the hallway, explaining the tradition of the bride not seeing the groom before the wedding day, suggesting their sons stay at her house, with her father Brian taking them to the club.

'So, Peter's brothers, how'd it go today, I purposely didn't check the football results?' asked Johnny, as they sat in the limousine.

'Bloody won!' said Stan. 'Promotion, great result! Long drive down, but our boss let us miss the celebrations this evening, so we could be here,' he added.

'This time last year we were relegated. Great feeling around the club now,' said Joe, adding, 'we've both had a great run for nearly eighteen years. Been amazing, made a really good living out of kicking a ball about, eh, Stan?'

'Too true,' said Stan. 'Now, Mr Fenton, can I ask you a question please?'

'Celebration tonight then, boys! So, what can I help you with?' said Johnny.

'Do you make a good living out of running your club, if you don't mind me asking?' questioned Stan.

'We certainly do,' he said, looking at Ruth, winking at her. 'Maybe not as much as you footballers,' he added, smiling at the twins. 'But, it was tough when we first started. Must've worked twenty hours a day, building it up to what it's been for, say, thirty odd years.'

'We took the club on when it was, let's say, difficult in the late 1950s. Took out a mortgage that was really tough to get, put our life savings into it, didn't we?' said Ruth.

'True. Worked bloody hard for everything. Don't have to now. You know why we still do it? Because we both love it,' said Johnny smiling.

'Right, get that bubbly open,' Ruth said.

In the limousine, there was a mini bar. Johnny opened a couple of bottles, saying, 'Champagne, ladies?'

'Yes, thank you,' said Janice, then Berny.

'Gentlemen?' asked Johnny, handing a glass to each of the twins.

'Yes, thank you, sir,' said Joe.

'Very kind of you, Mr Fenton,' said Stan.

Johnny poured a glass for himself and Ruth, then he raised a toast. 'To good living, good loving and most of all, happy families.'

'Cheers,' they all said, Joe adding, 'and especially now, to happy families.'

Johnny continued chatting away, asking Janice what she did for a living; a hairdresser was her answer. Berny was a teaching assistant. He asked them if they liked their jobs, both replying they did. He told them he loved his job, always did, telling them it was great working alongside his wife all these years.

Ruth told him not to be so soppy. He didn't listen, wishing them all a happy and prosperous life.

Joe and Stan told them all about their game, winning 2-1; neither of them could stop talking about football. Luckily, Janice and Berny liked football! Stan said they were going to have a great weekend; then another wedding in a couple of months when he and Janice were getting married. He invited Johnny and Ruth to their wedding in Manchester. They immediately said yes.

A little while after their limousine arrived at the club, Helen's father arrived, dropping off the Martinez's, explaining to Big Dave who they were. They were expected, so Big Dave escorted them into the club, pointing out Johnny to them. They went up to him, Martinez tapping him on the shoulder.

When Johnny turned to face him, he said, 'Ah, Mr Martinez, with your lovely wife. I recognise you from a photo Peter showed me and your visits to the club.'

'We are glad to be here,' replied Martinez.

'I remember you from a few years ago. Please, let me introduce you to everyone,' Johnny said, taking them over to Peter's family at the tables.

He introduced them all, telling Martinez that Peter would join them later; he was going to do his act on stage tonight, even though Johnny had asked him to have a break on the eve of his wedding.

They sat with Peter's parents; Jimmy and Dotty were there. They'd already left their son Charlie with Helen. Jim took over from Johnny, introducing the rest of the family to Martinez and Mina.

Johnny went over to the bar, coming back being followed by two of the waitresses, saying, 'Anything you want, just ask these two young ladies, folks, okay?'

'Thank you, Mr Fenton, for this,' said Jim.

Johnny sat down next to Jim, who had his walking stick to help him. 'Jim, let me tell you something, might not get the chance after tonight,' he said quietly, pausing. 'Your son is one hell of an amazing man. When I first met him, I wasn't at all sure about him.'

'Oh, well, thanks,' said Jim, Brenda listening in as well.

'My niece Helen, is like a daughter to me. Never had children myself. You folks are very fortunate, having four sons. Now, when he'd been here a few years, "the kid" took a shine to Helen. And she to him. I wasn't keen at first, neither were Helen's parents. But, he proved us all wrong. He's a great guy; seems to run in the family with you Johnsons!' he said, smiling.

'Thank you, they're very kind words, Mr Fenton,' said Brenda.

'Call me Johnny, please. We're all family here,' he said, waving his hand over the tables, before continuing. 'Now, enjoy the show. Your son will be on stage shortly. Order whatever you want – food, drink. Just have a good time. I'll be back shortly, going to find my little lady.' He got up, shaking Jim's hand, kissing Brenda on the cheek.

'Quite a guy, this Johnny Fenton,' said Brenda.

'He sure is,' said Jim, adding, 'I'm not drinking alcohol, Brenda, you know I've not touched it since that day.'

She smiled at him. 'Look, if you want a drink, have one, I don't mind.'

'No, I don't need it. This is all intoxicating enough,' Jim said, smiling at her, then leant over to kiss her.

'This is a great club,' said Martinez to Jim.

'It's the first time we've been here, Mr Martinez, we actually live in Manchester,' said Jim.

'Oh yes, sorry. I remember Peter telling us now.'

'So, you own clubs in Spain, we've been told?' asked Brenda.

'Yes. We do. We've our three sons with us for the wedding, they are at Peter and Helen's house at the moment.'

'You've been here before, our son told us?' asked Jim.

'Yes, it's where I saw him on stage. Fantastic act. Have you ever seen him?'

'No, this will be our first time,' said Brenda.

'Enjoy it. He is very good,' said Mina.

The twins had already ordered drinks, getting their mum a vodka and coke, their dad an orange juice, knowing he hadn't drunk for many years.

One of the waitresses asked Martinez and Mina if they'd like a drink, coming back over with them quickly afterwards.

'Cheers!' shouted Jim above the din of the noise. They all smiled, shouting cheers, raising their glasses. The twins had a few drinks that night. But they didn't get drunk, they both knew too much would affect their fitness levels, with a couple of matches still to play this season. Elly, Jenny, Jimmy and Dotty were deep in conversation themselves, breaking their chattering to raise their glasses.

After they'd all eaten, with the band still playing, Johnny turned up on stage. 'Folks, may I have your attention please!' as a hush went over the club. 'Now not many of you will be aware of this, but our star drag artist is getting married tomorrow. Yes, to a woman, none other than my niece and god-daughter.' He stopped talking as loud applause and laughter rang out in the club, then he held his hand up after a few seconds, to quieten everyone. 'As well as this, we have some very special quests with us tonight. They are none other than Petra Juno's – yes Peter Johnson's – family.'

Immediately, spotlights went onto the tables they were all sitting at.

Johnny said, 'I wouldn't normally do this, but as this is an exceptional couple of days for us here, I'd like to introduce two people to you in that group.

They are "the kid's" parents, Brenda and Jim Johnson. Please, show your appreciation for them. Without them, there'd be no Petra Juno act.'

The crowd rose to their feet, some of them knowing the story about Peter Johnson. The reason why Johnny did this, was because every person in the club tonight was a guest. It was a special free night Johnny and Ruth had planned, to say thank you to their guests, and to Peter's family.

When the applause died down, Johnny thanked them, wishing them all a good evening, going back to the tables, where Ruth had joined them. 'Sorry about that,' he said, shaking Jim's hand again. 'It's the only way I know of thanking you... all of you.'

Jim stood up, struggling. He looked at Johnny, still holding his hand, then hugged him. 'I know he's had a great family here, Johnny. Thank you, from the bottom of my heart for taking Peter in all those years ago.'

Johnny, for once, was speechless, and just nodded, putting his hand around Jim's shoulder.

The rest of the evening flew by. Peter was late on stage waiting for his brothers, Martinez and Mina to arrive. His act as Petra Juno was brilliant, they all said. When he had finished, he changed and joined them at their table.

'That was bloody great,' said Stan.

'Wow, baby brother!' said Joe. 'Amazing!'

'Ladies, did you enjoy it too?' Peter asked, looking at Janice and Berny.

They both nodded, Berny saying, 'You definitely looked the part up there!'

'Thank you,' Peter said, adding, 'Mum, Dad? What did you think?'

Brenda nodded. Jim got up again, hugging his youngest son, whispering in his ear, 'Fantastic. Not laughed so much in years.'

'Well, Elly, was it worth the wait?' asked Peter, his arm still around his father.

'Fucking great!' she shouted, everyone laughing before Peter spoke again.

'Jimmy, you and Dotty like that?'

Dotty nodded, Jimmy stood up smiling. 'You're a typical Johnson you are. Bloody brilliant, little brother!' he said, hugging him.

'Great show, yet again,' said Martinez, who hugged Peter, standing waiting to greet him.

'Glad you could make it, really good to see you,' replied Peter.

'You too, my friend,' said Martinez.

Mina hugged him as well, saying, 'Our boys are at your house, we were delayed by the plane.'

'No matter, you're here now, that's the main thing,' Peter replied, adding, 'would you excuse me for a few moments, I'll be back shortly.'

He walked over to a table, where two couples were sitting. It was Richard Leonard with his wife Grace, plus Arthur Dempsey and a young lady. He hadn't seen Dempsey for at least six months. He tapped him on the shoulder, as Dempsey turned round, Peter said, 'Long time, no see, old friend.'

'Peter, great to see you. Thanks for inviting us,' Dempsey said.

Richard stood up, walking round the table, shaking Peter's hand. 'Good to see you, my friend. Likewise, much appreciated for the invite. Great show up there again.'

'Thanks, guys, I just wanted to come over to say hi, and I'll see you tomorrow at the wedding.'

'It'll be our pleasure to be there,' said Dempsey. 'Someone I'd like you to meet, Peter. This is Audrey,' he added, winking at him.

'Very nice to meet you, Audrey. Hope you enjoyed the show. Is it your first time here tonight?' Peter asked, as she stood to kiss him on the cheek.

'Yes. You were wonderful, thank you,' said Audrey.

'Hello, Grace,' Peter said, kissing her on the cheek.

'Nice to see you again,' Grace replied, slurring her words.

'Gentlemen, ladies, enjoy the rest of your evening. I will definitely catch up with you all tomorrow,' he said nodding at Dempsey, adding,

351

'My family are here from Manchester, so if you'll excuse me, I've got some catching up to do.'

'No problem,' said Richard. 'You enjoy the rest of your evening too.'

'I will, thanks again,' Peter said, turning, then returning to his family and friends.

For the rest of the night, they all sat together. His twin brothers repeated Peter was great on stage, Joe telling him he had a real presence. There was much back slapping, Peter telling them all doing the act took his mind off the big day tomorrow. Elly hugged him, telling him he'd always been good at taking the piss out of people, in a subtle way! At the end of the night, after they all talked incessantly, it was time to leave.

When they went back to the houses, courtesy of Johnny and the limousines, nobody was drunk; they'd all been too busy talking.

As the others drove off to stay at their respective houses, going into Helen's parents' house, Jim said, 'Great night. Nothing like that in Manchester, well not that we've ever been to.'

'Just wonderful,' Brenda added, yawning.

They had a coffee, and a chat with Helen's parents. Brian told them it'd be another great day tomorrow, before they all went to bed.

Peter had stayed at the club, saying goodbye there, until the wedding day tomorrow.

34
Wedding Day

Waking up early, Peter knew he had to let in the extra caterers at eight o'clock.

They arrived, with Terry turning up at nine o'clock, to oversee everything. It had all been arranged courtesy of Johnny; he wanted them to forget about working, telling them to enjoy the day.

By midday, Terry had organised everything in the kitchen for their three-course dinner at five p.m., after the wedding ceremony. Peter helped put all the chairs in rows for the service. Helen's mother Joyce arranged the flowers after being delivered specially on a Sunday at two p.m.

'You okay, Peter?' Joyce asked him when she arrived. He was still in his shorts and T-shirt.

'Fine. Well, to be honest, a bit nervous.'

'No need, don't be daft,' she said, smiling at him, adding, 'you'd better get your suit on, it's nearly three o'clock, only an hour to go.'

'You look lovely, mother-in-law to be,' he said, as she gave him a curtsey.

'Thank you, son-in-law to be. Now go and get yourself sorted out, Ruth and Johnny will be here soon to help; not much left to do other than wait for the registrar, once I've sorted out the rest of the flowers.'

'Okay, see you in a bit,' he said, going upstairs to change. When he got there, he went into the room Terry used before he got married a few years ago, knocking on the door.

'Better get that suit on,' said Terry after he opened the door, Peter seeing he was in his morning suit already. 'You nervous, kid?'

'I am. Not like being on stage, I'm in control there, well that's how that always feels. Look, Terry, can I come in and have a quick word?' he asked.

'Yep, sure. You okay?' replied Terry.

Peter went in, closing the door behind him. 'Listen, Terry. I've got my twin brothers as ushers. I wanted them to do this, you know because I've kind of got my family back,' he said.

Terry could see and hear in his voice, that Peter was getting upset. 'Hey you,' he said. 'You know Johnny looks upon you as a son. As for me, well, you're like… like a brother to me… a younger brother. We're all one big family now. Come here,' he said, grabbing Peter.

'I know,' Peter replied quietly.

They hugged, both crying, before Terry said, 'Oy, don't you cry on my suit!'

They both smiled before letting one another go, as Peter said, 'Yep, you're an older brother to me, Terry.'

'Thanks, kid. Now, go and put that suit on, get back here, and you can check on my speech, okay?'

'Right, see you in a bit,' said Peter, turning and leaving.

Knocking on Terry's door a while later, he went in and they checked through one another's speeches. 'Don't know how I'm going to get through this, Terry.'

'Just be yourself. Pretend you're on stage, you're brilliant when you're up there. Told you that loads of times.'

'Will do,' said Peter, taking a big breath, as there was a knock on the door.

'That'll be the wife,' said Terry. 'Asked her to come up, make sure we weren't still sitting here going through these,' he said smiling, holding up his speech.

'Hi, Alice,' said Peter, as she came in.

'Come on, you two, not long now. You'd better get your jacket on, Pete,' she said.

Terry already had his jacket on, while Peter went next door to his old room, returning a few moments later.

'Need to get these buttonhole flowers in, gentlemen,' said Alice, putting Terry's in place.

'Right o' boss,' said Terry, laughing.

'You know who the boss is in our house, kid, don't you?' said Alice, looking at Peter.

'Knew that when you got married years ago, Alice. Great guy you married,' said Peter, laughing as she fixed his buttonhole flower on his jacket.

Then, they all went downstairs.

'You've got a great lady there,' said Alice, kissing Peter on the cheek as they got to the bottom of the stairs. 'Now, buttonholes in, go and welcome the rest of your guests.'

Ruth had the box of buttonholes, inside the front doors of the club. A few minutes after they reached her, more guests started arriving. 'You can stay here welcoming people if you want,' Ruth said to Peter, 'or just go and sit down with Terry?'

Then, his twin brothers arrived, with their ladies. 'I'll go and sit down with Terry, thanks, Ruth,' said Peter, getting his brothers to take over as the ushers. He showed Berny and Janice to their seats, telling his brothers to send their parents and Jimmy to where he'd be sitting.

Johnny had invited, with Peter and Helen's permission, some of the clients to the club. To them, they were almost like family.

When Elly came in with Jenny, she went straight up to Peter, who was sitting next to Terry. 'Want a word with you, Mr Johnson,' she whispered into his ear.

'Hey, Elly, what is it?'

'Stand up and close your eyes, right now,' she said.

'Why?'

'Just do it, Pete, got a surprise for you.'

'Oh, okay,' he said, putting his hands over his eyes.

'And keep your hands there, until I tell you to take them away,' Elly ordered.

As he stood there, he could hear his mother whispering, 'Come on. Come on.'

Peter said, 'What's going on?'

'Take your hands away now,' said Elly.

As he did, he got the shock of his life. Standing in front of him, were Elly's parents, who he'd not seen in almost twenty years. Behind them, he saw an old man and two old ladies. He knew who they all were. 'You, how, how, you're here!' he said, putting his hands to his head.

He walked towards Elly's parents, hugging them. Then he walked between them. Smiling in front of him, were his mother's parents, and his father's mum. His grandparents had made it to the wedding.

Peter put his hand to his mouth, as his only grandfather stepped forward, saying, quietly, 'Couldn't miss this, boy,' smiling at him.

Peter grabbed him gently, whispering, 'Grandpa', tears rolling down his cheeks. He did the same with his two grandmothers, whispering, 'Thank you,' to both of them.

As they stood there, Elly said, 'Think you'll be needing a hanky, Pete!'

Everyone around them laughed. 'You always say what you think, Elly,' said Peter's mother, adding, 'make sure you never change.'

'You know I won't, Mrs Johnson.' Elly replied, adding, 'Right all of you, we've got a wedding to attend. Let's stop all this crying, this is going to be a wonderful day!'

A round of applause rang out in the club. It wouldn't be the last that day.

When Helen arrived, she looked beautiful. Her best friend Kate was her maid of honour, with Tammy her only bridesmaid. The service went without a hitch.

Everyone had to help move the tables back in place, so that they could all sit down for the meal and the speeches. Terry got emotional, just like Peter. Helen's dad did as well.

When the speeches had finished and they'd all eaten, Jim got up from his seat. 'Ladies and gentlemen, just one more speech, if you'd allow it.'

Peter looked at him, saying, 'What, Dad?'

'It's okay, son, just a few words.'

Brenda leant forward, facing Peter, whispering, 'Don't worry.'

Moments later, Jim spoke. 'Ladies and gentlemen, I've written something here that I'll try and get through without too many stoppages, I promise you it won't take long.' He paused to sip his orange juice. 'My wife and I and our other sons and family, would like you all to know… that… that we'd like to wish Helen and Peter and their children, a most wonderful life together, for many, many years to come. Most of you will be aware of our background, I am not going to dwell on that. What I want to add is… is that we all know, that they have here, amongst all of you… amongst all of you, a family who will always be there for them.' Jim paused to take a breath, his voice quivering. 'We'd like to say simply, congratulations to the happy couple. Your family will always be in our hearts.' Jim wiped his eyes, as Brenda stood supporting him then, as he added, 'Please, raise your glasses one more time, to… the bride and groom… Helen and Peter.'

Everyone raised their glasses, then there was thunderous applause, led by Johnny, who left his seat still clapping, going over to shake Jim's hand. When the applause had died down, Johnny shouted above the din of voices, 'Right, you lot, celebration time continues, let's have a party!'

There was more applause, as the band on stage started playing.

Helen's mother Joyce and Brenda, had been looking after Tammy and Ronnie throughout the celebrations.

The tables were already in place, other than the top table where the bride and groom and the others were sitting; they were quickly removed, to allow room for the dance floor to appear.

The first ones up to dance were Dempsey and Audrey, Richard Leonard and his wife Grace. Peter joined them with Helen. Ruth joined them, as did Joyce and Brenda, carrying their children, handing them over to their parents. Brenda said to Joyce it had been a wonderful couple of days, but she was exhausted. Joyce agreed, saying she was also worn out, thinking nothing of Brenda's passing comment.

Dempsey said to Peter later, as they walked away from the dance floor, 'Think I've found the one,' smiling as he spoke.

'Lovely woman, Dempsey. I hope you'll be really happy,' replied Peter.

'We've spoke about having children already, Audrey wants at least three!' said Dempsey.

'They're a life changer. Made me grow up a bit when we had Tammy,' said Peter, looking at his daughter in his arms.

'We'll have to wait and see what happens on that score,' said Dempsey, as Audrey came over to them both.

'What are you two talking about then?' asked Audrey.

'Just congratulating, Peter. Told him it's been a brilliant day,' answered Dempsey, winking at him so that Audrey couldn't see.

Helen walked over to join them.

'I'll second that,' said Audrey. 'Thank you, both of you. This is a beautiful day,' then she kissed both Peter, then Helen, before adding, 'Now come on you, more dancing!' grabbing Dempsey's hand, pulling him back onto the dance floor.

'Nice dress Audrey has on, Pete, I like the dark green with the yellow flowers. Really different. I'll ask her where she got it later.'

'Not as nice as yours. You look fantastic, the new Mrs Johnson,' he said. They smiled at one another, kissing, still holding their children, as they walked over to where his parents, were sitting. Jim and

Brenda were surrounded by their sons. His dad was crying, with happiness, as they all said his speech was brilliant.

'Thanks, Dad,' said Peter, bending down to hug his father. Jim couldn't speak, the occasion overwhelming him. He just nodded.

The rest of the evening was fabulous. They danced, sang, drank and laughed. Even Jim attempted the dance floor with his walking stick.

Peter took time to speak to his grandparents, promising to carry on visiting them all with Helen and their children.

Kate was talking to Helen when Peter spoke to his grandparents. 'You looked beautiful today,' said Kate.

'And you too, Kate.'

'Don't think I'll ever find Mr Right myself. You know I've had no luck with the fellas in my life.'

'It'll happen, Kate, one day, when you least expect it. You look lovely yourself. Thank you for being my maid of honour,' replied Helen.

'My pleasure. You're my best friend, Helen, always will be.' They hugged, smiling at one another.

It was a great celebration. Stan told Peter at the end of the night, he had no chance of organising a wedding as good as this. Peter told him it doesn't matter, as long as they are all together; it could be in a pub for all he cared.

The new Mr and Mrs Johnson thanked everyone at the end of the night. Tammy and Ronnie were staying the night at Helen's parents. Johnny and Ruth had organised their wedding night, at the Savoy Hotel. Yet again, Johnny knew someone, who knew someone so they had the bridal suite for the night.

35
Stan's Turn, Then

Later in July 1987, it was Stan's turn to get married to Janice. He and Joe had been kept on at Middlesbrough for one more season, their new manager told them he was impressed with their professionalism. Their wedding was in Middlesbrough, where they lived. It was a church wedding, most of his football colleagues came. Joe was his best man.

By that time, Jim had improved, only using his walking stick occasionally. He'd taken the package the football club offered him. No need to work. Brenda continued to teach because she loved it, although the summer holidays had arrived.

Their reception was in a stately home. As well as Peter and Helen being invited, Stan and Janice had already invited Helen's parents, plus her uncle and aunt. It was another lovely celebration.

When it was over, Brenda knew there was no school for a few weeks. The break, she hoped, would allow her to shake off her tiredness or vanish for good.

Jimmy and Dotty saw his parents every week, as did the twins, who continued to pop down from Middlesbrough regularly. Peter and Helen visited every two weeks, staying over with their children. The picture his mother gave him was returned, with new ones of his family. His parents' house now had a sideboard full of new family pictures, some of the recent weddings.

That summer flew by. Before she knew it, she was back at school teaching in September. When she'd been back to work for a month, in early October, Brenda came home from school on a Friday, exhausted. Jim was there, having stopped working now. When she came in, he said, 'You okay, luv? You look really pale.'

'Been feeling tired for ages now,' said Brenda.

'I noticed weeks ago, just thought you were run down.'

'That's what I thought, Jim. Just a virus maybe. Can't shake it off. I'm shattered; going to bed, can hardly stand.'

'You want me to call a doctor?'

'No, leave it. No fuss, a sleep should do the trick, I hope.'

'Well, if you're sure?' asked Jim.

'Yes, I'll be fine,' she said, kissing him, before going up to bed.

Later Jim checked to see if she was okay; she was fast asleep, so he left her, resting. When he went to bed later, she stirred, waking. Jim put his arm around her waist, saying as he did, 'Hey you okay? Your belly feels bloated.'

Brenda sat up in bed, holding her stomach. 'Jim, I weighed myself a few days ago, I've lost weight,' adding, 'Oh no.'

'What is it?'

Her face reddened. 'I think I've wet myself.' She pulled the bed sheets back, checking herself. 'Oh, Jim!' she said, covering her mouth with her hand.

He looked at the sheets, seeing a yellow and green discharge. Slowly he helped her out of bed, sitting her on the settee.

'Jim, I'm scared. My back hurts, this looks like diarrhoea, I've been going to the toilet more lately and I'm knackered. Something's wrong, I know it,' she said.

'Right, I'm calling the doctor, this isn't right.'

She nodded, laying on the settee where Jim slept for a few years. While they waited, he cleaned their bed, then took Brenda downstairs. She fell asleep on the settee as they waited.

It was late at night, almost midnight before a doctor arrived. When he'd examined her, he called for an ambulance. 'Mrs Johnson, I cannot confirm one hundred percent what is wrong with you, I need to get you to hospital immediately for further tests.'

'You must have some idea?' asked Jim.

'I have, but I don't want to alarm you,' he said.

'Come on, Doc, even if you're wrong, we've got a right to know!' Jim shouted.

'I'm sorry. We need to do further tests, as soon as possible,' said the doctor.

'Look, if my wife's ill, you've got to tell us,' Jim said, more calmly.

There was a pause before the doctor spoke. 'From everything you've told me, there's a chance you have, maybe... a form of cancer. But I cannot say how far and at what stage it is, or if that's correct yet,' said the doctor, looking at Brenda.

She put her hand to her mouth, gasping for air.

'No!' shouted Jim.

'Listen to me, please. We need to get you to hospital. Can you tell me how long you've had these symptoms, Mrs Johnson?'

She stared at the doctor, unable to speak.

'Brenda,' said Jim, looking into her eyes. 'How long has it been going on?' He put his hand on her shoulder before she answered, looking at the doctor.

'A while. I started feeling weary at Christmas time, finally went to the GP in March; he thought it might be IBS. After tests it wasn't that, so he said it was likely a virus. About three or four weeks ago when I went back to teach at school, I was prescribed painkillers for my back and some vitamin tablets to get me more energised. You remember, Jim, don't you?'

'Yes, I do,' he said, 'but you never said it started that long ago.'

She didn't answer him.

'And what did he think was wrong with you more recently?' asked the doctor.

'Like I said, probably a virus still,' said Brenda.

'So, the fatigue has been going on a few months,' said the doctor.

'Yes,' said Brenda.

'But what about the diarrhoea, discharge, swollen stomach, weight loss and lack of urine control?' the doctor asked.

'Stomach and weight loss I noticed a couple of months ago. Back pain comes and goes, while controlling my wee has been going on a few months. I've not been drinking much lately,' said Brenda.

'Why didn't you say?' said Jim.

'Didn't want to worry you, with all you've been through,' she replied.

'Listen,' said the doctor, 'hospital and tests, Mrs Johnson. When the ambulance arrives, I will follow in my car.'

'Okay,' said Brenda.

Jim was standing, just about to sit down with Brenda, when there was a knock on the door. He shot off to answer it, being followed into the house by two paramedics. 'Can you walk to the ambulance, Mrs Johnson?'

'Yes', she said, standing up. As she did, she fainted, Jim and one of the paramedics catching her.

A few moments later, the second paramedic came back in with a wheelchair. 'Into the ambulance, onto the bed, please gentlemen,' said the doctor.

She woke, looking up at Jim and the doctor standing over her. 'You fainted, Mrs Johnson. Likely due to de-hydration, that's why you have a drip in your arm, for fluids. We'll be there in a few minutes,' he said.

That night, the doctor who was on call explained to the hospital doctor, Brenda's symptoms, updating him on everything he knew, before leaving. Within an hour, she'd had blood tests, the hospital doctor telling her, she would be having an X-ray and a biopsy operation in the morning. He explained that different areas in her pelvis and abdomen, plus lymph nodes would all be biopsied, allowing them to know at what stage it was and if she actually had cancer or not.

Jim sat with his head in his hands after the doctor had explained this to Brenda. He'd made almost a full recovery from his injuries.

'Why me?' Brenda asked the doctor, tears in her eyes.

'It's difficult to say. Maybe a trauma triggered your reaction: it could be many things.'

'Just the luck of the draw maybe?' she asked.

'I deal in science and facts, Mrs Johnson. Let's get the results before we proceed any further. Now, try and get some rest until the morning if you can,' said the doctor. 'One of my colleagues will be in to see you. If you need anything just call one of the nurses, or push the buzzer beside your bed,' he said pointing to it, smiling, then leaving the cubicle.

'Christ,' said Jim. 'I've almost got back to normal, now this,' he added moving his head side to side.

'Don't tell the kids yet, Jim, we've got to wait for the results?'

'Okay, but as soon as we know, I'm calling them all,' he replied. 'Why didn't you tell me about all this, I only knew you were tired and had backache?'

'Like I said earlier, didn't want to worry you. You're just getting over the accident yourself.'

'I know that, I know that. But if this is... you know... well, if it is, we might not...' he trailed off, putting his hands over his face.

'Jim, come here.'

He got off his chair, holding her in his arms, as both of them cried, quietly.

When they let go of one another, he sat on the bed, as they both wiped their eyes.

'Come on. Whatever it is, we'll deal with it, okay?' said Brenda.

He nodded, saying quietly, 'We will, we will.'

They sat holding hands for a few minutes, until Brenda, smiling, fell asleep. Jim sat in the chair next to her, nodding off himself.

It was a few hours later at six o'clock when he woke up, a nurse tapping him on the shoulder. Brenda was still asleep.

'Would you like something to drink and eat?' she whispered.

'Yes please,' he said quietly, following her away from the cubicle.

By ten o'clock, Brenda had had an X-ray and was in theatre. Waking later that afternoon, the doctor returned, saying that the results should be known in two days. He said he would chase the lab himself. That evening he discharged her, promising he would be in touch, or one of his colleagues would be.

That was Saturday evening. She called Mr Crawford, her school headteacher, the next day, having his home number, telling him she wouldn't be in at school. He drove to see her immediately.

Arriving, Brenda told him, with Jim's help, what had happened. Forget work, he told her. He will say nothing until she contacts him.

On Tuesday, she received a phone call from the doctor asking her to come to see him. Sitting down in the office with Jim, he gave them the results.

36
Dealing with It

'Mrs Johnson, Mr Johnson. I've received all of the results from the laboratory,' said the consultant.

'And?' asked Jim.

'I'm afraid the results of the X-ray and biopsies are not good. Let me explain where we are, exactly,' he said, pausing before continuing. 'There are different stages of cancer from one to four. You've told us your symptoms are pelvic pain, you've got abdominal swelling, frequently urinate, and have been tired for some time. These are all signs, pointing us to a cancer,' he said, pausing. 'I see from your records that many years ago you had a hysterectomy?'

'Yes, after childbirth quite some time ago,' said Brenda, looking at Jim.

'It's unusual for a woman to contract ovarian cancer after this, but I'm afraid that in your case, I'm sorry to tell you, that is what has happened,' he said.

Jim turned to look at Brenda, saying nothing, reaching out to hold her hand.

'So, so, I've got ovarian cancer, Doctor?' said Brenda.

'It is a difficult thing to be told, but yes, from all the test results, I'm sorry to tell you, that is exactly what it is,' he said.

As Jim held her hand, Brenda put her hand to her mouth, gasping.

'As I said, we have four stages of this,' he continued. 'Unfortunately, you are already at stage four. It's a very difficult disease to diagnose, that's likely why your own GP wouldn't have known.'

'What can we do, Doctor?' asked Jim.

'Well, although it's at an advanced stage, we can operate but this may not be successful. We'll only know afterwards, when we take more biopsies and X-rays to ascertain the results, as to how aggressive the cancer actually is and how far it may have spread,' he said.

'Fuck,' said Jim, quietly.

Brenda glanced at him, before saying, 'And when will this operation take place?'

'As soon as possible. We've a consultant specialist here at our hospital for this. He is in theatre as we speak. I'll contact him before the end of the day and be in touch. Please be aware, that because of the nature of the cancer it may have spread to other organs, like the lungs and liver. As I said, we'll only know when we operate as to what extent it is. Again, I'm sorry,' said the consultant.

'Thank you, Doctor,' said Brenda, wiping tears from her eyes, 'for giving me the facts.'

He nodded, saying, 'Let's see what happens with the operation. I will be in touch in due course, or my colleague will. It will be soon,' he said, getting out of his seat, leaning over to shake Brenda's hand, then Jim's.

They left the room in silence. When they got to the car, Brenda said, 'Don't tell the kids yet, Jim, please.'

'We've got to,' he replied. 'Look, I... we don't know how long... oh shit! You know what I mean: don't know how long YOU might have!'

She kissed him. 'Please, Jim, just a few days. I want to spend some time with you. Let's go for a walk later, down by the canal, like we used to when the kids were small. You can show me where you used to work, if you want?'

He smiled at her. 'Okay,' he said, kissing her.

They drove to a part of the canal where he used to work on the lock gates, sitting in the car. 'Jim, I've always loved you,' she said.

He turned to look at her, reaching over, stroking her face. 'This isn't fair.'

'I know,' she said, kissing him.

For the next three days, they went for short walks along the canal. Their children all called, as they always did. They didn't tell them. Jim promised her he wouldn't say anything to them; it would be her decision.

Five days after being told the news, she was being operated on again. The day before, she spoke to Jimmy and the twins, calling Peter afterwards, then Elly. Each time, she cried while talking to them. Jim took over the calls when she tried to tell Peter and Elly, later calling his mother and Brenda's parents.

After the operation, when she woke that afternoon, her eyes opened to see Jim, with Jimmy next to him. She looked towards the end of her bed, seeing Stan and Joe. Opposite her husband, she saw Peter and Elly.

'We all decided to be here. Spoke to one another after you called us yesterday,' said Elly, continuing. 'We'll help with anything you want.'

Brenda had never seen Elly cry, as she held her hand. 'You know you've always been like a mum to me,' she whispered, bending to kiss her.

'We don't know the full extent or results; be a while before they let us know,' said Jim.

'Look, Mum. We'll pay for the top experts in the country to check you over, we can afford it,' said Joe.

'Joe, it's okay. We've got one of the best men in the country here at this hospital. He's the one who operated on your mum,' said Jim.

'Well, it's not bloody fair!' Joe added, as Stan put his arm around him.

'I know. We know it's not, don't we?' Jim added, looking at Brenda.

'Said that already, son,' said Brenda smiling, adding, 'now listen you lot. I'm going to stick around as long as I can, okay? Got lots of living to do, see you lot and my grandchildren grow up. Just have to see, like your dad said, how long when we get the results.'

'Okay, Mum,' said Jimmy and Stan in unison.

'How long have you all been here anyway?' Brenda asked.

'I drove up this morning,' said Peter, leaning to kiss his mother.

'We got here a couple of hours ago, had training this morning,' said Stan.

'Got here an hour ago,' said Jimmy.

'Same time as me,' Elly said, looking at Jimmy.

'Well, I'm fine for now. As soon as we know, you'll all know, okay.'

They all nodded, before Jim said, 'Right you lot, go and get some drinks; there's only supposed to be two of us here at a time, you all know that.' They all left, apart from Jim and Peter.

'Dad told us all everything, Mum, about you fainting last week and all the symptoms.'

'We've just got to wait. Stay calm,' she said.

They did. Brenda stayed in hospital for the next two days, recuperating. When she was discharged she was weak and tired from the operation, using a wheelchair. Jim and Jimmy took her home; when inside, her other three sons were there.

They made a fuss of her. 'Drink, mum?' asked Peter, when she was wheeled in by Jimmy.

She nodded. Shortly after Peter passed her a cup of tea she said, 'Your birthday in a few days.'

'And I'm spending it right here, with you,' he replied.

'What about Helen and the children?'

'Coming up tomorrow. We're staying here or at Jimmy's if you want peace and quiet?' Peter said.

Brenda smiled, then Jimmy said, 'Plenty of room at my place.'

'We're going to sort out a rota between us, Mum,' said Stan. 'We can be around to help with anything you want.'

'Thank you. All of you. Just need a bit of time to get my fitness levels up!' Brenda joked, looking at Stan and Joe.

'You know we can help with that, Mum,' said Stan, laughing.

'That's more like it,' said Brenda. 'Now listen, all of you. I'm being serious. I honestly don't know how long I've got. None of us do. But I know my time is limited. So…' she paused, taking a deep breath, 'so, no dull as dishwater faces, right? You lot are so handsome, all of you. Just be your normal happy selves, for me. Okay with that?'

'Yes, Mum,' said Peter.

Jimmy nodded, saying, 'Okay, boss,' laughing.

Stan said, 'Yes, milady!' just like Parker out of the television show *Thunderbirds*.

Then Joe added, 'Anything for you, Mum,' smiling at her.

They all took it in turns leaning over her wheelchair, hugging her, before she spoke. 'Right, I'm a bit peckish, you lot making dinner?'

'Already under control. Just got to serve it up. Remember that day when we made dinner after them school reports?' said Jimmy.

'That's a long time ago, young man!' Brenda said.

'Well, can you remember what we had back then?' asked Joe.

'Crikey, let me think. Err… I should know, it never happened often with you lot!' she said, laughing at all of them.

'Is that what happens when you get in your fifties, Mum, your brain starts to go!' said Joe.

'Cheeky!' Brenda said, adding, 'roast chicken dinner and apple pie. There, see!'

They broke out into a round of applause, before Jim said, 'Just like old times.'

'Yes, Dad, you're right, it is,' said Peter smiling, putting his arm round his dad's shoulders.

'Right, you lot, come and give me a hand,' said Jimmy, going out to the kitchen, leaving Brenda and Jim alone as their sons all chattered away going into the kitchen.

'This is lovely, Jim, I couldn't ask for any more than this, right here.'

'Me neither.'

'Great kids, aren't they?'

'Yep, I reckon so,' he said, smiling at her, helping her out of the wheelchair, sitting her at the table.

'They're all special, aren't they?' she asked him.

'Course they are. Great boys – well men now. They can look after you now, for a change.'

She smiled at Jim, told him she loved him, saying, 'Just like it used to be.'

They had dinner, all chatting away. Elly arrived just as they were about to sit down. Peter had called her, asking her to come round.

That evening, there was lots of laughter in the Johnson house.

37
Results

Helen told her parents, then uncle and aunt about Peter's mother, taking their children up to Manchester. The day after she arrived, her father phoned. He told her that Johnny knew a couple of doctors who frequented the club. One of them knew of a specialist piece of equipment called an MRI, which was in St Bartholomew's Hospital, in Hammersmith, London. This machine could see inside a human body; it may help, the doctor suggested.

Within forty-eight hours, Brenda was at that hospital, lying in the MRI machine, having her body scanned. A couple of hours later, as she waited with Jim, Peter and Helen, the specialist called them into his office. Knowing that she had cancer already, the MRI confirmed it had spread to her lungs and liver. With what could be seen on the scan, and after her operation, the specialist told them the only thing left was chemotherapy. Even with this, her time was limited, the cancer being aggressive, in the last fourth stage. If he had to say how long, no more than three months. They left the hospital, all four of them stunned.

That night, they stayed at Peter's house. Brenda called her other sons herself, then her parents and Jim's mother. Peter called Helen's parents, Johnny and Elly.

'Right,' said Brenda after Peter had made the calls, 'no more tears, okay?' wiping her own eyes.

They all had tears in their eyes, when Peter said, 'What do you want to do, Mum?'

'Hmm, well, there's somewhere I'd like to go,' said Brenda.

'Where to?' asked Peter.

'I need the permission of your parents, Helen.'

'Why?' asked Helen.

'I've never been to the seaside on the south coast. How about a visit to Bognor?'

Helen picked up the phone, calling her parents. 'Yes, of course you can,' her mother said, before Helen put the receiver down.

'Tomorrow it is then, Jim. It'll give me time to think,' said Brenda.

'Okay, Bognor here we come,' said Jim.

Later that evening, Helen's parents came round. So too, did Johnny and Ruth, telling them he'd left Terry in charge at the club.

When they'd all gathered in the front room of the house, Brenda repeated what she said earlier. No more tears.

'Right,' said Johnny, 'who's for a drink?'

'Make mine a vodka and coke please. A double,' said Brenda, smiling.

'Coming up,' said Peter, going to the kitchen.

'Oh, and make another one for your father,' said Brenda, looking at Jim.

Nodding, Jim said, 'Go for it. It's about time.'

'Are you sure, Dad?' asked Peter.

'If my wife says so, then sod it, yes!' he replied, smiling. Everyone stared at him, knowing he'd not drank alcohol for almost twenty years.

'He'll only be having a couple, any more then he'll be flat on his back, after all this time!' said Brenda, laughing. Then everyone laughed. Peter turned into the barman. Helen put the children to bed. Brenda got drunk, finally falling asleep. Jim had to carry her up to bed, with Peter's help. But, they had a wonderful evening, laughing and joking about old times. Jim only had the two drinks his wife allowed him.

The day after, Brenda having a hangover, they said goodbye, driving off to the seaside and Bognor. They walked on the beach, paddled in the sea, wandered around the shops, relaxing.

She slept a lot more than usual, telling Jim she felt exhausted after walking on the beach, having pains in her stomach. But they kept doing it, because she told him she loved the smell of the seaside. They were together, she told Jim. And making memories for one another.

38
Decision Time

When they came back from Bognor after a week, going directly to Peter's house, Brenda sat them down. She'd made her mind up, after researching this ovarian cancer with Jim.

'Okay, here's the thing,' said Brenda, herself, Jim, Peter and Helen all sitting around their kitchen table. 'We've been looking at this chemotherapy. There are loads of side effects if you have it. It can't cure the cancer I have, but may prolong my life. Thing is, when the specialist told me, it could only be maybe three months, I've decided I don't want to be ill for the last part of my life. So, I'm not having chemotherapy. That's it.'

'But, Mum, it can help you live longer!' said Peter.

'Listen, I've already had surgery. That MRI scan has found it in other places. I am not going to maybe have rashes, mouth sores, being sick, or lose my hair,' Brenda said.

Peter stared at his mum. Then he looked at his dad. 'It's your mother's decision,' said Jim, quietly.

'It is my choice. My life,' said Brenda, her voice trembling.

Peter nodded. 'Okay, if you're really sure, Mum?'

'Yes, I am. I'm not going to suffer. When we get back, we'll go to the hospital and my GP, they'll have painkillers and know everything I'll need,' she said.

After a few seconds of silence, Helen said, 'Are you staying here tonight?'

'Yes, if we can. We'll drive up tomorrow,' said Jim, adding, 'we'll let you know what happens when we get back. We've got the phone to keep in touch.'

The next day, as they drove back home, they had to pull over every hour for Brenda to use a toilet. On two occasions, she told Jim, she had the discharge again.

When they arrived, she went straight to bed. The next morning, Jim called the GP, taking Brenda to see him. He already had all of the information about Brenda. No chemotherapy, she told him. He prescribed painkillers, which he said would ease the pain.

That evening, Mr Crawford from her school visited Brenda. He already knew she'd had surgery. Jim told him about the visit to London for the MRI scan. Anything he could do, they only had to ask. Jim told him she didn't have long…

Three weeks later, in the early afternoon, Jim called their GP. Brenda couldn't get out of bed and was in pain. He called his sons to tell them. Jimmy went straight round to the house as an ambulance arrived. The twins drove immediately from Middlesbrough. Peter was on his way, with Helen from London.

She was rushed into hospital. A drip was put in her arm with morphine. Jim went with her in the ambulance. Jimmy waited at the house for the twins, Peter and Helen to arrive.

The twins arrived two hours later, Jimmy telling them which hospital to go to. An hour later, Peter pulled up with Helen. They followed Jimmy to the hospital. When they found their mother, she was unconscious. Her own GP stayed with her, telling them the morphine would ease her pain. Dotty arrived half an hour after them, after Jimmy called her.

At two a.m., Brenda woke up. Jim was by her side. 'Hey, you,' he said.

She smiled, whispering, 'Sorry.'

'Don't be silly,' he said.

'I want to go home, Jim. Don't let it happen here,' she whispered. They all heard her words.

It was Helen who rushed out of the room, finding a doctor. She explained that Brenda wanted to go home. The duty doctor knew she was gravely ill. 'If we move her, the trauma may just finish her,' he said.

'She's not dying in this bloody hospital!' Jim told him, with menace in his voice.

'I'll see what I can do; try and organise an ambulance,' said the doctor, visibly shaken.

'Sorry,' said Jim, 'and thank you, Doctor,' he added, shaking his hand.

Within minutes, as they all stood around Brenda's bed, they were ushered out by Helen. Two porters arrived with a trolley bed. Jimmy and Peter helped their mother onto it, with the porter's help, as the twins held the doors to the room open. They did so, in silence. Helen held the drip. Jim held his wife's hand.

In the ambulance, Jim travelled with Helen and the doctor back to the house. When they got her inside, Jim carried her upstairs as Helen held the drip. Brenda was asleep.

As she slept, the doctor finally said, 'I know this isn't the time or place, but I've got to tell you, we've broken several rules here. I did this for one reason; your mother taught me at school, didn't mention it earlier. If it hadn't been for her, I would never have become a doctor. This is my way of thanking her,' he said, with tears in his eyes.

Jim shook his hand.

'If you don't mind, I'd like to stay. Have to make some phone calls first, if I can use your phone please?' said the doctor, adjusting the morphine drip.

'Yes, absolutely,' said Jim.

Everyone was in the bedroom by now.

Jim showed the doctor to the phone downstairs. When he came back up, he told them all he'd organised for palliative care, explaining what it was: end of life care. They all listened in silence.

'She's asleep still,' said the doctor looking at Brenda, continuing, 'when she wakes up, it'll help if you try and get her talking: old memories, play some music if she likes it. I know it's difficult but try and make her happy, if you all can?'

'We will, Doctor,' said Stan.

'Right, let's get some chairs up here,' said Jimmy.

Peter shot off to his old bedroom, having a chair in there. 'Here's one,' Peter said, 'plus we've got the settee there as well,' pointing to the place where unknown to them all, Jim used to sleep for many years.

Stan and Joe had already raced downstairs to get some chairs. When they came back up, Helen and Dotty were sitting on the settee, Jimmy and Peter next to them on the arms. Their dad was sitting on a chair, next to Brenda. They put the two chairs opposite their father, Stan saying one was for the doctor.

Nobody said a word, until the doctor spoke again. 'Does she like music?'

'Yes,' said Jim.

'Be right back,' said Peter. When he returned he had his old record player with him and some vinyl records he used to play. Plugging it in, he put on an old Beatles record. 'She loved the Beatles,' said Peter.

'You remember she was always dancing around the living room when we were kids?' said Jimmy.

'Yep,' said Stan.

'And she used to sing along to loads of songs. Must be where you got your singing voice from, Pete?' said Joe.

'Probably was,' said Peter.

They chattered away, all telling different stories about when they were boys, growing up. Dotty and Helen went to make tea, as daylight appeared.

When she came back, Helen told Peter to phone Elly. He'd forgotten. It was seven o'clock, so he called her. She was there ten minutes later, sitting on the empty chair next to the doctor.

39
Don't Go

At eight o'clock, a nurse arrived. This was who the doctor called; she would stay until their own GP arrived. There would be a nurse with Brenda twenty-four hours a day now, he told them, to control and administer her medication, helping her with anything their mother needed.

When the doctor left, he shook everyone's hand. Jim asked him his name, he'd tell Brenda when she woke; it would please her to know one of her former pupils had become a doctor. 'David Foster,' he said, bidding them all goodbye.

Elly decided she'd make them breakfast and some sandwiches. Again, Dotty and Helen helped.

When they came back up afterwards, they heard laughter. Brenda had woken up. Jim told her about the doctor. She joked that at least her teaching had been good for at least one person. And Peter told Helen his mum had joked they had to keep playing music, but she wasn't up to dancing.

Jim leant over and kissed Brenda. The music played on. Brenda waved her hand to usher them all closer to her bed. Peter turned the music down, but it could still be heard.

As they all stood around her bed, the nurse moved away. Brenda was breathing loudly now, struggling for air. 'I… I want to tell you all… all of you… I love you. Always have. Elly, you're the daughter I never had. Boys, my men. All of you. You all say you've been lucky.' Brenda took a big gulp of air, as Jim knelt next to her, stroking her hair. 'Well, I'm the lucky one. I had the gift of all four of you.' She took another deep breath, as the nurse put her hand over her mouth. Dotty, Helen and Elly were all crying. Jim and the boys had tears in their eyes.

'I love you, Mum,' said Peter, hardly able to get the words out.

One by one, her other sons spoke.

'I love you too, Mum,' said Jimmy.

'Me too, Mum, love you,' added Stan.

'Love you, Mum, you're the best,' said Joe.

None of them could speak properly, their voices croaking, trembling.

Brenda took another gasp of air, saying, 'Take care of our grandchildren, especially Ronnie. Love you all, Jim, you girls, our four boys. All as one.'

She sighed, smiling, looking up at Jim. He held her hand tightly. Brenda's grip and hand slipped from his. She couldn't squeeze his hand any more.

Jim sobbed, he cried and cried. They all began crying. The nurse had tears in her eyes.

Brenda slipped away, in their home. Where she wanted to be. She'd got her wish, thanks to the doctor she taught. With her family all around her. Now they had to deal with life without the one person who always held everything together...